MY LIFE
IN YOUR EYES

My Life in Your Eyes

Addyson's Story

PART ONE OF THE MY LIFE SERIES
ELLSIE BROOKS

iUniverse, Inc.
Bloomington

My Life in Your Eyes
Addyson's Story

iUniverse books may be ordered through booksellers or by contacting:

iUniverse
1663 Liberty Drive
Bloomington, IN 47403
www.iuniverse.com
1-800-Authors (1-800-288-4677)

ISBN: 978-1-4759-2885-3 (sc)
ISBN: 978-1-4759-2887-7 (hc)
ISBN: 978-1-4759-2886-0 (ebk)

Printed in the United States of America

iUniverse rev. date: 06/04/2012

ACKNOWLEDGMENTS

This book is dedicated to my Hero. The one person that has been there for me as long as I have been alive; supporting me, loving me, and helping me to grow into the women I am today. If I can be half the mother to my kids that you have been to me, I will be happy.
I love you mom.

To my husband and kids, who have encouraged me to follow my dream and never give up: thank you for believing in me, even when I didn't. I love you all.

To my new friend Jim Parsons: You are my miracle!

To Melissa Ramsey Atkinson, one of my real best friends and the first to read this book: your words and comments gave me the fuel to continue. Even when I didn't have the courage to share such an enormous part of myself with other people, you never let me quit. No matter where you go or how long we go without speaking, you're always there for me. I love you so much.

To everyone who is reading this: for whatever reason you are reading, I pray when you're done you will walk away with hope. I have been there, and I know what it is like to live in pain. I just want each and every one of you to know that God has a plan for your life and YOU will find your Braxton too. I love each and every one of you with all of my heart, and this story is for you.

Ellsie Brooks

To my Father and God, Jesus Christ, I praise your holy name. Thank you for never leaving me and never forsaking me. Thank you for the ability to write and for allowing it to touch so many people all over the world. Thank you for loving me, the world, and for all of your mercies and grace that I pray I never take for granted. I know without you I can't do anything.

Psalms 139:17—How precious also are thy thoughts of me, O God! How great is the sum of them.

CHAPTER 1

Summer was almost over, and it was time to go back to school. I could not say that I was ready to go back, but I did not hate school either—only because of Braxton. He made life so much easier for me whenever he was around. It was just the times that he could not be with me that were so hard.

That summer, Braxton and I had been to the beach together. Our parents were extremely close friends, so it was not unusual for us. We usually went on one vacation together, then one with our families, alone. Those were nowhere near as fun. There were a few things that were easier when Braxton wasn't with us at the beach, however. Like, I would never get into a bathing suit in front of him, and I did not like eating in front of him. Being a hundred pounds overweight, I was self conscious anyway, but I did not ever want Braxton to see me, especially in a suit.

He had never judged me. He stood up for me when someone said something mean or cruel to me when I was with him. If I told him of something that happened when he was not around, he usually had words with that person later, especially at school. Because of that, I tried not to mention things that happened. I felt like a burden to him sometimes, like the little sister he had to protect. He was only one month to the day older than me but, because of his constant protective mode, I felt much younger.

If being so fat was my own fault, I would say that I may deserve some of the picking and joking that I constantly received. It wasn't my fault. I ate healthy food, I worked out three days a week, I only ate junk food on holidays or festive events, like birthday parties. I had been to every doctor in North Carolina and South Carolina, and still no one could help me.

I had tried every fad diet on the market, had been to gyms, workout clubs, and even tried medications. I could not lose weight. I would never give up, in any case. My dream was to be proud of the way I looked. Even though Braxton had made it clear he would be my best friend no matter what, I would have liked for him to be proud of being my best friend. Maybe, if I were skinny, maybe, we could be more.

Nobody asked me to dances, on dates, and, I had never had a boy friend. I would not let Braxton take me to the dances and other social school events. I was too worried people would tease him and laugh at him, all because of me. I felt like I tied him down. A lot of the dances and other things, he said he would rather not attend, but I felt like it was certainly because of me. He knew I wouldn't go, and I thought he felt guilty that I was at home alone; he missed out on so much by babysitting me.

I did go to a home football game once, and spent the whole game talking to Braxton. We were laughing, and screaming for the team. I booed when the other team would score, and just had fun generally. Then the game had to end, and it was time to leave.

I was following behind Braxton, very slowly, watching my step. The bleachers seemed narrower on the way down, and I was anxious to make it to the bottom without falling on my face. It would be embarrassing to fall, no matter who you are. The fat girl falling, that is even worse.

As I was passing Gary Williams, one of the hottest guys in school, he looked up to see who was coming by him. He made eye contact with me, and I instantly blushed. As I was stepping to the next step, trying to regain my focus, Gary quickly stuck his foot out, and sent me rolling down the last four steps.

I wanted to die. It was unfortunate enough that I had fallen in front of the entire school, but I had also fallen in front of Braxton. I could not look at him. The tears streaming down my face added to my shame. I heard Gary and his group laughing loudly.

"Hey Addy, I thought we were having an earthquake!" yelled Gary. I moved my hair out of my face with my bloody palms, and glanced up at his group. When the perfect Kristen Hefner, sitting beside him, saw my face, she stopped laughing. I saw the remorse and pity flash through her eyes, but only for a second. She glanced back at her boyfriend, and simpered, "Good one, Gary."

I stared at the ground, knowing I had to get up, but my knees were hurting so badly I could hardly move. I tried to work myself to all fours, which made the jokes come rolling out from the same group of kids. "Elephant" or "Cow," and let's not forget "Fat ass"—that was their favorite one. Suddenly, there were two people at either side of me trying to help me up. I quickly began to get up on my own. I did not want someone feeling how heavy I was.

I finally reached my feet, after what felt like thirty minutes, and thanked the people who had tried to help me. I began to walk towards Braxton's car in the school parking lot. Although, out of embarrassment, I did not want to see him right then, he was my only ride home. I realized he wasn't anywhere near me. I searched for a moment, thinking maybe that had been the last straw for him. I had been waiting for the day that he would get tired of it all; the day that he would say our friendship was over. As I looked back to where I had fallen down, I noticed Braxton beating the crap out of Gary.

I ran back over there, as fast as I could run, and begged Braxton to stop. After three boys had finally peeled Braxton off of Gary, Braxton walked down to me, put his arm around my shoulders, and simply said, "Let's go."

I could only imagine what my face looked like at that moment. My eyes had to be as large as baseballs. "Braxton, do not ever get in another fight for me, ever," I scolded him.

"Don't ever get picked on in front of me then." He smiled that heart-melting smile at me. His crystal blue eyes held no regret. As a matter of fact, I thought he was pretty proud of himself. I walked off of that football field, with my head hung down, my long hair covering my face, hiding a massive smile.

That day held three firsts and one last for me: The first football game, and the first time Braxton got into in a fist fight over me. It also was the first time I had ever fussed at him for anything, as far as I could remember. However, it would also prove to be the last football game, or social event I would ever attend.

That was freshman year. We were going to be juniors this year. One would think the older we got, the older we would act, but that is not true. The older we get, the crueler people can be. Braxton always said when we graduated and went to college everything would be different. I wished I could believe him.

On this particular day, the day everything changed, Braxton and I were going to get our school supplies and some clothes. The clothes were for

Braxton; I would never try clothes on in front of him. If he had discovered what size I had to buy, I would have died of embarrassment.

"Are you going to get another UNC book bag this year?" He asked as he pulled into the mall parking lot. I sat there for a few minutes taking in the sight of Concord Mills. I loved this place. It had every store anyone could want to shop in. When it first opened, people said it had a roller coaster inside of it. It turned out to be a lie, but the place was capacious enough to hold one. "Do fish have lips?" I asked as I got out of the car.

The car was another issue for me. His parents had bought Brax a brand new Chevy Camero over the summer. It was jet black and felt like it sat slam on the ground. It was beautiful, and Braxton fit in it perfectly. I had always imagined he would get a hefty truck, but the Camero suited him; he made the car look hot.

On the other hand, I almost had to roll out of the flippin' thing, onto the ground to get out. It was terribly embarrassing at first. I had figured it out though; instead of putting one foot out and trying to pull myself out, I turned to the side and put both feet on the ground, and then pulled myself up. Two hundred and forty-five pounds was a lot of weight to try to pull anywhere.

We must have walked around that mall for three hours. Out of all the clothes he had bought, he may have picked out only two shirts; I picked out most of them. I always looked for dark or blue colors for him. When he wore them, his eyes would glow. Braxton's eyes were his most remarkable feature. They were crystal blue; just like a Siberian husky's. Everywhere we went at least one person would ask if he wore contact lenses. It had become funny to us. People did not believe him when he said he did not wear contacts. Some people would compliment him on how beautiful his eyes were, and quickly walk away from us. One girl beats them all. She asked him to prove it. After a few minutes of awkward silence, I was finally the one to ask, "How is he supposed to do that?"

The dingbat girl said, "I don't know. Just prove it." Braxton and I laughed at the poor girl. He threw his arm around my shoulders, as best as he could, and after we had walked off, he said, "How? Take my eyeballs out?" It was hilarious to us, but maybe you had to be there.

I like to relive that day over and over, not because of the look on the nitwit's face, or over Braxton's reply, but over the look of pure shock and jealousy when he put his arm around my shoulders as we walked off. As far as she knew, Brax was more than my best friend. In her mind, a boy as hot as Braxton could never have love for a fat girl like me.

I laughed thinking about it. "What's so funny?" Braxton asked as he paid for our paper, pens, binders, and all of the little items we needed for the next week. I did not realize I had laughed loudly enough for him to hear.

"Oh nothing," I lied. He gave me a strange look. "Do you want to go to the art gallery for a few minutes after we leave here?" I asked, quickly changing the subject.

There was no way I was admitting that I was reliving the look on the face of the "eyeball retard" from four years ago. Plus I truly wanted to go home anyway; my feet were killing me, and I did not want to tell him that either.

"Do we have to, Addy? I was hoping to go home." His eyes flashed regret.

"Of course, we can go home."

I noticed he had been acting strange all that day. He unquestionably had not been as happy go-lucky, or as laid back, as he usually was. We had no physical contact, which I never asked for or initiated, anyway; he usually put his arm around my shoulders. He looked tired and preoccupied, and I knew something was wrong.

Once we got back in the car, I looked over as he stared at the steering wheel. "Braxton, is everything okay?" I finished snapping on my seat belt. It was a bitty to reach; the belt seemed like it was in the back seat. For a normal sized person, it would not be a problem at all. Me having to reach over my stomach, well, it was a deed in itself.

"I am OK." He smiled. Did I see regret flash in his eyes?

With one quick motion, I reached over and yanked the keys out of the ignition, "Tell me Braxton." I crossed my arms, and he knew I meant business.

He let out a deep sigh, leaned back against the seat, and closed his eyes. His head lay against the head rest, allowing his black hair to spread out over the top of it. As he sat with his eyes closed, I stared at him. How could one person be so perfect all the way around? His skin was flawless, not one pimple or scar; his nose, his mouth, his ears, all perfect.

It was not just my opinion; every girl who met him apparently agreed. I had watched girls trip over their feet trying to watch him walk by. Some girls stuttered or rambled on aimlessly about nothing at all, and others had hit on him with their boyfriends standing right beside them. A couple of girls had walked up and groped him as if they were dating him. One person even walked up to him and said, "I am in love with you; marry me." Of course, none of them would have ever thought for one second that someone as handsome as Braxton would ever be with me. I did not exist, a ghost in the shadows; to them, I did not matter. And, of course, we were not dating, and I did not own him; I just felt like I did.

"I am not looking forward to this year, Addy. I do not know how you do it. How do you allow things to roll off of your back so easily? Nothing seems to bother you. I am not looking forward to the pointing and laughing, the jokes and sneers. This school supply trip always confirms it for me; our little vacation from Hell is almost over. Now give me my keys back." He stared at me with his hand held out for the keys.

I did not know what to say. My mind was rolling a mile a second, but no words would form. I was an enormous burden on him. The hottest boy in East Lincoln High should not be dreading school. He should be living it up, going out on dates with girls. Brax should be playing sports, especially football; I knew for a fact that football was something he had always wanted to do. He should have been hanging out with his friends, going to social events and parties—all of the things normal teenagers our age did. I looked at him one last time with my heart breaking for my self-proclaimed hero. I promised him, in my heart, that the last two years of his life in high school, were going to be the best two years of his life.

CHAPTER 2

A change came over Addyson when she gave me back the keys to the car. She became quiet and detached. I glanced over at her several times but she was not looking back at me.

"Did we forget anything?" I rotated my eyes from her to the road, waiting on a reply.

"No" was all she said. I finally gave up on getting her to talk. Maybe she was thinking about next week and everything that came with a new school year. Maybe she was secretly dreading it as bad as I was. One of the things that always amazed me about her was she never let her pain, anger, frustration, or fear show on the outside. The last time she showed any kind of emotion about being teased, we were in seventh grade. At the time, we were still bus riders. My parents would drop me off at the Michaels' house every morning so I could catch the bus with her. This particular morning wasn't any different from the rest. The bus pulled up at fifteen minutes 'til eight. Addy followed me onto the bus as I guided us toward our regular seat. Addy took the window seat, and I sat on the aisle.

Matthew Henson sat right behind us with Jerrod Finley and Billy Maxis. I had a terrible feeling that something was going on, something was brewing. After so many years of endless pranks and jokes, you start to recognize the ones that are the cruelest; you could almost feel it like an invisible force in the air. I could hear laugher and hushed whispers coming from behind us. I kept glancing back but, when I looked, all three were crunched in the seat talking to each other.

"Are you going to be at the water fountain?" Addy always seemed nervous on the bus and at lunch. Those two times of the day, I would trade bodies with her. I would trade forever if I could.

"Ain't I always?" I smiled at her, trying to lighten the mood.

The bus pulled into the parking lot. I threw my book bag over my shoulder and stood. Addyson's terrifying scream startled me, and my protective instincts flew into action.

I focused on Addy. She was still sitting against the window with her hands held flat out in front of her. Milk was dripping out of her hair and into her lap. I looked behind the bench seat and noticed Jerrod and Matt laughing wildly. Addyson looked up at me and the tears spilling from her honey brown eyes had me spinning into outrage. My blood ran cold in my veins and all I could think about was punching those boys in the face, making them hurt as bad as she did.

"What the hell is wrong with you?" I directed my anger towards Matt the most. I knew he was the one who did it. Jerrod and Billy weren't mean enough to do that, but the laughter was almost as bad as the act itself.

Matt stood up from the bench and his head almost touched the roof of the bus. He was in high school and three times my size. I knew he would beat me to a pulp, but I tried to hide my fear. "Why do you mess with her? What did she do to you?" The laughter had ceased and I realized that the entire bus was watching us.

"I thought the cow would want some milk." Matt's face looked as stern as his words. "What are you going to do about it?" He stepped over the other two boys in the seat and was now standing in front of me in the aisle. Before I could answer him, the bus came to a stop and the bus driver was walking towards us, to break up the fight that was about to happen.

"Braxton, I am okay; just let it go," Addyson whispered as if no one else could hear her. Matt laughed. "Yeah, listen to your girlfriend." Matt pushed me out of the way, and I fell into a girl who was sitting in the seat across from ours.

"Break it up, High school kids get off first and transfer to the shuttle bus. Everyone else sit down . . ." The driver's words trailed off as he noticed Addyson and the milk all over her and the bus floor. "What did you do?" He asked Addyson.

Her eyes went from the driver to the trio. "It was an accident." Addy didn't tell on them; she took up for them. Even after all they put her through, they never broke her personality.

"Clean up this mess before you get off, and no more food or beverages allowed on the bus from now on." The driver stepped off the bus and went into the building to look for cleaning supplies.

Moans of protest came from all corners of the bus. Kids filed off, needling Addyson as they passed for making them lose their food privileges. Mike Brennan curled his lip and said, "Thanks a lot, Addyson; you ruined it for everyone!" My eyes made contact with the brown, hate-filled eyes behind thick glasses. Fear spread across the short boy's face and he suddenly was at a loss for words. He quickened his step, and got off the bus without another word.

I tried to relinquish the anger and frustration before I turned back towards Addy. "I will clean this mess up; you just go in and get cleaned up." She didn't look at me. Her lap was a puddle of milk. Her hair was sticky and matted together. Her eyes were swollen and red from crying. "Why didn't you tell the driver the truth, Addy? Why did you let them get away with it?" I whispered so softly I wasn't sure she even heard me. She looked out of the window and took in a deep steadying breath. When her eyes finally met mine, the pain and hurt were gone; something was there I had never seen before.

"It wouldn't do any good, Braxton. You know that already deep down. Matt would have gotten into trouble and he would have been ten times worse the next time. It only makes it harder on me." A small smirk came across her face and she knew I understood.

Addy slowly stood from the seat; milk drained from her lap, down her pants and onto the floor. To my surprise, she laughed. "Well this is a first." She said simply, and got off the bus. I watched her walk into the building while I waited on the bus driver and the cleaning supplies. No matter how hard I tried, I could not stop her pain. I would never stop trying to protect her; even if it did feel useless.

That was the last time I saw Addy cry in public over something a bully did to her. It was like it was the last straw, the one thing that made all the rest not matter anymore. Matt destroyed a piece of her that day; he hardened her heart forever. I regretted more than anything not throwing a punch that day. I was ashamed that I didn't have the guts to fight him back then. He may have beaten me half to death, but I would have died trying. We took the bus for another week or so and then our parents started taking us to and from school.

I think about things like that, on the last week of every summer. They were real life nightmares that I wouldn't believe, had I not been there to see them. It never ceases to amaze me how downright heartless people could be. Every year I vowed to myself to try harder to protect Addyson, but every year something or someone would get to her. She never sheds a tear.

I pulled into Addyson's driveway and parked the car. "I will be here in the morning for our walk around the pond." I noticed her face was pale looking. After the one word responses I had been receiving all the way home, I just let it go.

"Pop the trunk, Brax, so I can get my bags, okay."

I reached down, out of habit, and pushed the little silver button on my door. Before I could ask if she felt okay she was out of the car, and opening the trunk. I focused on her in the rear view mirror. She was acting really strange. I waited for her to shut the trunk so I could see her eyes clearly in the mirror.

"I can't go walking tomorrow; I have plans with Mom." I could barely hear her. She wasn't looking at me. Something didn't feel right.

"Oh well, text me when you get back home, and I'll come over and take you for your hair cut." I watched her intently in the mirror.

Just as I grabbed the handle to get out, she said, "I will Brax. Bye."

I searched her eyes for the split second she looked at me. She must be having a really hard time with going back to school. Why didn't she talk about it? Did she think I would judge her? She obviously didn't want to talk about anything right then, but I would bring it up that night over the phone. She should have known I was always there for her; we were going to talk about that too.

CHAPTER 3

The ride home was quite. Country music was playing in the back ground, which made it even harder for me to hide the tears that were threatening to push their way out. Country music could be so depressing, Tim McGraw was making it almost impossible to stay calm as he sang "Live Like you are Dying" straight to me. This feeling came with the realization that, if I genuinely cared about Braxton, I would have to leave him alone. Seeing how I spent every free moment of my life with him, seeing how he was not only my best friend, but my only real friend, my whole life was about to be turned upside down.

I could not get out of the car fast enough. "I will be here in the morning for our walk around the pond." He shifted the car into park as he spoke to me. I turned to get out.

"Pop the trunk, Brax, so I can get my bags, okay." No matter what, I refused to look him in the face. I knew if I did, I would have a complete mental breakdown. I heard the trunk pop as I pulled myself to my feet. I shut the door without saying a word. Just a few more minutes, Addy, I repeated over and over in my head; hold it together, just a few more minutes. My chest was on fire. I felt like screaming. It felt like someone close to me had just died, and I had not even been away from him yet.

I grabbed the bags out of the back, "I cannot go walking tomorrow, and I have plans with Mom." I strained to keep my voice straight.

"Oh, well, text me when you get back home, and I'll come over and take you for your hair cut." He looked at me through the rear view mirror; I felt his eyes on me.

I was pulling my famous Addy move, hiding my face behind my long black hair. I was more than sure I was pale, and my eyes had to be bloodshot. Braxton knew me better than anyone, even my parents.

Quickly, I pushed my hair behind my ear and looked Brax in the eyes to say goodbye. If I did not, he would get out of the car and confront me, and I would break down for sure. "I will, Brax. Bye." I shut the trunk, made myself smile, and took off up the sidewalk to my house.

The Camero came to life and sped down the street. I hardly made it to the steps as the ball of raw emotion came flooding out of me. I dropped the bags, not caring about anything in them, and clutched my chest, scared I was going to explode. I began to sob.

Why was I so hurt? Why did I feel so lonely, I knew this day was coming? I had expected it for years. To be honest, I would not have blamed him if he had been the one to call our friendship off years ago. He spent his days defending me at school. He spent his nights with me, out of pity, I'm sure, and I had taken up his whole life. If he was not going to be the one to step up to the plate, and live his life, I would do it for him. No matter how badly it hurt me to do it, I would have to.

I sat on the steps for several hours, long after the tears had subsided. I leaned up against the brick wall that sat on either side of our stairs, staring out into nothing. I imagined how Braxton's life was going to change—the friends he would have, the sports he would play, and the parties he would attend. The life he would finally begin to live; the one he deserved. The hardest thing to imagine was the girls he would date.

Then, I began to think about how my life would change. I would have to start driving myself to school. I'd have to change where I ate my lunch, and the halls I walked. Finding a route around our normal meeting places between classes would prove to be a challenge. I would have to study in the library, find new places to visit that Braxton would never think to look for me; I would have to build a whole new life. I would be utterly alone. The tortures would be tripled. What about the simple fact that I would not see Braxton anymore. I would not have his protection, his affection, or his attention anymore. I would not have the one single person that I have always had in my life. This would be the hardest thing I had ever done.

I watched the sun set, ending the day, and my way of life, as I knew it.

CHAPTER 4

"Mom, has Addy called?" I sat at the bar and watched my mother fly around the kitchen as she cooked our dinner. Dad was on his way home, and Mom always wanted dinner to be ready by the time he got home. The smell of lasagna made my stomach growl and my mouth water.

"No, Sweetie, she hasn't." Mom tossed her wooden spoon in the sink and stopped to look at me. "What is going on?" She asked in her concerned mother voice. Before I answered, she was back to tossing the fresh salad she had made.

"I honestly have no idea. I let Addyson off at her house two days ago and haven't heard from her since." I played the day over and over in my mind. I could not figure out what I did wrong.

Mom was silent for several minutes. "Just go to her house and talk to her." Mom made cooking look like an art; the way she glided around the kitchen doing three or four things at once.

"I have, and I can't catch her at home."

"Hey ya'll, something sure smells good." Dad tossed his jacket over the back of the couch and loosened his tie. "Hi, Son" Dad walked past me towards my mother. I knew they would spend the next ten minutes being mushy; I quickly slid out of my seat and went to my room.

My cell phone had no missed calls or texts. I flicked the mouse of my desktop computer, and the screen came to life. I pulled up Facebook and checked Addyson's page. There were no new posts, no new emails either. It was as if she had fallen off of the planet. I would send her one more message, just one more. I would beg if I had to. I just had to know what exactly I had done to deserve this. She owed me that at least.

"Braxton, dinner's ready." Mom's voice was full of laugher and happiness; I did not feel like being around happy people, not when I felt so miserable.

—◊◊◊—

It was Sunday morning and still not so much as a text from Addyson. I was done with this; I had not done anything wrong. I made a commitment, to myself that, if she wanted to end our friendship for no reason at all, it was okay with me.

I pulled on a shirt over my pajama pants and walked into the kitchen. Mom and Dad had planned to spend the day in the mountains. Addyson and I were supposed to go with them; I did not want to go without her. I thought about taking a trip of my own; I just did not know where.

"I am not driving all over Denver looking for her. I will not go to her house; I will not beg her anymore!" I whispered to myself as I went towards the shower. As I stripped in front of the sink, my eyes caught my attention in the mirror. My face was showing anger, but my eyes deceived me. The red streaks of busted blood vessels and dark puffy circles around them made it clear that I had no sleep the night before. I had tossed and turned all night long. When I did sleep I had dreams of past events at school, things that had happened to Addyson that I could never prevent.

I leaned in closer to the mirror and pulled the bottom of my eye down to examine them closer. The bright red smeared all through them was not enough to overwhelm the transparent crystal blue. They were the color of a blind man's eyes. I hated them. I had tried contacts before. I could not wear them; my eyes burned and watered the whole time. I wanted a normal blue, as my father's, that people could look into and admire; not look away from like they were scary.

The shower was steaming hot. The scalding pellets hit my back and made me tense up for a moment. Once I had adjusted to the heat, I rested my head against the wall and tried to shush the memory my eyes brought to my mind.

Addyson was eight years old which made me seven. Mrs. Michaels had taken us to the Lincoln County courthouse for the annual Apple Festival. Everyone looked forward to this day, especially the small town business owners. Cheerleaders preformed in the streets; live bands played on the green grass of the court yard, and tents were as far as the eye could see. They had every food one could imagine, not to mention art work, handmade crafts, and unique things never seen before. Kids ran free up and down the streets, spending whatever monies their parents had given them. Laughter and joy, smiles and handshakes of long time friends; everyone looked forward to this day.

Addyson was chubby, even back then, but things were a little different. No one seemed to notice it as much as they did as we got older. Our parents had given us twenty dollars each; to us it was a lot of money.

"Look!" Addyson took off into a tent filled with 5x6 hand-painted pictures of scenery. Her eyes floated over each canvas with such respect and admiration.

The owner of the tent walked over as soon as he noticed two small children close to his items. "Can I help you two find something?" He did not want to deal with us at all.

"How much are your paintings?" Addyson was holding one in her small hands. The picture of the sun setting over the ocean was beautiful, but I did not see why she would spend her money on it. We had a hundred photos just like that from our summer vacations.

"Twenty five dollars apiece," the man said with disdain.

"I don't have enough." Addyson's face showed her disappointment so clearly.

"She only has twenty dollars," I said to make the guy understand. He reached over and took the painting out of her hand and placed it back in the metal rack.

"Sorry, kid," he said as he turned to walk away.

I grabbed Addyson's hand and held it tight as we left the small blue tent. "You will find something else you want Addy; don't be sad." I noticed the man that we always looked for—homemade apple cider man is what we called him. "Look, Addy!" I pulled her by her hand and ran towards the cider machine.

"Two cups, please." I said, never letting Addy go.

"Grab your apples, there, out of that pile." The man was always smiling.

"You go first, Addyson," I said, looking the pile over for my two apples. Once Addyson picked two out, the man began to pump the large metal pedal at his feet. A large round wheel began to spin, and Addy dropped her two apples, whole, into the spout on top. After a few seconds, the plastic cup underneath began to fill with fresh green apple cider. It only took a few minutes to fill the cup to overflowing. Addyson reached down and picked up the cup and took a small sip.

"Your turn, son." The man grabbed a cup out of the plastic bag, dipped it in a chest of ice, and stuck it under the drain.

"I found two perfect apples," I said to Addyson, but the man answered, "Yes, you did!" I dropped the apples in and waited for my sweet and sour treat.

Addyson was looking over towards the art tent. When she noticed me staring at her, she turned back towards the apple cider machine. "You picked the best apples, Brax." She smiled and took another sip of her drink.

I paid the man two dollars for both drinks and pulled Addyson towards the live band on the grass. We sat underneath one of the towering oak trees that cluttered up the court yard. Addyson sat so close our knees were touching. I let go of her hand; hers went to hold her cup, and I ran mine over my shorts to clean off the sweat. I reached up and grabbed her hand off of her cup and held it tight again. She didn't act as if she even noticed, and I felt comfortable holding her hand, so I never asked; I just grabbed it whenever I wanted to.

Bluegrass music was being played by the older men on the makeshift stage. Everybody was clapping their hands and swaying to the music. In the shade of the tree, the wind made my sweaty body cool. I knew from the stinging on my cheeks I was sun burnt.

Three boys, a lot older than us, walked by. "Oh, look at that . . . love birds," the giant one with long nappy hair said to the other two. They laughed and looked towards Addyson and me; neither of us responded. Addy tried to let my hand go, but I held on tighter. I tried to keep my eyes on the band, but the more the three bullies talked, the angrier I was getting. When Addy would not look at them, the giant bent down on his knees to get closer. I felt scared suddenly, as if he was going to hurt Addy. She leaned in closer to me and squeezed my hand tight.

"Leave her alone!" I yelled, facing him for the first time. The smile slid off of his face, and he stared at me with shocked eyes.

"Hey, look at this kid's eyes; holy shit, he is a freak!" He laughed as he pointed towards me and stepped back between the two guys with him. All three were staring at me. "No wonder he is with the chubby girl; no one else wants the freak!"

What did he mean? My eyes, I had the eyes of a freak? Why? Why would he say that? My feelings were hurt, and I could not think straight. After the initial shock of the remarks, I became angry. I was about to express my opinion of them, when suddenly Addyson scrambled to her feet. Her little hand jerked out of mine.

"You have a lot of room to talk about someone else. You . . ." She stopped and pointed to the giant. "You are as tall as the jolly green giant and as skinny as a bean pole!" She pointed to the next one, "You have so many bumps on your face you look like you have chicken pox, and you—are in desperate need of a toothbrush!" She looked down at me and reached out for my hand. I got to my feet and grabbed her hand. Addy looked back one last time. "Braxton's eyes are beautiful; you are just jealous," she finished and pulled me towards the main street.

I stared at her like I did not know who she was. She had never spoken out like that before. She had never stood up to anybody for any reason, but she stood up for me. I wanted to do something for her. I wanted to make her happy.

Mrs. Michaels was browsing through the sidewalk sale BonsWorth was having. We ran up to her, and Addyson showed her mom the cup of apple cider in her free hand.

"I forgot mine, I'll be right back." I let go of Addyson's hand, and ran back towards the court yard. It was not but a block over.

The blue tent came into my view. I pulled out all of the balled up dollar bills I had left in my pocket. My mom had given me twenty dollars the night before to spend at the festival, but I had seven dollars of my own. After buying the apple cider, I had twenty-five dollars exactly.

I saw my cider sitting on the grass, but I knew if I stayed gone too long Mrs. Michaels would come looking for me. I really wanted to surprise Addyson with the painting she wanted. I ran to the tent as fast as my legs would carry me. The same long-haired hippy who was there before was standing behind the small card table in the corner of the tent. Without speaking, I searched for the right canvas. I grabbed it up and took it to the hippy.

"I want this one please." The guy looked the picture over and looked back at me.

"Didn't you just come in here; where is your girlfriend?" He took the price tag off of the painting and placed it in the middle of a sheet of newspaper to wrap it up.

"She is waiting on me with her mother; I want to surprise her," I said, mentally hurrying the guy up. The guy just watched me with unasked questions; I was getting impatient.

"Twenty-five dollars, kid" the guy said, looking at me as if I did not have that much money. I pulled the balled-up money out of my pocket and placed it on the table.

"Twenty five exactly," I said, and took off out of the tent.

My mouth protested as I glanced one last time in the course of my cider.

"There you are I was starting to get worried." Mrs. Michaels and Addyson were walking towards me. I smiled at Addyson and handed her the bag.

"I had to pick something up. This is for you." I watched her eyes hit the bag; without opening it, she knew what it was. "Thanks, Brax!" Her arms came around my neck, and she squeezed me hard. It was the best feeling in the world.

—◊◊—

The water was losing its heat. I stood straight up and quickly washed before the water went totally cold. So many years ago, on that day at the festival, I promised to always protect Addyson. She was my best friend, and I loved her. Up until three days ago I thought we would always be best friends. How could she just let me go after sixteen years of friendship? I stepped out of the shower and dried off. Wrapping the towel around my waist, I walked to my room to get dressed. "I have to see her." I whispered to myself. I was going to the Michaels' house.

CHAPTER 5

Sunday! School started the next day. It had been three days since I had seen Braxton. It took a lot of explaining, lying rather, to my mom about why I would not accept Braxton's calls, or why I refused to see him. Mom knew something was wrong when she had to take me to get my hair cut. I joined yet another gym. I had to get my workouts in, since I would not be walking around the pond on our property daily, and I did not go over to Braxton's house with my parents for dinner Friday night.

He texted me thirty times in one day. I would read them and weep; I would cry until my stomach hurt. I cannot describe in words the pain that I felt. The last night I saw him, after he dropped me off, Braxton called for our nightly talk. I did not answer. The texts that broke my heart did not start until the next day. The abuse started on Friday afternoon, when I was supposed to text him to get my hair cut.

- Addy it is after five, where are you?
- Since I have not heard from you all day long, I am guessing your mom has kept you busy?? call me
- I just called your house and your mom says you are in bed. I know better, Addy, you're painting or reading, what is going on? Are you okay?
- Are you mad at me? Whatever I did I am sorry, just call me k?

I could not take it any more and cut my phone off. That was the first day. I told my soul it would get easier, but Sunday was the third day, and it was harder than the first.

—⁓—

I was on my way to the library, not the public library I would normally go to, but the university library. Braxton would not think to look for me there. On my way in, I ran into Mandi. Mandi was the closest thing to a friend I had. I had never called her, and we had never hung out, but she was nice to me at school. If we had classes together I would always sit beside her, and we usually had an enjoyable time together.

The way I felt when I saw her walking towards me was as if she was a best friend that had moved away for many years, and I was seeing her for the first time.

"Hey girl, are you and Braxton ready for school tomorrow?" The sound of his name rolling out of her mouth made my heart beat faster. I wondered how long it would take before people would stop mentioning us as if we were a married couple.

"Yeah, I am ready. How about you?" I was silently praying that she would not mention Braxton again. "Are you heading into the college?" she asked to change the conversation, thank goodness.

"Yeah, I am going to check out the library; want to come?" I asked, walking towards the entrance of the college.

"Sure" she said, almost eagerly.

After finding the library, we spent hours looking at books, talking about nothing, laughing, and I was having a fabulous time with her, until she spoke of him again.

"Where is Brax?" She was still giggling from the last painting we had seen. It certainly is unbelievable the things people label masterpieces. The pain hit me again, like a transfer truck.

"I don't know" I said simply with as little emotion as possible. I tried my best to play it off as though it was not a big deal.

"I am not used to seeing the two of you apart" she stated flatly.

"I am not used to being without him." I struggled to keep the tears back. *Do not destroy this, Mandi; I need you more than you will ever know*, I thought to myself.

I had decided an hour earlier that I was going to try to replace Brax with Mandi in my life. I had laughed, and felt more normal with her, than I had felt in days. Like the rest of the school, she was going to ask me questions about Braxton until she either figured it out, or drove me to another meltdown. Because I had not replied, Mandi was facing me, with her book closed, and an eyebrow arched, waiting for an answer.

"Do you want to have dinner at my house tonight? If you can stay for a while, I will tell you all about it." I managed to get the issue out without tears falling.

"Sure! That will be great; let me call my Mom." She pulled her cell phone out and walked towards the doors. I walked to the counter and checked out four books.

I found her outside, sitting on a bench in front of the college entrance. "OK, it's all good. Let's go." She seemed genuinely excited about coming over. I wondered if she was excited because I was going to tell her what was going on with Braxton and me, or if she was really excited about hanging out with me.

We walked to my house. On the way back, we talked about school and our class schedules. I was so happy to find out I had three out of four classes with her. Being with her would make being without Braxton bearable.

As soon as I walked in the house, Mom yelled out, "Braxton just left a few minutes ago; he is looking for you. He told me to tell you to call him." My heart broke.

"Okay, Mom. Come here for a second. I want you to meet someone," I yelled back.

Mandi whispered, "Are you going to call Braxton?" She looked so confused.

"No," I replied. "I'll explain after dinner." Mandi stared at me with utter disbelief and shock. I turned to face my mom as she walked into the room. "Mom this is Mandi. She is going to have dinner with us tonight, if that is okay with you." I knew it would be.

"Well, of course, it is so nice to meet you, Mandi. I am not used to Addy having a girlfriend over; it is nice to see that she is spending some time with more people." Mom was already walking back towards the kitchen. The questioning look she gave me didn't go unnoticed.

I threw my books on the couch and followed Mandi into the kitchen. Well, at least Mom would be happy about seeing a lot of Mandi. Hopefully I would feel the same. I introduced Mandi to my dad, right before we sat at the table to eat. Over all, I would say that my parents actually liked her. We laughed and talked like we had been best friends forever.

Mandi seemed to be shocked when she saw what I ate for dinner. I was used to it. People saw the size of me and expected me to eat four or five plates of food, and a whole cake or pie for dessert. When I ate a garden salad with a piece of toast and ice water, though she did not say a word, I could tell she was curious. Everyone else had spaghetti. On the other hand, I was surprised when I watched Mandi eat two full plates of food. She could not weigh more than 130 pounds, maybe less, and was eating like a horse.

Mandi's most astonishing feature was her eyes. Like Braxton, her eyes were so unique; they were as green as a blade of grass and seemed endless. I made a mental note to ask her later if she wore contacts.

Why couldn't I be like that? Why did this have to be me? I hated me. I hated my body. I hated what I was. I was exactly everything those mean kids called me at school. I wished someone could help me. I felt I was falling into self pity and depression . . . again. I pushed my almost full plate of salad aside. I was no longer hungry.

Mandi and I cleaned the kitchen, washing, drying, and putting away the dishes. Then we took off to my room. "Follow me." I said kind of excited to share my room with someone else. I knew she would be impressed. Well, Braxton and I always thought it was extremely cool.

We walked out of the patio doors to face our underground swimming pool. My parents had it installed when we found out swimming is one of the best ways to work out; I spent hours a day in that pool during the summer. Usually at night, once Braxton had left.

"You have a pool!" Mandi squealed in delight.

"Yes, we can go anytime you want," I said, suddenly panicking about getting into a bathing suit in front of her.

We continued to walk around the pool to the far side of the fence. There sat a miniature house. It had a mailbox by the porch that said Addy. We walked up on the porch; I took my keys out of my pocket, and opened the front door. Mandi walked in behind me "This is your room? This is so awesome, Addy; you have your own house!" She liked it; I could tell by the huge smile lighting up her face.

"The people who owned this house before us, kept a tanning bed in here. They had told my parents they put it out here because they had three very small children. They were scared one of them would get in it and get hurt." I threw my keys on my desk. "Well, it has almost everything except a kitchen. I do have a mini fridge over there with cold water in it if you want one." I could not help but smile; she was so excited. She made me excited about it, and it was my room. "We call it the play house," I said letting myself drop on my bed. Mandi belly-flopped onto my black and yellow beanbag chair.

I think she asked me a hundred questions about my room: "Is this your only room? Do you not have a room in the house? Do you have to go through the house to get out? Do you have a T.V., a computer? Did you paint all of these paintings?"

I am not sure if she took a breath at all. "Yes this is my only room; no room in the house. There is a gate to the side of my porch that lets me out to the street, I do have a T.V., I have a laptop, and, yes, all of these paintings are my own work, minus a few I have collected over the years." I took in a deep, exaggerated breath.

Her voice became low, and her face became serious, "Tell me about you and Braxton, Addy." She never looked at me. I felt a lump come into my throat. I composed my thoughts and began to tell her everything. I explained what he went through every single day of his life, because of me. Everything he missed out on because of me. I explained to her why I had to let him go and everything I would have to do to avoid him. I felt guilty for not calling him, for not telling him why. I hated that he thought he did something wrong, or that I was mad at him.

If I did not know anything else, I knew Braxton. If I told him the truth he would get angry with me, and never let me go through with it. He would have never left me. If he was going to, he would have done it by now. I felt like I had taken up enough of his life.

I had tears running down my face. I could not stop them from flowing. My breath was catching in my throat from sobbing so hard that I was jerking. I closed my eyes and took deep breaths, trying to calm down. I was so embarrassed; I honestly did not know Mandi well enough to be sharing those emotions with her. I could not help but wonder if I would ever see her again after that night.

When I finally found the nerve to look Mandi in the eyes, I noticed she was crying too. She stood from the beanbag and wrapped her arms around my neck, and hugged me for a long time. I tensed up at first. Only a second later I was grateful. I did not feel alone. I felt like I had someone who would help me get through it all. Again, she had no idea how badly I needed her. I wrapped my arms around her and hugged her back. As far as I knew, that was the first time in my life I had been hugged by another girl my own age.

I genuinely did not want Mandi to leave, but we both had to get up early and go to school. She left around 11 p.m. After she left, I remembered I had to go ask Dad to take me tomorrow and pick me up from school. I hated the idea of driving my beat-up car; like I didn't have enough to deal with already. I wanted to throw up just thinking about it. The bus wasn't an option. I would rather walk. The bus held more of my bad memories than even the lunch room did. I lied, again, and told Dad I had to be at school early to go to the library and sign up for painting classes. I lied about how Brax would not want to be there that early. I knew he thought something was strange, but he never said anything about it. Even Dad knew how Brax took care of me—used to take care of me.

I said goodnight to both Mom and Dad, and headed back to my room. I locked myself in my mini house, put on my night clothes, and turned the lights out. Working up the nerve; I finally turned my cell phone on. After a few minutes, my cell phone started repeatedly alerting me of new text messages. I closed my eyes and waited for the "Droid" to stop. Every time I got a text my phone would scream DROID in a transformer voice. Brax always used to say that he was waiting for it to transform into an evil transformer, like on the movie. Everything in my life reminded me of him. Everything . . . even my flippin' ringtone!

After a few minutes, silence fell over my room. I wanted to read his messages, I wanted to answer them I just did not want to hurt, and I did not want to hurt him either. I knew how selfish I seemed, but was it not more selfish to hold him down, to keep him from all of the chances he had passed up for a normal life?

I just could not find the courage to erase them without reading them. Fifteen new text messages to be exact; I touched the small envelope and began to read:

1 I haven't heard from you or seen you in 3 days Addy I have been worried. Can't you at least tell me what I did wrong-
2 I found your binder in my stuff, do you want me to give it to you at school, or can I bring it over there now? -
3 I don't deserve this Addy-
4 Where the hell are you at, you are not at home-
5 Please-
6 Damn Addy do you want me to beg-

My insides hurt so badly after reading that much I did not think I could read any more. I just wanted to text him. I wanted to go to his house. I wanted to beg him to forgive me and stop this from going any further. I made myself read on.

7   Fine I can do this too~

8   Don't you think I deserve to know why~

9   So I guess you don't want to be friends anymore~

10   You are just going to let me go . . . after all of these years~

11   Will I see you at school~

12   Do I still come and get you in the morning~

13   Damn it Addy I am getting pissed~

14   Do you care at all anymore~

15   Please Addy I will beg then, please just text me one letter to let me know your okay, call me and hang up, come over, do something . . . please~

I ached from the sobbing. I cried until I fell asleep. I was so exhausted I did not even hear the phone ringing.

CHAPTER 6

When Addy did not come out to the car Monday morning, I decided to knock on the door before I was late for the first day of school.

"Hey Mrs. Michaels, I have been waiting for Addy; do you mind if I go see if she is ready?" I knew she was going to tell me she was not there before she answered me.

"Well Braxton, she told her father and me that she had to be at school early this morning, and you didn't want to go that early, so her dad took her. They left about a half hour ago, I'm sorry." Mrs. Michaels was dressed for work, and obviously about to leave. She locked the door, shut it, and walked down the steps with me.

I was not going to lie; I was confused as hell, and hurt. This was not like Addy. We had two fights in our whole lives, and she did throw the silent treatment on me, but it did not last but about three hours. "Thanks Mrs. Michaels, I will catch up with her at school." I tried to smile at her. I saw the confusion on her face. I wanted to say, yeah, me too, but I did not. I just got in my car and headed to school.

Addyson was like a sister to me. She truly was my best friend. She knew me better than anyone else did. Until four days ago I thought I knew her. I replayed the last day I was with her in my head over and over again. Other than not going to the art museum, I could not think of anything I could have done to her. It just did not make sense. I realized how much she meant to me, and how much I needed her in my life. She was more than my best friend; Addyson made my life better, worth living. I had realized she was my life.

I pulled into the school parking lot fifteen minutes later. I had to almost the last one there. At that point, I did not have time to try to find

Addy. I had to go to homeroom straight away. When I walked in I was greeted by a few of my friends—Mandi was there, Dom and Tony were in there too. No Addy. I did not even know if I had any classes with her.

The teacher came in and greeted us all, took roll, and said we had fifteen minutes to chat before first period. I stood up and walked over to Mandi. I bent down beside her desk, so that we would be closer to eye level, and so that our conversation could be semi-private.

I could not help but grin as I noticed her face turn a bright red color. She had been crushing on me for a long time. Mandi was a genuinely sweet girl. She was pretty too. I loved her eyes. However, I only meant to be friends with her.

"Have you seen Addy?" I tried to hide my concern, but my voice failed me. "Yeah, I spent the day with her yesterday. I went over to her house and had dinner with her. She showed me around her house. She really has an awesome room, well mini-house really." She would not look into my eyes anymore. My freaky blue eyes had that effect on some people, on most people, actually.

"Sunday, did she say anything about me?" I could honestly say I was scared to hear her response. I was not sure what the hell I had done, but it was awful, really serious this time.

"Yeah, she talked about you a lot actually. I can't tell you what she said; I'm really sorry." Mandi looked into my eyes then quickly pulled her attention back to her desk.

"Please, Mandi, I just want to know what I have done to her. Can you tell me that?" I pleaded, and was not trying to hide it.

"Oh no, you didn't do anything to her. You have done nothing wrong, Brax. She said you wouldn't understand, and it's all her fault, but that's about all I can say. I promise she isn't mad at you in the least. I know she misses you."

I thought I saw a tear form in her eyes, and was about to ask her what was wrong when the bell rang, indicating time for the first period. "Thanks, Mandi. When you talk to her again, tell her I am begging her to call or text me." For some reason, I did not feel ashamed, or embarrassed at all about begging her. I mean, I was a guy; most guys would not do that, right? With Addyson everything was different.

I walked to my desk, grabbed my backpack, and took off to the water fountain down the hall. That is where she was supposed to be, waiting on me. People did not dare pick on her in front of me. I had beat up a few boys for doing it, and told off several girls for it. I could not stand it, it was not even Addy's fault; she ate better than I did. I did not think she would admit it, but she was embarrassed to eat in front of me. Not just me either, I mean anyone at all, minus maybe her parents.

Over the years, I had been around Addy so much for so long, I could see past the weight; to what she was supposed to look like. I saw her brown and yellow eyes; they seemed to look through me. In them, I could see the real Addy. She was funny, caring, loving, and passionate; sometimes she was wild and crazy. She was so brave. I looked into her eyes, and she made me want to be an upstanding man. I wanted to protect her from all the assholes around her. I wanted to listen to her when she needed to talk, and hug her when she needed to cry. I wanted to be her best friend.

We had never gone that long without talking to each other, ever. I did not see her every day, especially in the summer. We both went on separate vacations with our families. We always did text, even if it was just to say good morning or goodnight, but we had never gone more than a few hours without contact.

I had almost made it to the water fountain when Carri Richards stopped me. "Braxton, how was your summer? I sent you an invitation to my summer bash; I was really hoping you would show up." She squealed at me. Her hand was rubbing all over my chest. I felt abused for a second. I grabbed her wrist lightly to stop her.

"Hey, Carri! Yeah, sorry about that, but Addyson's must have been lost in the mail, because she didn't get one. So I took her to a movie that night." She could not look into my eyes. I hated my eyes; they were so freakish. People never held a real conversation with me; it was usually with my forehead or my lips, and some people would even look away altogether. Except Addy. She said God gave me my eyes to be unique. She would stare into my eyes and it seemed she could see straight to my soul. She was not scared of me or intimidated. I would even say she liked them. Besides my mom, she was the only other person that did though. My dad would not even look into them.

Carri's voice turned low, snapping me back to the moment. "No, it didn't get lost; I didn't send her one. She wasn't invited. I only invite my friends and she is not my friend." She tried her best to look into my eyes for more than a millisecond to make sure I understood fully.

Disgusted, I replied, as cold as I could, "Then neither am I."

Carri had no problems staring into my back; I could feel her gaze like hot daggers, as I walked off towards the water fountain. Addy was not there. She was going to talk to me, whether she liked it or not. I would find her, and she would give me an explanation. I walked back the way I had come, back to my own class. I was blazing mad, and I knew I was not hiding it well. Between Carri and her ignorance, and Addy not being there waiting on me, I was furious.

My heart broke thinking about how many people might have picked on her. Did people not consider that, if she could help her weight, she would? Did people think that Addy wanted to be overweight and tortured every single day? It was the same with freckles, glasses, braces, and birthmarks; all things people could not change. People who are overweight because of their eating habits, I am sure, if they had their choice, would not have the problem. Nobody is perfect; me and my freak show eyes are no exception.

What amazed me the most about Addy was she never called any of them names back. She could have easily found an imperfection with every single person that picked on her. Like Carri, and her oddly shaped ears. They looked like saucer plates. She could have put ten earrings in one of those ears. Addy never said a word.

I hoped to catch her at lunch; I had an awful feeling she would not be at any of our meeting spots. I walked into English with only one thing on my mind, finding Addyson.

CHAPTER 7

The first day of junior year was the worst first day of school I had ever had. It wasn't so much because of the teasing and picking, but because I had never, never, started a school year without Braxton. Thank God I had Mandi; she had actually stepped up to the plate. I told her where to meet me, so we could walk to our classes together. We had the first three classes together and first lunch. Fourth session was going to be the worst.

I did not have many places to hide in school. I had a feeling I would run into Braxton eventually. I played the scene out in my head over and over again. What would I do? I had a plan. If I saw him, I would just keep walking and act as if I hadn't. The problem was I did not know if I would be able to go through with it.

I had to go the long way to first period, so that I would avoid the water fountain where I was supposed to meet Brax—assuming he was still trying to catch me. I knew him; he would not give up, not until he got a convincing enough reason for my disappearance. I still had not figured out what to say to him about that. The truth would not be strong enough for him. I hated to lie to him. I did not want to hurt him. I just wanted him to live a little. I felt that once he realized how happy he would be, he would understand.

"Hey girl, have you seen Brax?" Mandi asked as she turned to walk in the other direction towards our first period class.

"No, not yet anyway." I looked down at my feet as I walked.

"Well, I have homeroom with him. He told me to tell you something." She had a grin on her face.

I knew that Mandi had a long time crush on Brax. Of course, a lot of girls did. Her face turned a light shade of pink. She must have been thinking about him. I smiled too, as his face flashed before my mind's eye.

"He said he wants you to call or text him. He wants to know what he has done wrong." I could see the pity come across her face as her words burned holes in my heart. "I told him that you said he had done nothing wrong, that it was your fault, not his. I also told him I knew for sure you missed him." I could have hugged her right then.

"Oh, Mandi, I am so glad you told him that. I have wanted to tell him that for days." I walked in silence for a moment, rolling her words around in my mind.

"Did he ask me to call him before or after you told him it was my entire fault?" I asked with high hopes that it was before. That would mean he had enough information. If he still asked after she told him, he was not satisfied with Mandi telling him and would still expect an explanation from me.

"After . . . why?"

I moaned, Nope it was not enough for him. "Just wondering," I replied, standing in front of the class room. I took a deep breath and walked in with my head hung, Mandi following, almost stepping on my heels. "I will explain it all to him one day, when he will understand, but until then, I don't know what to tell him."

"Well, you better come up with something quick." Mandi grabbed my shoulder "Like right now!" The sudden pull on my shoulder made me stop, and I turned to look at her. She was staring in front of me. I turned around quickly to be face-to-face with Braxton.

"So we have English Literature together this year. Of course, if my best friend had called or texted me in the last four days, I would have known that already." To anyone else his voice would have been cold and hard. I knew what it undoubtedly was—hurt. I looked into his beautiful crystal blue eyes, trying hard to think of what to do next. Mandi ended up being not so much help, after all. She ran to the back of the classroom and held two desks, side by side.

What was I going to do? All the plans, the idea I had come up with just flew out the window. The pain in those eyes and strain in his voice made my voice break. "Braxton, I can't talk to you right now. I just . . . I mean . . . I need to . . ." I took a deep breath and tried my best to get my heart to quit racing. I held his gaze as long as possible without busting out crying. I finished, "I just can't right now, Braxton."

I walked to the back of the class and sat in the desk that Mandi had saved for me. I looked down, glaring holes into my desk and refused to look up; I knew I would look straight at Braxton.

"He is just standing there in the middle of the class; he is just staring at you, his mouth hanging wide open . . . oh . . . he is walking back here." Mandi was whispering through her teeth, trying not to let her mouth move. My whole body began to tense up at Mandi's words.

The teacher's voice boomed over the chatter of the class as the door slammed shut behind him. "Good morning, class and welcome to English Literature. I am Mr. Soesbee, for those of you who do not know me . . ." I had finally found the nerve to look up, thinking Brax must have gone and sat down in his desk by then. When I looked up, he was still standing in the same spot, staring right at me.

"Addy, come and sit beside me," he said with pleading eyes. The teacher stopped talking, realizing for the first time that Brax was standing and talking in the middle of his classroom. The whole class had their eyes on him, but his eyes were only on me. I wanted to slide through the floor, and under the school. I knew I turned every shade of red ever created, maybe even some purple.

"Braxton is that you, son? Sit down. It's time to start class," Mr. Soesbee said, grinning. Everyone knew Braxton, and everyone loved him, including the teachers. Anyone else would have had a good, hard scolding for pulling a stunt like that.

"Mr. Soesbee, I mean no disrespect, but I will not sit down until Addyson comes to sit beside me." He never took his eyes off of me, even while speaking to Mr. Soesbee. Every person in the classroom made some kind of noise. Most of the guys said, "Gross!" or "Sick!" while all of the girls said, "Oh, how sweet!" or "Why the hell does he want to sit beside her?" One girl even said, "Braxton, come sit beside me." She didn't skip a beat as she told the boy sitting beside her to move.

Braxton finished with: "Like you always do." I didn't know if anyone else heard him, due to all of the noise.

Mandi whispered, "What the hell is wrong with you? Get up and go sit with him."

I glared at her and said "What a lot of help you are!" I could hear my heart beating in my ears. I was shaking, and honestly I thought I was going to throw up. I could not stand this attention on me. All of those people and their judging eyes. They were not just on me right then; they were judging my Braxton too. I started to get angry.

I looked back into his eyes, taking my flashing eyes off Mandi.

"Brax, please I am begging you. Please go sit down." The internal explosion was coming; I felt my chest burning and tears rising in my eyes with every rise and fall of my chest. He stood there still. His gaze filled with pain, anger, confusion, questions, pleading—with so much care and compassion.

"I will not sit down until you come and sit beside me, Addy, where you always sit." The sternness was gone from his voice, and it reminded me of when we were about nine years old. A person, possibly the only person ever, had said something mean about his eyes. As I witnessed the incident back then, the pain and questions in his sweet, beautiful, eyes were apparent; just like today.

Defeated, I stood from my desk; I jammed all of my stuff back into my book-bag and stomped past him. He smiled from ear to ear, fueling my anger. The whole class clapped, much to my surprise. I wasn't sure if they were congratulating or mocking, and which one of us or both.

Once Mr. Soesbee began to talk again, I leaned over to Brax and glared into his eyes. "That is the first time in our lives you have ever embarrassed the T-Total shit out of me, Braxton; not to mention yourself. Do you know what people are going to be saying about you now? People used to think you just felt sorry for me; they used to think you were just protective, because you saw me as your sister, now . . . Good Lord God . . . now people are going to be saying . . . Braxton, the sexiest boy in school, is in love with the fattest, ugliest, girl in school. The one thing, the very thing I did not want to happen to you, is sure to happen now!"

I was yelling. The whole class had heard me. "You think I am the sexiest boy in school?" His words seemed to bounce off of every wall in the school. You might as well have given him a megaphone and let him yell it over the whole city. I looked into his eyes; he was serious. Out of everything I had just said that was the only thing he heard? He had no idea how beautiful he was.

I grabbed my backpack and stood up. "Brax, if you would stop spending all of your time with me, out of pity for the fat girl, you would see that every girl in this school wants to be with you . . ."

I couldn't stop the tears from streaming down my face. I did not know what was more humiliating, the whole class hearing me tell Braxton he was the sexiest boy in school or the raw emotion my eyes were displaying.

"You can have a normal, happy life, Braxton, that I will not have any time soon. I can't give that life to you, and you can't have a life being associated with me." I was down to a whisper, trying with my whole body to steady my voice and calm the tears. "I refuse to be the cause of it any more, Brax. Please, I am begging you to live . . . for me. Go to parties, play sports, hang out with your friends, go on dates, fall in love, be happy and stop worrying about me. I love you too much to be the cause of you dreading school, having to protect me, and walk me to classes, so these assholes won't be cruel. You have done your time. Now live."

I darted towards the door as fast as possible. Mr. Soesbee was asking me where I was going. I knew he didn't think I was staying in that class. I was going home and, after that day, I wanted to quit school altogether. I had my hand on the door knob, when a guy I didn't know in the back of the class yelled, "Like anyone could ever love your fat ass!" I didn't even bother to acknowledge the statement.

Braxton was on his way to the back of the class room, apparently to come to my rescue yet again. Had he not heard anything I had just said? Brax grabbed the guy's shirt and had his arm reared back in the air to punch him in the face. Mr. Soesbee's voice never rang out to stop him. "Braxton don't! Just stop, Brax. You cannot win a losing battle. Just stop, please!"

His eyes were so beautiful; I stared at him for only a second longer. He let the boy go. The boy pulled his shirt down, trying his best to wipe Braxton's fist print away. He laughed nervously, trying to relinquish his embarrassment. "*I* love her," Braxton said to the red-faced punk.

I walked out of the door. I walked out of school. I walked home. I went into my mini-house and shut the door behind me. I lay on my bed and rolled the whole morning over in my head; every single word, every single look, every single action that anyone made. It was like a broken record freshly burned into my brain. I told him. I told him the whole truth. It wasn't exactly what I had planned, but he now knew my disappearance was not his fault. At least, at that, I was satisfied.

I was waiting for my parents to get home. I was going to come clean with them. I was going to tell them the truth. I would beg them to let me quit school; beg them to home school me. I just prayed they would listen to me.

CHAPTER 8

I wanted to go after her. I wanted to comfort her and ask her the many questions that ran through my scrambled brain. I stood over Josh, with his agitated face, and punk attitude, which gave me no pleasure. Who was he to judge her? He had braces, but not just normal metal braces with little rubber-bands on them. He had these enormous rubber-bands that seemed to be connected from his top jaw to the bottom. When he talked, his mouth would snap open and shut like a robot. He was so self-conscious about his mouth that he had learned how to communicate with his teeth clenched shut nearly all of the time. To Josh it seemed more normal; to everyone else it was the freakiest damn thing ever.

It was something Josh could not help—his braces, or whatever the hell they were—something he had no control over. If he had not had that contraption in his mouth, he would be walking around with an overbite from Hades. Something Josh could help was his asshole attitude. I had no sympathy for him. Pity . . . all of the heartbreaking words that Addy had screamed at me came rolling back into my brain.

I looked around, still standing over Josh. I glared at him. I bent down eye-level with him, allowing him no choice but to keep eye contact with me. He was more nervous then, more so than when I had my fist prepared to pound in his face. I guess sometimes my freakish eyes were a blessing.

"The next time you say something hateful, cruel, or mean to Addy, I will beat your face in, until it is unrecognizable to even your own mother. Do not look at her, do not think about her, don't talk to your scum bag friends about her; she is a better person than you will ever be." I wanted my words to seep into his skin and burn like liquid acid. I wanted him to hold the revulsion I felt for him at that moment.

I pushed off of his desk with both of my hands; my mind was already repeating everything Addy had said before she left. I wanted to go after her. I walked back to my desk and sat down, trying so hard to separate my thoughts.

I apologized to Mr. Soesbee. "I am sorry for the interruption." I had a considerable amount of respect for Mr. Soesbee; he was also the football coach and had been after me for a few years to play. I had taken his weightlifting class for the previous two years, counting that year, and I would admit I had considered playing football. I just did not want to be like the football freaks. Most of them were the cruelest people in the school. After watching the horrible things they had said and done to Addy, it was hard to be associated with them. It was not just Addy they would tease; it was every person, male or female, in the school, that they thought deserved to be teased. I am sure they had talked about my eyes, but never to my face. I would have liked Addy to come watch me play, but I knew that would never happen.

Mr. Soesbee smiled at me and nodded as if to say, 'hey he deserved it', but said, "Open your books to page fifteen." His words trailed off in my mind. I could not focus on anything but what had just happened.

It hurt me more than she would ever know that she thought I was her friend out of pity. "Pity for the fat girl" she had said. I was almost seventeen years old. I made my own decisions, and could not have given a rat's ass what anybody thought about it. I was proud to be her friend. If anyone else had taken the time to get to know her, they would have loved her, too.

I smiled to myself as I thought about some of her words. I could not help it. I wished she had talked to me alone about it, and I hated that she was so upset. She thought I was the sexiest boy in the school, did she? She never said anything to me about thinking that. She thought I did not go out and do more things out of pity for her. I stayed with her, because I would rather be with her than any other person in that school.

Addy was quick-witted and made me laugh until my sides hurt. When she laughed, it was contagious; you could not help but join her. She would do anything to help a person; all you had to do was let her know the problem. She loved to play in the rain, and still, at sixteen years of age, would make a mud pie. She was so smart and hungered for knowledge; she loved to read and knew a vast array of useless information, and, when she would paint. It was phenomenal. She could capture the emotion of a scene. It was like looking through her eyes at how she saw the image in front of you. Addy made everything beautiful. These were just a few things those complete morons would have known about her if they had just given Addy a chance.

The class went by in a blur. When the bell rang, I ran to the bathroom that was on the west side of the school. I knew she would not be there, but I had to make sure. She was not.

I slowly walked to the other side of the school to my next class. I made it to History class, walked in and sat down in the first desk I came across. I texted Addy a half a dozen times, with no response; I was not surprised.

"Did you see Addyson?" Mandi's voice was so quiet and cautious I thought, for a second, I had imagined it.

"No, I didn't," I replied. She seemed to be worried about Addy. It seemed she was going to be a loyal friend to her. She spent all day Sunday with her. I could not pretend I was not a little jealous of that. Was Mandi going to take my place in Addyson's life?

I glanced back at her, noticing that she had picked out a desk in the very back of the room. This was our second class together plus homeroom. I did not know why she was so shy with me; Mandi was pretty. She had a lot of friends, and from what I could tell, I could not see anything wrong with her at all. Personality-wise, I mean, nor physically. She was a lovely person. She saw me looking at her and blushed. I grinned at her.

Addy had said that, if I would take the time to notice, a lot of girls liked me. To be honest, I had not noticed any. Other than Carri, who was blunt, running up to me, putting her hands all over me like we knew each other, and Mandi, who turned red every time I looked at her.

I heard two voices, talking crazy loud, in the hall. They sounded as they were getting closer to the door. "Yeah, he told me that Brax said he loved her! That is so gross," one whiney voice said as the other laughed loudly.

The other girl replied, "Well, I would have him in a heartbeat. Josh told me that Braxton did not seem to know how many girls liked him, and can you believe that. I do not know anyone that would not date him . . . hell; some guys might even go out with him! Everybody knows that Addyson wants him . . . like Braxton would ever be more than her friend . . . Please, he just feels sorry for her!" Laughter exploded from both voices.

I glanced back at Mandi. "This is what she did not want," she said as she shrugged and shook her head.

The two people the voices belonged to appeared in the doorway. The laughter stopped when they met my glare. Both girls turned a burning shade of red. They knew I had heard them. They quickly walked past me, whispering and giggling like immature fifth graders.

What was I going to say to them? The same things I had been saying for the last twelve years? I heard Addy's voice ring through my ears, "You cannot win a losing battle", followed by the images, the look on her face, the sadness, the pain. It ripped through me, and I forcefully stood from my desk.

I walked over to the two bimbos and smiled. I stared at them. I tried my best to act as if I wanted to talk to them; I kept my face straight. I took long deep breaths to calm the anger long enough to get what I wanted to say out calmly.

They looked at each other, blushing from embarrassment. As soon as they realized I was not going to cuss them out, they began to flirt. "Well, Brax, it's good to see you. How was your summer?" said 'Barbie' as she leaned over her desk, allowing her gigantic, blonde curls to fall around her shoulders. She batted her eyelashes at me, pouted her lips, and acted as if she had never said those terrible things seconds earlier.

I went down to my knees and smiled as sweetly as possible. I noticed she did not look away from my gaze, not even for a second. This girl was confident, that was for sure. A growing laugh began to form on the inside of me as I noticed that her nose was beefy close up. To add to the size of it, there was a Herculean pimple scar right at the end of her nose that was covered with layers of makeup, which made it look like a blood red mole. No one is perfect.

Before I could say anything, she handed me her phone number, written on a scrap of paper, with a giant heart and a smiley face on it. "Call me sometime; maybe we can go out," she said in a deep voice.

I raised an eyebrow and stared at the number for a moment. I ripped the tiny paper into a thousand miniature pieces and put it back in her hand. "I just wanted to let you know that I would rather be with a man, than to be with either one of you fake fronters. Addy has more to offer a person than the two of you will ever possess in your whole lives put together."

The anger was impossible to hide, in my voice, in my eyes; my whole body was showing the disgust and hatred I had for these two, and everyone like them.

I smiled as her jaw dropped open in total shock; she kept looking back at Barbie number two, she could not think of what to say. She frantically looked around the room to see who else had witnessed the display of pure rejection. The only other person was Mandi, and she was laughing uncontrollably in her seat, with her hand plastered over her mouth. I smiled at Mandi. It felt pretty smart; I felt pretty solid.

Barbie's real name was April, and her friend was Della. I never would have thought either of them would want to go out with me. I know that I would have never considered going out with either of them. I am not into the whole slave relationship.

You know what I mean: When you date a girl that just wants to show you off; as the man, you have to put her on a pedestal. Dress in polos and khakis, only the most expensive and most popular of name brands, of course, and accompany her to every social event that is ever planned. You do not talk; you just silently stand behind her, and look handsome. You laugh at all of her jokes, all the while, she talks about you as if you are not even standing there, bragging to her superficial friends about all of your accomplishments. All of this just to prove that her man is better than yours—slave relationship . . . not for me.

The classroom began to fill up with students, almost as if they had timed missing my perfect rejection. It would have been sweeter, if all of those people had been in there to witness it too, and not just Mandi and me.

I sat at my desk, looking through my cell phone. I looked through all of the pictures, though not one of them had Addy in them, only because she refused to allow me to take her picture. It was pictures of things we had done together. So many pictures; a decade worth of memories: like the ducks on the pond at her house. The water park inside of concord mills—we did not go swimming, but I would have loved it. Christmas, birthday parties, her mini-house, her paintings, my room, my house, and the beach. All of the pictures tugged at my emotions; I wanted to laugh at some of them, thinking of something that had happened. There are extremely few of my memories that do not include Addy.

I felt as if I had lost my best friend. The look on her face as tears ran down her cheeks was burned into my brain. I felt tears running down my cheeks in History class. I frantically wiped them away and tried my best to focus on the pictures. I was going to our meeting spot after that class . . . God, I hoped she would be there.

The teacher finally took roll. "Addyson Michaels . . . Addyson Michaels . . ."

Giggles filled the room, along with whispers and glances at me. I looked back at Mandi. She had her head bent down into her desk, and she was texting on her cell phone. That was why she sat in the back. Addyson had this class too. I knew she must have left school altogether. I picked up my book-bag and headed out; it was only a few steps to the door.

"Mr. Carmen, where are you going?" asked the teacher, looking at me over the frame of his tiny glasses. "Home," I said, as I shut the door behind me.

I was running through the halls. My heart was beating out of my chest. I had never been this emotional over anything. I did not even bother going to the office—no, I was going to Addyson's house. I was almost sure she would be there, and her parents would be at work. I smiled. She would not be able to get away, and she would have to talk to me. I deserved some answers to my questions.

I was in my car and on my way to Addy's house.

CHAPTER 9

I don't know what to do from here. I didn't know that one basic thing would cause my life to spiral out of control. I am so tired of fighting Brax, much less my own feelings. I am just so tired.

I am sitting on my bed, staring at a blank canvas. I want to paint Braxton's eyes, the deep, endless pools of turquoise blue that I personally can fall into and drown peacefully. I pull my paints out, and mix the various shades of color together to make his specific shade of blue. I took all of my brushes, and sponges, cloths, and a razor blade and spread them all out over my desk. With the first stroke, as the perfect shade of blue bled across the canvas, I could see my vision.

I spent the next hour desperately working to finish what I longed to see. Tears started to stream down my own face as the picture of his in class came to my mind. I never wanted to hurt him. The more his beautiful eyes came alive on canvas the faster I worked.

As I stood back and stared at my piece, it was no longer an empty canvas, but the picture of perfection, at least in my opinion—Braxton Carmen's eyes. The image of his eyes, the bridge of his nose and his eyebrows; I think I could paint him with my eyes closed. The only difference in this painting is, his eyes held no pain, no confusion, no regret, no questions, no shock, or anxiety—no, just happiness, peace, and the caring love I witnessed today in class.

I didn't hear the door open. I stumbled over to my desk and began to clean up my mess. I feel drained and exhausted. I noticed I ruined my shirt and my Capris. I am used to that. But I genuinely like this shirt. "Crap monkey," I whispered.

I turned towards the bathroom. "Braxton . . ." my words trail off, staring at him as he is staring at the painting I had just finished. I had painted that painting with such raw emotion, it was powerful. But I was not sure how he was going to take this painting. I honestly had rather him not see it at all.

I became exceedingly self conscious of it and rushed to cover it. He put his hand over the top of the painting to stop me from hanging the blanket of white silk over it. "Is this how you see me, Addy? I mean, I know that is me. But I see my eyes as a curse, not . . . well, not anything like this." He pointed to the canvas, still staring at it.

I waited a few seconds longer and moved his hand to drop the silk. "No, this is not how I see you, Brax; this is how I want to see you."

His eyes turn towards me at my words. His mouth went into a flat line. Before his thoughts could run wild, I continued.

"Now I see those same eyes, full of pain, and sorrow, confusion and maybe even a little regret, but more than anything I see pity." I close my eyes, I refuse to cry. I refuse to go mental.

"You have no idea what it's like Braxton. To be the butt of every joke, to feel self conscious about everything you do, everything you say, the clothes you wear, the way you walk, the things that are normally embarrassing to any normal person are triple embarrassing for me. I refuse to eat in front of just about anybody; I don't know why, I just feel like I am being judged by every single person around me, no matter what. It is hell, Brax, and I do not want this life for you. Why can't you understand that?"

He stared at me with angry eyes. I waited impatiently for him to pull his thoughts together. "Why can't you understand that I am with you because I want to be with you? I don't know what it feels like to be overweight, Addy, but I know what it's like to have an imperfection."

I interrupted him. "Wait! What? What are you talking about, Brax? What imperfection?" I asked, laughing from the shock that he could think he was anything less than perfect.

He laughed. "My eyes, Addy, I have the eyes of a damn dog! People will not even look into them—well, most people—for more than a few seconds, like they are looking at some hideous birth defect, something gruesome, or a horrible injury that turns their stomachs." He looked straight at me to prove his point. I stared right back, as if he was the dumbest person alive. I could not believe what I was hearing.

"You are so stupid. Obviously this is very real to you, but it is not the truth. People cannot stare into your beautiful eyes because you are intimidating, Brax; you are smart and confident, you are not judgmental, usually, and have morals, and demand the same respect as you give. There are so many people, including myself, that cannot do that. Now I know there are people who are scared of the abnormal. Your eyes are very abnormal. But there are many, many more that can't return your gaze because you stare through to their soul; they are afraid you will uncover the real person hidden inside of them."

I broke eye contact and put my hand on the back of my neck. My eyes were glued to the floor. His words had me shaking my head, and I was trying to control my temper. I noticed I was shaking from head to toe. Was it because of his words, or the absolute fact that he was standing in my room after such a raw and embarrassing display of emotion?

"The reason I can hold your gaze is because I know you." I finally looked back up at him. "I know everything about you. The happiness and peace that is in that painting has been long gone; every great once in a while I will see it for a flash, but not often."

I grab the painting and easily place it against the wall on the floor. I made my eyes focus on my feet and closed the distance between me and the edge of my bed. I want to relax for just a second before I explode.

"I know you have a million questions, Brax. I can't answer all of them . . ." He tried to interrupt me and I stopped him. "Let me finish okay?"

He sat on the chair at my desk. He ran his hand through his hair and let out a sigh of exasperation. He turned to face me and rolled so close our knees were touching. He bent over with his elbows on his knees. His eyes were crystal clear and unconditionally focusing on me. I had his full attention. I couldn't blow this opportunity, but I had no idea how to make him understand. I said the first thing that came to my mind. I was not thinking of the consequences or anything else. I just blurted out, "I am leaving, Braxton."

His eyes flashed fear. His warm hands covered both of mine and squeezed harder than he would mean to. I squeezed his hands back nervously trying to think of what to say next. "I am going to my aunt's house in New York until the summer." I felt his face on our hands. I closed my eyes begging myself to stay strong. "I will be gone for ten months. I hope that when I come back, I will see the painting in reality." I sat quiet, waiting on a response from him.

"Why, Addyson? I don't want to be away from you. You are my best friend; I have never been away from you for more than a week! Let me go with you. I know your aunt Mae wouldn't mind; she loves me, and I love her. Please just let me go too. We will have a blast together."

He finally looked up, and I saw the tears I thought I had heard in his voice. I broke and the tears came flowing down my face. I instantly wrapped my arms around his neck and hugged him as tight as I could. The force of his arms wrapping around me was shocking, and instantly I was embarrassed. How many fat rolls did he feel? Did he have to stretch his arms as far as he could to get all the way around me? Were his hands even able to do so?

I pulled away quickly but not forcefully. "You can't go with me, Braxton. I have to go alone," I lied.

"Promise me, Addy that you're going to keep in touch with me; Call and text me." He stood to his feet, changing from upset to angry. "This is not fair to me, Addy; you are not going to just leave me for ten damn months as if we never existed!"

His eyes are alive and almost on fire. He moved quite close to my face, eye to eye. "I promise you, if you don't keep in touch with me, and I mean every day, I will . . . I swear to God . . . I will come to New York." He was like two people in one. He was going from pleading to angry with every sentence he spoke. I will not lie, it almost sounded as if he thought of us as a couple, and, for that, I loved him more.

His eyes were soft. "I love you, Addy; you are my best friend, and you're like blood to me. I am not going to let you end our friendship because you think I can't handle what people think about me. If I wanted to go do things without you, I would. If I wanted to go out on dates, I would. If I wanted to play ball, I would. You say you know me, Addy, but I am starting to think you don't!" The anger was draining out of him, and he looked like a young boy again.

His words seeped into my insides. I felt a little stupid, a little embarrassed, but mostly relieved. There was a small part of me that thought if I hadn't been here he would do all of those things. "I promise I will keep in touch with you every day . . . okay?" I lied again.

I did not even think about going to New York. It was the first thing that came to mind. But the more I thought about it, as hard as it would be to leave him, the better the idea was sounding.

Braxton's phone started ringing—*Simple Man* by Lynard Skynard. He stood straight up, never taking his eyes off of me, and answered his phone. I could actually hear his mother screaming at him all the way over here on the bed. He was getting fussed at for leaving school today. He turned around and walked closer to the front door, glaring out of the window. He finally said through clenched teeth, "I am on my way now." Frustrated, he slammed the phone shut.

He turned back to face me. "I have to go." He grinned slightly, pointing in the direction of his car. I could see how frustrated he truly was. To be honest, I didn't want him to go. If he didn't leave soon, there was no way I would be able to go through with this New York thing. Totally assuming Mom and Dad weren't going to freak out at the idea of me going for the whole school year.

I stood from my bed and walked over to him. "I'll see you tomorrow at school. It's not like I will be leaving in the morning." I was suddenly curious about how soon I would have to leave; I couldn't complain, as I have gotten myself into this mess.

"So you will be in school tomorrow?" His voice was hopeful but skeptical.

"Yes I will, but you don't have to walk me to my classes. You don't have to sit beside me in class, and you don't have to sit with me at lunch. I am also riding with Dad from now on, so don't come by here in the morning." With everything I named off, his hope faded away.

"I will still talk to you; of course, I just want you to spend some time with some of your other friends, okay? If you want, you can come to the house for dinner the night before I leave?" I regretted it as soon as I said it, but what did I expect? He might love me as a sister, but my feelings had changed, into seeing him as something much more than a brother; I was head over heels in love with him. I would easily have chosen the teasing, and torments over having to spend every single minute of my life, staring into the eyes of the boy I could never have.

"I am going to be here in the morning to pick you up and you better be waiting on me. I am also going to eat lunch with you. I will not walk you to class if you insist, but I honestly want to. So, if you change your mind, text me. I expect a text tonight too, by the way. I text you every night and tell you goodnight; I have not received one back in four days."

He moved closer, putting his hands on both of my shoulders. I tensed up under the feeling of his warm hands. "Promise, Addy?"

I would do anything for him, anything. "Okay, Braxton . . . I promise."

—∾—

I spent the next three hours thinking of what the hell I was going to tell my parents. I had already called Aunt Mae and talked to her about it. To my relief she was totally excited about it. A small part of me was hoping she would protest, and I could back out of this whole foolish thing.

"Yes, yes, I am so excited!" I almost dropped the phone on the floor. Aunt Mae was screaming into the phone. "Greeeaat . . ." I tried so hard to sound excited; I mean, it was my idea. I threw up a little, realizing this was actually working out—so far anyway. I still had to get through my parents; there was still a fifty-fifty chance of not going.

I walked into the kitchen; Mom had not started cooking yet and Daddy was sitting at the table looking over some mail.

"I need to talk to you both. Mom, can you come and sit with Daddy and me?" My stomach flipped, and my voice cracked a little. I noticed I was wringing my hands in circles remarkably fast. Dad pushed his mail to the side, and they were both looking at me with a concerned look on their faces, waiting on me to speak.

Before I started I said a silent prayer. God help me! I screamed. "I want to go to New York and stay with Aunt Mae for this school year." Well . . . that was blunt, more than I had hoped it would be, but it was out in the open, and sucking all the oxygen out of the room.

Mom and Dad looked back and forth at each other. Dad was stammering, and Mom looked like I had hit her in the stomach with a baseball bat. I quickly spoke up. "It doesn't have anything to do with you two at all. It's for me." I suddenly remembered two doctors I had found on the Internet that specialized in unexplained obesity. "There is a doctor in New York that specializes in hard-to-diagnose weight gain. I really want to go and see him." I was telling the truth for the first time in four days. "I also have checked out the painting programs in the new school I will start." Oh. My. God. I had not even thought about having to start a new school, A NEW SCHOOL. Do you know how much attention a new student gets? Imagine being the new student and weighing over two hundred pounds! I know my face turned green. I picked up mom's water and drank almost the entire glass; that way when I threw up my guts later, it wouldn't be acid!

"I have seriously thought this through," I lied yet again—I was making a habit of this. "What if this doctor can help me," I said, thinking for a second about that possibility . . . all of this would be worth it, if I came home a new person . . . right? We all three sat in silence.

I was turning over the idea of telling Mom and Dad about what happened today at school, but I decided against it. Mom would think I just wanted to run from the problem and Dad would say to take a few days to think it over. If I did that, I knew I would back out all together.

Dad was the first to speak. "Addy, let your mother and me talk about this, and we will give you our decision after dinner. That's more than fair, don't you agree?" I have my dad's eyes. When I look into his eyes, I feel loved.

My mom is beautiful. I often wondered, if I ever lost this weight, if I would look like her; I so hoped so. "I know I am asking a lot from the two of you. But I will be back. And please consider that this could change my life forever." I felt slightly guilty for using their love for me to convince them to let me go. Especially when I was not a hundred percent sure I could even go through with this. I felt the heat rising back up in my throat, threatening to spew out at any moment. That was an understatement; my life was going to change alright.

I stood from the table and walked back to my room. My laptop was on; I looked up loads of information about the area Aunt Mae lived in, what school I would attend, the address of the doctors I would see, and a blog about New York.

I have been to so many doctors, I had learned over the years to never get my hopes up too high. But I couldn't help but think that if this doctor could help me, it would be worth all of this.

I also found tons of museums, and so many art programs it was unreal. New York is enormous compared to North Carolina and I felt myself getting terribly excited about that part. I had only been to Aunt Mae's once, when Brax and I were extremely young. He was right; she loved him to death. I am not sure why, as he spent the whole time making fun of her accent. But she made fun of his just as quick. We both have that southern drawl; it's unmistakable and impossible to hide.

Maybe this would be the best thing that had happened to me and Braxton.

—∾—

All three of us ate dinner without speaking much at all. After the dishes were washed, dried, and put away, we all sat at the table in the same spots as earlier. "We have talked about it, and we have come to a decision."

Dad grabbed Mom's hand. She glanced at him and smiled, recognizing his concern for her feelings.

"We have decided that you can go, under a few circumstances, of course. First, I expect phone calls every day. I want mailed or emailed copies of your report cards and progress reports. The same rules you have here apply there. You will do your part at Aunt Mae's house. I will send a credit card with you for your weekly allowance and any emergencies."

Mom was crying now, making me rethink all of this for the thousandth time. "I don't want you taking your car, or renting a car there. It's a lot different from what you're used to." I didn't say this, but I wouldn't want to take that old, crappy car that far anyway. Dad insisted that my first car be a piece of junk until I was an experienced driver. Braxton drove us everywhere. Can you blame me?

"Mom, if you don't want me to go I don't have to . . ." I honestly felt disappointed saying that. I was starting to think this might be a frightfully pleasant thing.

"Addy, I want you to go and see this doctor. Maybe, please Lord, this is the answer to all of our prayers." Mom smiled, assuring me she was going to be fine.

"We have already called Aunt Mae and talked to her about all of this. She is in total agreement. She seemed real excited too, by the way. I will call tomorrow and set your flight. You will leave in two weeks. This will give us time to get everything set up: school, doctor appointments, flights, credit card, packing, medical records, and more." Dad smiled at me for the first time. "We are so proud of you, sweetheart, this is a very brave thing you are doing."

I thought, if you only knew I am about to throw up all over this table you would not be calling me brave! "Thanks, thank you both for everything. I know I am asking a lot." I stood from the table and walked back to my room.

I was happy—at least, at this moment. I pushed all the thoughts that scared the hell out of me to the back of my mind. I would deal with that as it came. I had sort of hoped it would be sooner. I had two whole weeks to fight with my mind. I was sure it would go fast.

I texted Brax goodnight like I promised I would do. I fell asleep dreaming of going shopping for size eight pants instead of the size twenty four I was currently wearing. How glorious would that be?

CHAPTER 10

"I don't know what is going on with you lately, but you had better get your act together, son. I have never had any trouble out of you, and it isn't going to start now! Do you understand me?" Mom stood as I sat on the edge of my bed biting my bottom lip. If I talk back to her it will only make things worse.

"Yes ma'am." I squeezed the response out of my lips with as little contempt as possible. She stood in the doorway just staring at me and not saying a word. I felt more uncomfortable now than I did when she was yelling at me.

Her hand slid off of her hip, and her shoulders slouched forward. "Braxton, I am always here for you." She sat beside me on the edge of my bed and ran her hand over my back. "I will help you, but you have to talk to me, okay?"

I focused on the floor and decided to stay silent. I nodded my head; my mom and dad had always been here for me, but I didn't know what the hell was happening so how can I ask them for help?

"Okay, son, I am going to cook dinner." She stood from the bed and walked to the door. Before clicking it shut behind her, she said, "I'll call for you when it's ready." I could hear the concern or maybe disappointment in her voice.

I pushed myself back on my bed hard. There was one spot on my ceiling that my eyes always focused on when I lay down. It looked like a black spider on an all white ceiling. I didn't know what it was, but it had never moved. I turned to my side and slid my cell phone out of my pocket. Maybe I should call Addy. I wanted to, but I had come such a long way today I didn't want to push my luck. I scrolled through the contacts;

I really wanted to talk to someone. "I give up," I whispered, just before Mandi's number popped in view. "Mandi . . ." I sat up and pressed call.

"Hello?" She obviously hadn't recognized my number. "Hey Mandi, its Braxton." I waited for her response.

"Oh hey, Brax . . . is everything okay?" I guess she wondered why I would be calling her; after all, I had never called before.

"I guess. Do you have a minute? I just wanted to ask you a few questions." If it's possible, I think I heard her blush. I laughed under my breath; it truly was cute how nervous I seemed to make her.

"Yeah, sure, just hang on for one second and let me go to my room for some privacy, ok?" Before I could answer, I heard her hand come over the phone. In a muffled voice, she told someone she was going to take the call in her room.

"Ok I'm back." She sounded a little out of breath. "I am sorry for calling you without permission like this. Your number must be on your Facebook page, because your profile picture is also on my phone under your name, as well." I didn't want her thinking Addyson gave me her number without asking.

"Yeah, I do; yours is the same way in mine," She said shyly.

"Listen, I was just wondering when Addyson decided to go to New York?" I stood from my bed and sat at my computer. I hit the mouse and brought the computer to life.

"Um, well, I am not sure." Mandi sounded a bit surprised. I guessed it was because I was not supposed to know.

"Addyson told me about it today, so, unless she told you not to, you can talk to me about it." I clicked on Addyson's Facebook page and scrolled through her recent posts.

"You really know as much as I do."

Addy must have told her not to talk to me about it. "Ok, I guess I'll let you go. I just wanted to know what made her decide to do this." The frustration came out against my will.

"Sorry, I wish I could have been more help."

I felt guilty for snapping at her; it's not her fault. "Really, its okay, Mandi. I am sorry I put you in the position. But I'll holler at you at school tomorrow, okay?" My eyes stopped on the latest post from Addyson on Facebook.

"Okay Brax, have a good night . . . bye." I shut the phone and threw it on my desk.

My heart was speeding up. This was actually happening. She was actually going to New York for ten months. Why would she do this? Was it because of me? I still didn't know what the hell I had done to make her feel like she needed to leave me alone. Why would she think I wanted her to? Didn't what I want matter? Didn't that matter at all?

New York City here I come; two weeks and counting. I read her post under my breath over and over again. She truly was leaving, and apparently I could not do anything about it.

CHAPTER 11

Braxton was there on time to pick me up for school. As I walked closer to his car, I could see the smile of satisfaction that I was actually there like he had demanded, spread across his perfect face.

"Good morning. I will be going to Aunt Mae's in two weeks." I wanted to get this out of the way first thing. I knew it wasn't going to go over extremely well and didn't want the subject hanging over our heads for the whole fifteen minute ride to school.

"Well, at least we will be able to spend the two weekends together." He was expecting me to protest, I guess, because he kept looking at me, then the road, then me, like he was waiting to argue.

"Yeah, we will," I said simply and grinned. I wanted to tell him about the doctor so badly. But I thought I might curse it somehow and didn't say a word.

The rest of the trip to school was normal; we talked like the last five days had not happened at all. We were laughing and singing music, which I didn't sing as loud as him, and for a minute everything felt normal again. Then we pulled into the school parking lot. Both of us looked at each other. I believed he may have dreaded that place more than I did. The concern swam into his eyes.

"I'll see you in first period." I smiled at him and got out of the car. He went towards his homeroom, and I went towards mine. As I was walking to my locker to pull out the books I never got out yesterday, a group of girls came walking up to me—the cheerleaders.

They always had lovely things to say to me, things I could live the rest of my life without ever hearing again! I focused hard on my locker, trying not to make eye contact with any of them; maybe they would just walk on by without picking on me.

Jennifer Gripply walked up beside me. "Hi Jennifer." I tried to sound as pleasant as possible.

"Addy, the girls and I wanted to know if you want to eat lunch with us today." She stared at me, waiting on a reply. What was the catch, the punch line; they had never been nice to me before in my life? Why now? Something weird was going on.

"Really?" I asked, unable to hide the look I was giving all three of them.

"Yes, really. We would love to have lunch with you." She smiled so sweetly.

"Um . . . okay . . . sure." I was still waiting on the joke.

"Okay, we will see you then," she said, and all three girls walked off.

What the hell was that? I watched all three girls walk down the hall and around the corner. The bell rang informing me I was late for homeroom. "Crap Monkeys!!"

I loaded my book-bag with all the books I needed and ran towards my homeroom class.

—◊◊◊—

Homeroom and first period went by fast. In first period, Mandi, Brax, and I sat together. Braxton was happy, and so was I. Mandi stayed red the whole class. I couldn't help but laugh at her. She would get to spend so much time with him while I was gone. If she thought she liked him now, before long she would be in love with him.

Wow, I hadn't thought about that! How hard was it going to be to come home and have to watch Braxton with girls? I was jealous of the thought of Mandi getting to hang out with him. What would happen when I see him kiss a girl for the first time, hold her hand, or her sit on his lap, or touching him—period? I felt a sharp pain explode in my heart.

I found out that I also have History with both Brax and Mandi, which is cool. In History, Mandi texted me and said, "We need to talk ASAP." I wondered what that is about. I just didn't need anything else right now. What could it be? I replied with a simple "Ok."

Then it was time for lunch. I hadn't told Braxton yet about me sitting with the cheerleaders. I was curious about what the other cheerleaders were going to think about this. I had an awful feeling that I was going to end up tremendously embarrassed.

I walked through the line and picked out my usual—a carton of orange juice and a pack of cheese crackers. I walked out into the sitting area and saw the cheerleaders waiting on me.

I silently inspected the table. I looked at each of the girls, and they all were waving me over in their direction. For a split second, the movie Carrie popped into my mind and, without thinking, I looked up at the ceiling for the bucket of pig's blood. Of course, there was nothing there.

My hands were shaking so badly I am afraid I was going to drop my juice. "Hey, everyone, are you all sure it's okay if I sit here?" I waited for the insults and degrading remarks. You can imagine my shock when they all said "Yeah, have a seat."

Two girls moved over and let me sit down beside them. I don't know if the girls noticed, but I noticed that every eye in the room was on us; even the teachers were staring. They probably pictured the movie Carrie too.

"So where is Braxton?" Jennifer asked. The whole table looked at me waiting for my response. Oh, so that was what was going on here. They wanted Brax to sit here with them, not me. They knew if I did, more than likely he would too.

"He had to stop by his locker; he is on his way," I replied, amused at how stupid I could be. Well, give me credit; I did realize something was going on. I just didn't think of the obvious.

Jennifer quickly stood from her seat and yelled across the lunchroom. "Brax, she is over here with us. Come on over; we have room for you too." She was beaming from ear to ear. All ten girls began to fix their hair, sit up straighter; one girl even took her lip gloss out, and drenched her lips, leaving the greasy wet look behind.

Two girls on the other side of the table, across from me, slid over and made room for him. He had a tray with enough food to feed the whole table. I never understood how he could eat so much and stay so fit. But he would eat every bite of it, and would probably finish my crackers too.

He walked up to me. I turned and looked up at him. "They made room for you right there." I pointed across the table.

"I want to sit beside you." I couldn't help but feel proud. I know I was turning red. The smirk that ran across his face proved it.

The girl sitting to my left, without any warning, slid to her left. The girl on the end of the bench fell off into the floor, with her sweet tea in her hands. I heard the yelp and looked over at Carri. She was sitting in the floor with sweet tea all over her shirt and pants. I bit my lip until it almost bled to stop from busting out laughing at her. I stood from the table and walked over to her with a fist full of napkins I had grabbed off of the table.

"Here let me help you." I said and helped her to her feet. She ripped the napkins from my hand and stomped off towards the bathroom. I genuinely felt sorry for her, but I was glad it wasn't me. I know it's terrible to admit, but it was true.

Brax and I sat down at the table. "I hope she is okay. Are any of you going to go check on her?" I asked. They all looked at me like I had lost my mind. What kind friends they all were; how did I live without them?

Every girl at the table took turns asking Braxton questions—really stupid stuff and Brax was giving short and quick answers. When had he got his car? What did he like to do on the weekends? Was he going to try out for any sports this year? I looked at him when he was asked this one. He looked back at me.

"Yeah, football, but only because Addy wants me too." I felt the glares like hot pokers stabbing into my skin.

"I am so glad to hear that, Brax; you are going to be excellent." I couldn't contain my happiness, and allowed a genuine smile to prevail. I looked back at my crackers, and the questions fired back up.

I had been waiting for it, and I am sure Braxton was, too. "Do you wear contacts?" asked the one on the end now. She said it so low I could barely hear her. But when she asked it, I was taking a drink of my orange juice and almost spewed it out of my nose. Thank God I didn't, though. My eyes were watering from laughing so hard. Braxton was laughing too. But everyone at the table was looking at us, and between each other, totally confused.

"No, he doesn't wear contacts. His beautiful eyes are his gift from God." I spoke up first. I could hear his laughter fade, and, for the first time ever, I realized that he was truly self-conscious about his eyes; they actually bothered him a lot.

"Don't you agree with me, ladies?" I asked and looked around the table. Their voices chimed in together: "Good Lord, yes," and "Beautiful" or "Mesmerizing," and my favorite—"Peaceful." I actually looked at her. She had her elbow on the table, her head resting on her palm, staring at Brax languorously.

I leaned into him and whispered in his ear, "See, I told you." He looked at me, then back to his plate and smiled. After another fifteen whole minutes of this quite amusing, but overly irritating, event, I was ready to go. "Thank you for letting me eat with ya'll today. I am going to spend the last ten minutes of lunch out on the patio. I will see you all later."

I didn't wait for responses, but was surprised when they all thanked me for sitting with them. I smiled, then grumbled under my breath, "You mean thank you for Braxton." Then I walked away.

I felt an arm come around my shoulder. "Brax, that was . . . eventful wasn't it?" I asked without looking up.

"What?"

I looked up at the strange voice ringing back at me. "Jason?" My whole body tensed up when I saw his face, smiling at me. He was so tall I had to look up at him. I looked around, worried. What was about to happen to me? I began to shake. I knew he was going to do something to me. I just didn't know what. I was panicking now.

We were walking through the double glass doors to the patio. I was frantically looking around for his friends. My breath was speeding up, and my heart was beating out of my chest. We were the only two out here, apart from two girls sitting in the far corner; they didn't look at us at all.

"Do you want to sit here?" He pointed to a table under the tree planted in the middle of the concrete. He sat down before I answered him. I sat down cautiously. I still hadn't said a word. "I just wanted to apologize to you for all of those mean things I have said and done to you over the years." He stared at me, waiting for me to reply.

My eyes were about to pop out of my head; my jaw was hanging wide open like a human fly trap, and I forgot how to breathe. He laughed kind of loud, shaking me out of my own thoughts of horror film incidents that this could turn in to.

"Oh, I'm sorry. Thanks," I said, stunned to my bones. What the hell was happening? I had decided to go to New York for ten flippin' months, and the whole entire world flipped upside down. I turned around one more time to make sure someone wasn't sneaking up on me. I saw Braxton standing at the doors. I looked at him and felt as confused as he looked. Two cheerleaders walked up either side of him. They were talking, but I couldn't hear what they were saying to him.

"Here is my phone number. Why don't you call me sometime; maybe we could hang out?" I turned around to look at Jason. I couldn't say anything. I felt like a complete fool. I reached for his number and held it in my hand. I looked from him to the paper several times. Finally, feeling like a four year old, I spoke. "Okay" was all that slid out. I am not sure whether I blinked at all.

"Okay. I look forward to it; call me soon, okay." He stood from the table and walked back into the building.

"Okay, I will," I whispered, way too late.

I stared at the tree to my right. I looked around, and the two girls at the end of the patio were staring and whispering. That confirmed it for me: everything that had just happened, in fact, actually did just happen. I looked at the number in my hand one more time. I saved his number in my cell.

I had to go find Braxton and tell him what had just happened. I thought the world was about to explode or something. Besides, I was sure he was worried to death that Jason was being nasty in some way. I needed to make sure he knew I was okay.

When I walked inside the lunchroom, I stopped dead in my tracks. Braxton was sitting at the same table. There were him and four cheerleaders left. He was laughing. He looked so normal, so happy. I felt like I had been punched in the stomach . . . repeatedly.

When Jennifer reached over and put her hand on his arm, feeling his muscles, I am sure, he blushed. Braxton blushed! Why did I feel like knocking the bitch off the side of the table? This is what I wanted, right? This is what I had asked for?

I was about to walk away when Brax noticed me. I tried so hard to smile at him. I began to walk off quickly before I went over there and pulled him away from them by his shirt. I heard him say, "Bye" and heard his footsteps rapidly approaching.

"So what did Jason want? Was he mean to you?" he asked, as his arm come around my shoulder. I didn't answer.

"Did you have fun with the cheerleaders?" I tried to hide the jealousy. I wasn't doing too well.

"It was, strange. What made you sit with them to begin with?" Again I didn't answer.

"Jason wants to hang out; he gave me his number." I pulled the paper out of my pocket to prove it.

"What? Well, are you going to call him?" Was that jealousy I heard in his voice?

"I don't know—maybe," I said, smiling. I couldn't help myself. I know it was stupid. I mean, Brax just had four girls, four cheerleaders, who have always wanted to be with him, hanging onto his every word. Beautiful girls, skinny girls with the bodies of runway models, no brains whatsoever, but beautiful nonetheless.

Why would Brax be jealous that Jason gave me his number? I was not going to tell him this, but I still felt like there was something sneaky and underlying going on here. I doubted I would ever call him. I mean, if I did, what would I say? 'Hey Jason, I have thought of about a thousand different ways I would love to see you suffer. How are you today?' Come on.

"Are you still riding home with me? Or would you rather Jason take you?" He was jealous. I grinned a little, hiding behind my hair.

"I am walking. I don't think there will be enough room in your car for you, four bimbos, and me." I was trying to make him laugh; you could hear the laughter in my voice.

"I will leave my car here and walk with you, before you walk home alone!" He was getting defensive, and protective.

"I was only kidding Brax; lighten up a little. I am really glad that you have made friends with them. Maybe now you will see what I was talking about. That you can truly have any lady in this school you want. Live, remember?"

I began to walk down my hall. He had weight lifting, which was on the other end of the school. After a few moments, he yelled "I am with who I want to be with, remember?" He was so pissed.

I shook my head and walked into my class.

—⁂—

The ride to my house had been silent. He was so mad he could have spit flames. We were sitting in the car in the driveway.

"Are you really not going to talk to me at all?" I was laughing at him. "I was only joking about walking home. You were giving me hell about Jason, and I retaliated."

He looked at me, his eyes softening. He looked down into his lap, turning his key around and around his finger. "Can I come in?" He didn't look at me. He knew I was going to say no before I answered.

"No, Brax. Don't be angry; Mandi is coming over, and we are going swimming." He looked at me now. "I like to swim; why can't I come?"

I tried to think of something to say other than the embarrassing truth. "You just can't." I was the one looking down at my hands now.

"So Mandi is going to take my place as your best friend, is that it?" He was still angry but now he was hurt on top of it. "We have been best friends for ever, and you're just going to push me away, Addyson. It hurts; it hurts more than you will ever know."

I tried to speak. "No Brax . . ."

He cut me off. I'm not sure I had ever made him this angry before. "I have protected you, been there for you—hell, Addy, I love you—and all of a sudden you are letting Mandi and Jason come between us?" He honestly thought something was going on between me and Jason? Hell, as far as I was concerned nothing between Jason and I had changed at all. He looked back down in his lap, shaking his head and making hissing noises as if to say shame on you.

"First of all, Braxton, I have never asked you to protect me, I have never asked for your pity once, never once, and if you must know, if you're just going to flip the hell out if I don't tell you . . . then hear this! I don't want you to see me in a bathing suit! OK? Are you happy now?" I was screaming at him so loud my dad came out of the house. I climbed out of the car and slammed the door as hard as I could. I wanted the glass to bust out, but it didn't. I was so embarrassed, hurt, and just pissed off.

"Addy wait!" I heard his car door open. I turned around and took three steps back towards him. I knew I sounded colder than I had ever been towards Braxton. "GO HOME!" He stopped at the sound of my voice. He watched my dad walk up to me, asking me repeatedly what was going on. I couldn't talk to my dad. I wanted to talk to my mom; I had to talk to Mom.

CHAPTER 12

I watched Addyson and Mr. Michaels walk up the sidewalk. Mr. Michaels looked back at me with questioning eyes, but I couldn't think of what to say. I shook my head and got back into my car. "Damn! Damn! Damn!" I put the car in drive and turned the volume up on the radio as loud as it would go. Instead of taking the next right, to go home, I went straight towards the interstate. I needed some speed and this car could give it to me. "What the hell is wrong with girls? I mean what do they want from you?" I took the next right and hit the Highway sixteen on ramp. "You do everything you can think to do to make them happy . . ." I slapped the car in overdrive and hit 80MPH without blinking. "Begging isn't enough! Hell no, not even begging is enough . . ."

I passed five cars, swerving in and out of traffic. I could feel the tension releasing, but I only wanted more speed. I pushed the pedal to the floor board and sat back in the seat. "Goes MIA for four days, then when I do see her, she says she is going to New York for ten damn months. Ten months!" The sound of her voice was louder than the roar of the car's engine. "I don't want you to see me in a bathing suit, ok? Are you happy now?" My foot reluctantly pulled back from the pedal and the car was drifting at 120MPH, gradually slowing down. I didn't think about her being uneasy in a bathing suit. I knew she has never been in a bathing suit in front of me. What did she think? Did she think I wouldn't be her friend anymore, if I were to see her in one? Did she seriously think it would change our friendship?

The siren and blue lights flashing in my rear view mirror jerked me out of my thoughts. "Damn it!" I glanced at my speed—75MPH. "My dad is going to kill me!"

"I just lost it. I'm sorry, Dad." Dad was staring at me over his reading glasses, while Mom sat on the arm of the chair with her arms crossed over her chest.

"You do know you could have killed yourself or someone else?" Mom was past angry. "Go to your room and we will let you know what we decide to do about this." Dad put one hand on mom's knee, and took his glasses off with the other.

I knew to go, so I stood and walked to my room. I wanted to slam the door so hard it would break the hinges, but thought better of it. I pulled out my cell phone to text Addyson. More than likely I would lose this phone, so I had better do it now. All I said was, "I'm sorry, Addy. I didn't realize. I hope you will forgive me." Then I turned it off; I doubted I would get a response anyway.

I could smell the fragrance of mom's cooking and my stomach growled. It made me think of lunch that day at school. Addyson was certainly acting strangely, sitting with the cheerleaders and Jason . . . Jason. I wondered what that is all about. I didn't even know she liked him! I wondered if she called him. Does she text him back? Does he listen to her as I do? No—hell no—I know he doesn't. He is one of the assholes I have tried to protect her from!

My blood ran hot through my body. The thought of Jason taking my place is ten times worse than the thought of Mandi taking my spot in Addyson's life.

"Okay fine . . . she wants me to hang out with other girls . . ." I turned on my computer and pulled up Facebook. I scrolled down through all of the friends in my friends list. I looked at every cheerleader I had as a friend: Jessica, Sara, Bailey, Tinsley, Carri, and Jennifer. Jennifer was the prettiest one by far. ". . . then that's what I will do!"

—◊◊◊—

"We have decided that if we are not going to punish you." My eyes shot from my plate to my Dad's face in disbelief. Had I heard him right? Mom sat beside Dad and filled her plate up with food. "If . . ."—oh, okay here it comes—". . . you tell us exactly what is going on with you." Dad looked back at me with his elbows on the table and his hands clasped together. I had their full attention, regardless of whether I wanted it or not. Was I supposed to tell my parents about stuff like this? Did Addyson want them to know our business? What choice did I honestly have? "We know something is going on, son. You have been in more trouble in the last week than you have in your life time." Mom was right; I had made some terrible decisions in the last few days. But I had never been so confused in all my life either.

I stared at my empty plate as I rolled the choices over in my head. I certainly didn't want to lose my car, and I knew I was going to. I could live without the phone, and even the computer, but I needed my car. "So what's it going to be?" Dad asked as he put some carrots on his plate. Who knew, maybe, by some miracle, they could tell me what to do about Addyson.

"Okay, I'll tell you everything." I sat back in my chair and started from the day I dropped Addyson off at home after school shopping. Throughout the story, no one took a bite of food and by the time I was finished everything was cold. Mom and Dad talked to each other with eye language and a few times I wondered what they were saying; neither said a real word.

"I felt like I was going to explode and I just wanted to get away from it all. I turned the radio up and let the car out. It was stupid, dangerous, and irresponsible. I didn't feel bad for getting the ticket or for any of it really. Not until Mom said I could have killed someone; I never even thought about that. I promise I will never do it again. I wouldn't be able to handle it if I did hurt someone."

After a few moments, Mom spoke first. "Son, Addyson is in love with you." My dad smiled at my mom and looked back at me. "Yes, she is, and it sounds to me that you may love her a little more than as a sister too."

I laughed out loud at this. "Addyson loves me like a brother, and I love her like a sister. We have been like siblings as long as I have been born. She doesn't love me like that. And I don't love her like that either. As a matter of fact, I have been thinking about talking to a cheerleader." My stomach turned at the thought of hanging out with Jennifer. Just the way she acted over me saying hello on Facebook was repulsive. I said Hi, and she said, about time you said something. The thought of Jason and Addy sitting out on the patio at lunch today made me determined to suffer Jennifer . . . no matter how torturous it was.

I took a bite of the stone-cold biscuit from the table. I figured they couldn't help me either.

CHAPTER 13

The last remaining days had gone by so fast, and things had gotten so weird. Jennifer and the cheerleaders had been to my house twice. They went swimming. You can imagine there was no way in hell I was getting in a bathing suit in front of them. I didn't trust them. They couldn't care less about me, but put on an exceptionally terrific show. I had to give them credit for that.

When Braxton wasn't around, I didn't exist for them. I sort of just hung around in the shadows. I listened to their conversations. I secretly wanted the lives they led. They all looked perfect to me. They all had long hair in their own color—mostly blonde, but, out of the ten, there are three brunettes; they all wear a size three or below. Jennifer is a size zero . . . really? I was born bigger than that. Of course, come to think of it, I have never seen her eat anything more than an apple, ever.

They did not talk to me, but they still included me in everything. In the mornings when I got to school, they usually came to my locker. They didn't say a word to me; I just knew to walk with them. No one dared to say a word to me when I was with them. The girls wanted to *be* them, and the boys wanted to be *with* them. So, saying something about me, or about me being with them, was out of the question.

They walked me to my classes. If Braxton was in those classes they all would say bye before I slipped into the room, making a point to ensure Brax saw them with me. I had all four classes with at least one of them. If Braxton was in a class with me, the cheerleader would sit with me, talk to me—I was so her best friend throughout that entire class. I had absolutely nothing in common with any of them. I hadn't been able to sit with Mandi in weeks. She didn't return my phone calls any more. I honestly couldn't say that I blamed her at all.

We ate lunch together, Braxton included. So again, I was the most popular one at the table . . . that was the whole point, right? They all had my number and texted me, often. Usually it was stuff like:

- Party at my house 7pm . . . Bring Brax~

I never went, and rarely responded to any of the texts. With every day that passed by, the more I dreaded to see them, any of them, but one more than the others—the one that seemed to spend the most time with Braxton, even when I am not around, Jennifer.

Jennifer drove me home from school a couple of times. I had to put up with Braxton's complaints; the last time was the worst. So I walked home from then on. I needed the exercise, anyway. I had known since the first lunch I had with the cheerleaders that Braxton was the only reason they wanted to hang out with me, so why did it still hurt?

Oh, and Braxton, good Lord, what a mess! I was totally in love with him, but acted as if I was not. I wanted to be with him every second of the day, but acted as if I didn't. I wanted to call him, I didn't. I wanted things to be the way they used to be; I was not sure it ever could be again.

The torturing and name calling, picking and pranks, had certainly calmed down, because of the cheerleaders; the torturing I endured now was much worse, hands down. I watched those girls hang all over Braxton. They texted him and called him. They hung out with him. They made him laugh, and he seemed genuinely happy. Until, of course, he looked at me, then I saw the pain.

At least two of them walked with him to his classes, and now that I walked home from school, he usually took Jennifer home every day. Since the fight, things had been different between Brax and me. I still rode with him to school, but so did Jennifer. So I couldn't talk to him about much of anything. He made her sit in the back seat, and she hated that with a passion. I loved it!

I encouraged him to hang out with her, though, I knew I sounded like a contradictory crazy person. Hell, I felt crazy! I honestly wanted Brax happy; I wanted to see him live a normal life and enjoy every minute of it. At the same time, I couldn't make myself stop loving him.

You better believe I wanted to be selfish. I wanted to run to him and tell him, I want us to go back to the way it used to be. I dream of just the two of us again. But I knew that things would never be the same again.

When my feelings changed, everything changed. It felt so terrible to love someone with my entire self, knowing I will never have him that way.

He would say a thing sometimes, which made me think maybe he did love me that way. He did things that boys only do for girls that they love that way, right?

I had a daily fight with all of these thoughts. He had always made it clear he loved me like a sister, and that he wanted to protect me, like a brother. He wanted to spend time with me like best friends. Never, had he ever mentioned anything deeper than that. And I couldn't blame him.

But I should have been grateful for that, and have taken what I could get. After all, I knew about twenty girls that would have loved to just be his friend, or have his brotherly love, his protection. What was I supposed to do? I was supposed to go back to the way it used to be and torture myself worse, right? I knew it looked like I was being a complete and total bitch to him. God only knows what he thought about me at that point. He probably thought I was crazy, too.

I was just so tired of thinking about it. I wasn't able to spend much time with Mandi, the cheerleaders had taken up most of it, and Mandi would not hang out with them. I missed her. I probably had lost the only real girlfriend I had ever had.

I stood from the pool and walked into my room. I got my cell phone off my desk and called Mandi again. I left a message; I was not sure why. I knew she wasn't going to call me back. She hadn't yet anyway.

"Hey Mandi, call me when you get this, please. I want to apologize to you for everything. I wanted to know if you would like to hang out. I miss you, Mandi. Please call me back."

I hung up and sat on my bed. I dialed a number I haven't dialed in a long time . . .

"Hello?" He answered on the first ring; his voice sounded shocked.

"Hey Brax, do you want to come over for a little while?" I was honestly scared that he was going to say no. But what he said was much worse; well, half of it anyway.

"I will come over in a little while; Jennifer and I are at the mall. WE will be there in a little while, okay?" He sounded so happy.

"Well, I am going . . ."—I am such a crappy liar—"to . . . to buy new luggage for my trip. I wanted to see you before then. I will call you later and see if you want to get together, okay?" So they are spending a lot more time together than I thought. This was what I wanted, right? Then why did I feel like I wanted to die—first kill Jennifer, and then die.

"Addy, are we still going to spend the weekend together?" I could hear Jennifer in the back ground; they must have become remarkably close to each other. He probably had his arm wrapped around her shoulders; he could wrap his arm around her twice. "But, Brax, we are going to Carri's party tonight, right?" Jennifer whined. I could imagine her lip poking out and her eyelashes batting a mile a minute, with her perfectly manicured hand on his chest.

I closed my eyes and squeezed the tears back, and strained to keep my voice light and careless. My fist was clenched so tight I had crescent moon shaped marks in my palm, from my finger nails digging into my flesh. "I am leaving in two days, so I want to spend the weekend with my parents. You know I consider you family. So, if YOU want to come you can. Just a cook-out and hanging around the pool."

My screaming at him that I didn't want him to see me in a bathing suit, flashed through my mind, and I felt awkward and embarrassed again. I wanted off of this phone. "Dinner will be at seven if you want to come; if you have plans, I understand." I was hoping so badly that he understood that when I said YOU, I meant only him. Right then, if I had been face-to-face with Jennifer, I might have got into the first fist fight I had ever been in, ever!

But, how could I be mad at her? How could she not want to be with him? After all this was my entire fault. "Bye Brax." I hung up as I heard his voice in the phone. "Addy . . ." I hung up anyway. I was sure he had plans; if not, Jennifer sure as hell did. I threw my phone across the room and screamed as loud and as long as I could. I fell on my bed and screamed into the pillows, letting the tears flow. After my twenty minute temper tantrum, I felt better.

On my back, staring at my ceiling, I was thinking, thinking too much, like always. How did you make yourself fall out of love with someone? How could I have just been his friend again and watched Jennifer hang all over him, spend time with him . . . and what if he fell in love with her? What if, as his friend, he wanted to talk to me about their relationship? How was I going to act like I actually wanted them to work out and that I was actually happy about their relationship.

I hadn't perfected being a successful fake like the cheerleaders. I had a lot yet to learn. This was the last weekend I would spend with my family.

I sat up on the edge of the bed, deep in thought. I was going to make this a good memory, no matter what. My parents didn't deserve to have to deal with my bipolar brain. I was determined.

I was going to Mandi's house. I was going to apologize to her and, if she still didn't want to accept my apology, well, there was nothing I could actually do about it. But I would at least leave North Carolina knowing I had tried everything.

—◊◊◊—

This is only the fifth time since I have had this car that I have actually driven it. My glorious 1989 Nissan Maxima; It's so old. The paint job is okay, but I haven't decided if its light blue or light gray. It's faded just enough to not be able to tell. But the inside is actually falling apart. The cloth on the ceiling, whatever that is called, is hanging down inches from my head. When it gets hot, like it is today, the rear view mirror falls off when I shut the door, which you have to slam, or it won't click shut. I have to roll the window down to open the door because the inside handle is broken. It's so old, you have to manually roll the window down, and nothing is electric. It smells like oil and gas no matter what I do. I have had every piece of cloth in the thing shampooed, and it still reeks. It totally sucks, but my parents say that it's my first car, and if I keep my grades up, and have no accidents, they will buy me a new car for graduation. So far I am doing fantastic on the accident free part. I mean, I used to ride with Brax everywhere. When you don't drive, you can't have accidents.

I pulled into Mandi's drive way. Her car was there, so hopefully she was home. I got out of the car, slammed the door as hard as I could, and watched the rear view mirror jump off of the windshield on the passenger's side floor. I rolled my eyes. "Crap monkey."

I walked towards their front door. I heard the door bell ring out all through the house. I didn't hear any noises; maybe they are not home. I was about to walk off, when the door opened. Mandi saw that it was me and tried to slam the door. "WAIT, WAIT! PLEASE, JUST GIVE ME ONE MINUTE." I pushed against the door just enough to keep her from shutting it. When I put all of my weight against the door, there was no way she was going to shut it.

She pulled the door open quickly, with no warning, and I almost fell inside the door, on my face. I caught myself on the door frame. I looked up at her; she was standing with her arms crossed around her tiny body, and her hips cocked to the side. She was so not happy about this.

"Mandi I know you're mad at me, and you have every right to be." I stood straight up and tried to get my thoughts together. I took one step closer and finished. "I just wanted you to know that you are the best girl friend I have ever had. I am so sorry, for me, that I ruined that. You don't deserve the way I have treated you. You do not have to accept my apology; I certainly will understand, but I wanted to thank you for trying to be a real friend to me."

I turned and began to walk out, not expecting her to respond. I mean, after all, we hung out for weeks and became real friends quickly. She is the first person I have ever gone swimming with, other than my parents; I even ate a candy bar in front of her. If you're not overweight, you will never understand. And then, just as fast, I fell off of the side of the earth, so to speak. I was hanging out with people that couldn't care less about me, so I could believe I was part of the 'IN' crowd. Jennifer had what she wanted now; I wouldn't be surprised if I never heard from her again.

"Addy, wait!" I heard her voice as I was about to get into my crappy car.

"Yeah?" I yelled back.

"What are you doing tonight?" She smiled at me, and I quickly ran to her and hugged her as tight as I could without breaking her.

"Spending it with my best friend, if you want to come over?" I asked with the biggest smile I had worn on my face in days, weeks—hell, maybe ever.

"What time again?" she asked smiling back at me.

"Seven, and bring your suit, okay." I realized, from day one of our friendship, how much I needed her around but, if there ever was a question, now I knew I needed Mandi in my life. I would never let her go again.

—◊◊◊—

I had just finished setting up the patio for the cookout; thank God for Mandi. I had so much fun with her. And it was like I didn't have to be worried about anything. I still felt awkward in a bathing suit, in front of her, but it was different. I just knew she would never hurt me, or judge me; I knew that, no matter how awful I looked, it wouldn't change anything between us.

Maybe the reason I hadn't wanted Brax to see me is because it would have change the way he saw me. I mean, clothes hide a lot. A bathing suit is cruel and brutal. It shows everything. Maybe I was afraid that it would have confirmed for him that he could never be with me, that way. Maybe he would have seen me as repulsive or disgusting; I couldn't handle that.

"Addy, can I help you get the drinks?" Mandi skipped up beside me, and every time she jumped up her beautiful hair would swing around her face like in those shampoo commercials.

"That would be great." I said, laughing at her silliness. I was so glad she was there.

Mandi had come over early, so we could do some catching up. I told her everything, and I mean everything. From being madly in love with Brax, to the cheerleaders, Jason Harden, and going to New York. I hadn't even realized that she didn't know.

"Brax actually called me and asked me about it, but I didn't know what he was talking about. I just assumed it was another lie." Mandi looked away from me as her words reminded us both of my own stupidity.

"I am so sorry, Mandi." The guilt was still overwhelming—guilt or embarrassment, I was not sure. Maybe it was both.

"Don't worry about it. No worries." She meant it to.

Brax, my parents, and now Mandi, were the only four who knew about it, not counting Aunt Mae. It felt so good to tell someone. She was the only person that knew I was in love with Braxton. I felt as if a towering building had been lifted off of my chest and for the first time in weeks I could breathe.

I think she was glad to hear that the cheerleaders were just using me, at least for a second, I couldn't blame her. It was ten minutes to 7:00 p.m. I knew in my heart that Brax wasn't going to show up, but I will admit I was still hoping he would show up.

I had my bathing suit on. I certainly knew he was not coming; I wouldn't have been wearing this, if I thought there was even the slightest chance of him showing up. He was never late for anything. So, if he was not there in ten minutes he wasn't coming.

We had music playing, anything but country; I wanted upbeat, happy, feel fabulous music. We ate, and I actually ate a cheeseburger. It was so yummy. I could not get into a habit of eating food like that or I would have been 400 pounds before the end of the month. I got terribly sick of salads, and two ounces of grilled chicken breast. It would have been so easy to just give up and eat like a normal teenager every day.

We laughed, and joked; I threw Mandi into the pool, and she tried her best to do the same to me—wasn't happening. She finally decided to push me while I was standing at the edge, but I took her with me. I was truly having a marvelous time. Mandi and I were in the pool, with our arms on the edge, talking to Mom and Dad. Dad was helping Mom take in the left-over food. It was after 8:00 p.m. He didn't come. I can't believe he didn't come.

I climbed out of the pool, pushing the depression to the back of my mind. I had had a fantastic time today with my family and my best friend. I guess Mandi was going to take Brax's place in my life for sure. She just had, and, for the first time ever, he missed something significant to me in my life. My first memory without my Braxton; it hurts so badly.

Mandi and I pulled the patio chairs together and were talking. We had enormous beach towels draped over our waist and legs, allowing our feet to dangle. The crisp night air touching my skin gave me chill bumps. I knew without looking I was sunburnt; I could see Mandi was; her face was red, and so were her shoulders.

I heard the door open; Mom and Dad must have been ready to re-join us. Mandi and I were singing at the top of our lungs: Neither of us could sing but it was fun. Mandi looked at me, laughing, and then her face turned an exceptionally deep shade of red almost instantly.

"Looks like you two are definitely having fun," Brax said, laughing. I clung to my beach towel like it was a life preserver. I turned to see him. I looked around. He was alone. Mandi stood up to walk away, pulling her towel all the way around her body. Did she actually not like her body? She was beautiful; I wonder what she would have done if she had looked like me? She would be grateful then, I guarantee it!

"Mandi, you don't have to leave; you are welcome to stay here with us." I meant it too. There is nothing that he or I could have said that I would have minded her hearing. She blushed red all over again, with Brax's gaze on her.

"I will be right back; do you guys want a drink, too?" she asked, looking at her feet.

Both of us replied "Sure" and she quickly ran off.

"Chair's wet, but you can sit" I said, pointing to her chair.

"I am good. I thought this was just for family." His voice sounded offended.

"Where is Jennifer?" I replied, avoiding his statement.

"I didn't bring her because you said this was just for family, I was going to, but . . ."

I cut him off. "So are you two dating then?" I prepared for the blow. His eyebrows rose, and he grinned at me. I couldn't help but smile at him. The smile faded though with the thought of them officially being together. "I hope you're happy, Brax." I meant it. I honestly did.

"I am not dating Jennifer, Addy. She is just a friend."

He sat in the wet chair and looked down at his hands. I looked away from him and let out a deep breath of relief; I couldn't help it. "I am sure you only have to say the word, and that could change quickly." All of the sarcasm left my voice, and I was being sincere.

"Oh, I know, Addy; I am only hanging out with her, going to these repulsive parties, football, all of this for you. I want YOU to be happy, Addy, and, for some reason, in order for you to be happy, I have to stay away from you. You won't listen to me. I am going to show you . . ."

Mandi walked up with our drinks. Brax stopped talking; obviously, what he wanted to say, he couldn't say in front of her. We both thanked her for the drinks, and she sat on the chair on my other side. There was no way I was going to ask her to leave; I would never hurt her again. I didn't want to hurt Brax either. He was quiet, looking at his Diet Pepsi can as if he had never seen one before.

"Do you want to stay and hang out with us awhile?" I wasn't sure he heard me it came out so low.

"Do you really want me to stay?" he asked, looking at Mandi. It was actually directed towards her more than it was me.

"Sure, I don't mind at all," Mandi said, looking off into the distance at the stars.

He smiled at her. "I'll stay then." He chuckled when she turned purplish, and I laughed too.

We spent the rest of the evening and the biggest part of the night together. After Mom and Dad had called it a night, I went swimming. Yes, Brax, Mandi, and I went swimming. Okay, so I put on a large and remarkably long shirt, which Mandi went into my room and got for me, without me asking her to. I could have kissed her for that, but, yeah, I went swimming.

When I got out, everything clung to me, no matter how many times I would pull the bulky heavy shirt away from me; you could still see every inch, every roll, of my disgusting body. Mandi saw my shame. She walked up to Brax and began to talk to him about something crazy. I think I heard her say something about blueberry muffins, or something.

I quietly slid into my room and changed into a T-shirt, Capris, and flip flops. I walked back out, brushing the wet tangles out of my hair. I wondered how long it was going to be before Mandi stopped blushing around him. She already was laughing more and didn't seem as self-conscious. Self conscious? Please. Why didn't she know she was beautiful? We were going to have to talk about that later.

"Bathroom is free if anyone wants a shower," I announced as I pulled an ice cold Diet Mountain Dew out of the cooler. Mandi stood and grabbed her towel. She had decided to stay the night, which was totally acceptable to me. When Brax wasn't looking, she winked at me. I smiled a grateful grin in return and she took off to the shower.

"Brax, do you think Mandi is pretty?" I wasn't sure where that came from as it flowed off of my lips. He was shocked at my bluntness; I was too.

"Yeah, I do. Her eyes are amazing," He said, looking back towards the door Mandi had just walked through.

"Well, tell her, will you? I don't know why she is so self-conscious, but having the finest guy in school tell her she is beautiful will probably help fix that problem."

"Finest guy in school, huh?" he asked, staring at me.

"Why do you seem so shocked when I say that, Brax? You're just as bad as her. It's not a secret; you're the only one that seems not to know!" I held his gaze with no problems; after all, it was just the truth.

"Well, I don't care what EVERYONE else thinks, Addy, just you." See what the hell I mean, right there; you just don't say that to your "sister", do you? Now what am I suppose to think?

"Well, I think you're the best person, period, in that school," I replied.

"I think you're be . . ."

Mandi walked out of my mini-house and yelled, cutting Braxton off, "Who is up for some cards?" She was holding up a deck of playing cards in her hand. She was so cute in her SpongeBob night pants, and purple tank top. I kept staring at Brax. What the hell was he about to say? Finish, by God, before I explode, finish.

Brax leaned forward "I will, if Addy doesn't mind me staying longer?" It was a question directed towards me.

"Of course I want you to stay," I replied, disappointed not to hear the rest of his statement.

We spent the rest of the night playing cards, laughing together, having a genuinely lovely time. By the end of the night, Mandi was relaxed with Brax; the blushing was gone, probably for good. Once you get used to his eyes, you don't want to look away; all you want to do is get lost in them.

We ended up in my room. Brax was looking something up on the laptop, and Mandi was painting her nails. I was drawing in a notebook, listening to a movie playing on T.V. I stopped for a second. I looked around. I loved them both. I had everything I could ever want right here in this room. In less than a day now, I would be leaving for New York for ten months. Why did everything have to change so quickly?

I couldn't stop wondering what he was going to say before Mandi came out earlier. Was he about to tell me I was the best person in that school, or maybe beautiful? If he had, I would have laughed in his face. I am not blind. I know what I look like. Beautiful is not the word to describe it either.

Maybe he would have said some cliché' thing like 'I think you are beautiful on the inside'. That does me a lot of good. It has been proved, you can be a damn beauty queen, Miss flippin' America, on the inside, and you will still be hated, picked on, laughed at, pranked, ignored—and that is just the way it is.

Don't patronize me, I wanted to say; I am not that naive, that stupid, I know the truth. Telling me I am pretty in any way will not make me feel good; it will only make me never trust you again.

—∽∾—

When I woke up this morning, with my face on my drawing pad, the T.V. was still on. Brax was still at the computer, leaning back in the chair facing the laptop, sound asleep. Mandi was stretched out on the floor, wrapped around my hot pink body pillow, with a thin blanket covering her. I was covered too; Brax must have done it.

I walked into the bathroom, trying to be quite. I took a nice long shower. The hot water helped wake me up. Once I was ready, hair dried, and clothes on, I walked back into the room. I got my cell phone out of the desk drawer. It was almost dead. 1:00 p.m. My God, we had slept all day.

I woke them both and told them what time it was; Mandi panicked and had to run home. Her mom had expected her home over an hour before. They had things to do that day. Brax ended up staying. He took a long shower; he had clothes that he kept here for after swimming.

While he was in the shower, his phone, sitting beside me on the bed, was ringing and getting texts like crazy. I was waiting for smoke to start coming out of the edges. God, I wanted to read those texts so badly. I knew who it was—Jennifer, for sure. I couldn't do that, right? I wanted to, though, so bad.

I heard the water shut off. He was getting out. I quickly stood up and walked over to my laptop and pulled up POGO, pretending to be playing LOTTSO. "I heard your phone ringing a minute ago." I didn't turn around.

"Who was it?" He was walking towards my bed.

I turned around to start cussing him for thinking I would be so nosey and look through his phone, which not even two minutes before I was thinking extremely seriously about doing, when my heart stopped beating. It was a scene I had viewed a hundred times before. But now I was in love with him. Now everything was different.

He stood with a towel wrapped around his waist—no shirt on and water glistening on his chest. He reminded me of one of those lusty Harlequin books; I mean, he was picture perfect for it. His hair was wild, in all direction, even his back was beautiful.

I was straight staring. My brain shut down entirely; I think I just had a mini stroke. If it was possible, his eyes glowed even brighter. He saw me in all of my lustful, drooling, disgust, and smiled from ear to ear. "You like what you see?" He loved this.

Rapture!!! Now!!! I wanted to disappear into thin air. "Shut up and put some clothes on!" I turned back quickly to my laptop. My damn hand was shaking. I quickly slid it under the desk.

I heard him dialing his phone as he walked back in the bathroom. "Hey . . . no, not today . . . I stayed the night with Addy, and I am taking her and Mandi out. I plan on spending the whole day with them, No, just the three of us. It's important to me, whatever. Bye."

What was that about? I didn't know he was spending the day with us, but I was not going to pretend I'm not terribly happy about it. He walked out of the bathroom, fully clothed, looking great. I wanted to ask who that was on the phone, but didn't.

"Come on, let's go; we are already late"

I looked at him, confused. "Um, what?"

He smiled and grabbed my purse, and his wallet and phone. "Let's go, Addy. It's a surprise." I hate surprises. And he knew it. Must have been Mandi's idea. I stood reluctantly and headed for his car.

CHAPTER 14

Last night was incredible. I felt like I had my life back. The life I never thought I would lose. The life I took for granted.

Addyson was in a bathing suit when I got here. I understood then. I see why she didn't want me to see her in a bathing suit. Seeing her didn't make the world stop turning, or the way I felt about her change; if anything, it made me understand the hell she goes through even more. I wished I could have helped her. On the other hand, it didn't change who she was. It didn't change the way her eyes glowed more yellow than brown. It didn't make the constant need to hear her laugh, or see her smile, fade in the least. It changed nothing at all.

I knew she hated surprises, but today was all about her. Today she would be with me all day long, and all night if I have my choice. I had a plan, and nothing would stop me from going through with it. Not even Addyson.

I stepped out of the shower. I brushed my teeth and smiled to myself; today was going to be epic. We would never forget this day. I washed my mouth out with mouth wash, and the happiness began to fade at the thought of today, possibly, being the last day I would see Addy for ten months, assuming she would not let me be with her tomorrow; I had to make it exceptional. Opening the bathroom door, the chilly air of her room made small chill bumps spread across my body.

Addyson was sitting at the computer playing a game. "I heard your phone ringing a minute ago." She didn't bother to look at me as she spoke. I opened her closet and rummaged through the clothes I have here. I threw a shirt and some pants on the bed.

"Who was it?" I shut the closet door and ran my hand over my chest. Between the cold air and the water dripping off of my hair, I was freezing.

Addyson turned towards me quickly; she was pissed that I would think she looked through my phone. I knew she wouldn't, but couldn't have cared less if she had. I wondered if she would get mad if she knew I would read hers in a heartbeat. I noticed that she still had said nothing. Her face had changed; her eyes went from shock and annoyance to, well, to me. I couldn't help but feel proud of the way she was looking at me. She liked the way I look.

I chuckled. "You like what you see?" Addyson didn't usually blush, but, man, she was right then! I loved that. I tried to tighten my chest muscles without her noticing. The amazing thing about her for me is, even though blushing, she never broke eye contact with me.

Her eyes quickly changed, and she said, "Shut up and put some clothes on!" I grabbed my clothes and my phone and headed back towards the bathroom. Jennifer called. I dialed her number and made sure everything was still as planned.

I glanced one last time at Addy before entering the bathroom. I wished I could tell her the surprise, but I know she would never have gone through with it. Today was her day; today would be added to one of the best memories we had together, I hoped.

CHAPTER 15

This was it. This was my last full day in the Carolinas for ten whole months. I could honestly say I wished I had never done this now. Things were finally back to normal with Mandi, and . . . well, no, things are still screwed up with Braxton.

But today, today was going to be great. I had just found out I was spending the day with Brax and Mandi. Surprise? I hate surprises. That meant I was going to be the center of attention. I was not happy with that.

We, Braxton and I, were going towards Mandi's house, obviously to pick her up.

"Give me a hint, Brax. Come on, you know I hate surprises." I was looking out of the window at this beautiful day.

"I can't do it, Addy; I promised I wouldn't tell you." He quickly glanced at me with a smile on his face. "I am just really glad that I could be a part of this today." He pulled into Mandi's drive way and parked.

"I am going to miss you, Addy; hell, I already miss you, and it feels like you're already gone sometimes." He was facing me, allowing me to lose myself in his eyes. He waited for a response; he deserved a response, and after a long moment, he put his head down and laughed, shaking his head. I didn't know what to say. I noticed my hands were shaking. "I guess you don't miss me, huh, Addy. Will you miss me at all?" His voice was shaky.

"Hi, guys, are you ready to go?" Neither of us had noticed Mandi walking up to the car. I almost jumped slam out of my skin. I had been so bewitched by his gaze, nothing else in the world mattered. Braxton sat straight up and looked out of his window, obviously disgusted. I pulled myself out of the car.

"Do you want to sit in the front or the back?" I asked to be nice; I would have had a hell of a time getting into the back seat of this car, and cannot imagine what it would be like getting out, but it would have been rude not to offer. Before Mandi had a chance to reply, Brax spoke up.

"I am not trying to be rude or mean in any way, but I want you to sit in the front with me, Addy. It's just . . . it's just were you belong, you know?" He smiled so sweetly at Mandi, he could have said he was going to kill her dog, and she would have agreed. Mandi jumped into the back with ease. I flopped back into the front and shut the door.

At first the trip was silent. I could tell Mandi was a little uneasy. Brax looked into the rear view mirror at her. I think he felt guilty for telling her to sit back there. "Mandi, you look beautiful today. I wanted you to know, by the way, your eyes are as unique as mine; they are really beautiful."

Well, so much for the "no more blushing thing" I had noticed last night by the pool!

"Thank you so much, Braxton." The tension was totally gone, and she had an enormous smile plastered on her face.

Brax looked at me and grinned. I smiled back at him, very happy with his compliment. After all, it was what he honestly thought, it's not like he lied to her to make her feel good about herself. It was totally the truth. I thought she needed to hear it.

I reached up and turned the radio on. A song that we all knew was playing—Gary Allen—Songs about Rain. We all sang it, very loud, and absolutely none of us were any good at singing, but we all three enjoyed it.

We drove for almost an hour. I had no idea where we were or where we were heading. And neither of these two was even dropping a hint. We finally pulled into the parking lot of the Bechtler Museum of Modern Art. I had always wanted to go there; Braxton knew that too. So this must have been all his idea.

"I can't believe you, Braxton!" I was smiling from ear to ear.

"You haven't seen the surprise yet." He smiled, and I rolled my eyes. "Come on, Addy. Hurry up! We are already so late" He was so excited. He was genuinely happy, and it wasn't because of Jennifer, or sports, or some party. It is all because of Mandi and me.

We all jumped out of the car. Brax was almost pulling me into the building, and Mandi was doing her skipping about six feet in front of us. When we walked into the building, my jaw dropped open. Mom, Dad, Aunt Mae, Mandi's parents, and Braxton's parents were all there.

"What is going on?" I asked, laughing and hugging everyone.

The whole group walked down a hall towards a wide open room with about 150 people in it. When we walked in, everyone turned and stared at us. I instinctively grabbed Braxton's hand and held on to it with both hands.

"It's okay, Addy. I am right here." He had no idea how glad I was.

We walked to the front of the room. There were six paintings on easels in front of the room. Each had a silk sheet over it, hiding the contents.

"OH MY GOD, WE ARE AT A PAINTING INDUCTION?" I beamed.

When a painting is adopted by this institution, it is considered a real masterpiece of modern art; it is one of the most prestigious honors an artist can hope for. As an aspiring artist, it is even an honor for me to be able to watch this ceremony in person.

We walked to the front line of seats and all the joy I felt drained immediately.

Jennifer came running up to Braxton and gave him a hug. I tried to let go of Brax's hand, but he squeezed tighter, not letting me go. I wanted to punch her in the neck.

"Hi Addy, you all have kept us waiting long enough," she snapped with venom in her eyes. When she looked back at Brax, she smiled her beauty queen smile and took his other hand. I tried desperately to pull mine free.

I looked back at Mandi who was right behind me. She mouthed, IM SORRY. I wanted to cry.

After sitting and listening to the lady behind the podium welcoming and thanking everyone for coming, Brax leaned into my ear and said, "Jennifer's dad runs this place. She is the one that did this for me, so I could do this for you. Please, Addy, don't be angry." He squeezed my hand tight.

"I am not mad, Brax; I am so thankful for all of this." It wasn't a lie; I wasn't mad. Maybe disappointed, but not mad.

We spent the next hour watching each painting being unveiled. The artist stood, and we all clapped for the artist. They had to walk up on the stage and receive a certificate, a photograph was taken with their painting for the newspaper, and they shook hands with each person on the board of Modern Art.

There was only one painting left. I wasn't ready for this event to be over. I squeezed Braxton's hand and smiled at him shyly. I felt strange holding his hand with Jennifer sitting right beside him. I couldn't help but notice he wasn't holding hers. I will not lie, I loved that.

The lady behind the stand's voice shook me out of my gloating. "Our last painting of the night is a very special one, to say the least. My Life in Your Eyes is painted by the youngest artist to ever be recognized by this institution, Addyson Michaels . . ." The sheet was ripped from the painting to reveal my Braxton's eyes staring back at me.

My mouth wouldn't shut; my heart was either beating so fast I couldn't even feel it anymore or may have stopped beating altogether—either way, I was speechless.

"Come up here, Miss Michaels, and accept your award." I heard her voice, and knew I had to go up there, but I couldn't move, I couldn't blink, and realized that fear had me squeezing the blood flow off to Braxton's hand.

"Go, Addy, you have to go up there." I felt his warm breath on the side of my face. I understood what he was saying, but there was no way I was going up there in front of all of these people, by myself. I stood somehow.

"Come on, you're going with me." I pulled on his arm as hard as I could pull. He was trying to let my hand go.

"I can't go with you, Addy; you have to do this." Pity and concern covered his face.

I saw something I had never before realized; this moment revealed more than just my painting, it revealed me. I had *made* Braxton protect me. I had made him do things with me or for me and never even realized it. I didn't mean to. I didn't see what I was doing, until now.

I forced a smile, even though the tears of sheer fear were attempting to stream down my face. My legs began to shake, and I made myself let go of his hand; he couldn't feel the tremors I was beginning to feel or he would go with me, no matter what.

I could do this. I slid out of the aisle. Mandi gave me a knowing smile; she knew how hard this was for me, and she was proud of me for doing it alone. I watched my feet, expecting the crowd to whisper or make fun of me. After all, I had on Capris, a t-shirt, and flip-flops. In my defense, I would have dressed better had I known about this.

As I walked up the steps to the stage, the crowd stood and clapped for me. It shocked me so badly, the wide-eyed, dumbfounded look planted itself right back on my face as I watched people of all ages, cultures, male and female, stood and cheered for me—even Jennifer. I found my Braxton. His blue eyes, like a beacon, caught my gaze. He was standing, as well; he had an enormous smile on his face. For a second, just for a second, with the crowd's loud cheers and whistles, I felt as if I was hidden, and that no one but Brax was able to see me. I stared and didn't move an inch. I felt the tears coming back, but it wasn't from fear or shock; it was from the overwhelming feelings of love I felt for Braxton Carmen.

He laughed out loud and crossed his arms over his chest. Still smiling, he looked down at his feet and shook his head as if to say, only ADDY, and, when his eyes landed back on mine, the soft, tender affection that has always been there had returned. Finally, he brought the painting to reality.

"Thank you so much for this honor." It was simple, but was enough to get the crowd revved back up as I accepted my certificate and stood with the board of the museum, and the painting that explained why I live, for the picture and the paper.

I walked off the side of the stage with such pride, not for my painting, but proud of who I was, and feeling like the luckiest person in the world for having the two best friends anyone could ask for.

—m—

"Mandi is riding home with her parents. I am taking you to dinner." He had a sly smile cross his face as he took his eyes from the road to me.

"I bet you are pretty proud of yourself for this; sneaky, sneaky!" I looked at the certificate housed in a red oak frame. It was still hard to believe that one of the most well known institutes in North Carolina had recognized me, Addyson Michaels; I was officially a real artist.

My dream was literally coming true. I had always dreamed of being a real artist, but never actually thought it would happen. I glanced at Brax and watched as he turned his cell phone off and threw it in his console. He didn't notice me staring at him. I wanted to hug him. I wanted to slide my hand back into his and never let go.

He leaned back in his seat and held onto the steering wheel with one hand. His eyes scanned the road as he drove. In the dark, he still hadn't noticed me staring. I loved him so much it hurt my insides. Part of me hated it. The pain and frustration that came with knowing I would never have that love back from him.

But what if this doctor would help me? What if I came back to North Carolina in ten months and the real me was visible, the me that lived inside of this hideous costume? Would he love me then? Or would it be too late; would he love someone else?

I refused to lose hope now.

—⁓—

Dinner was nothing out of the ordinary. I had my usual salad with two ounces of chicken and water; Braxton had his usual too—enough lasagna to feed a teenage football team. I spent most of the dinner staring at him. I had never felt these feelings before, and I had no idea what to do with them. He looked exactly the same as he always had, yet, something was different. He looked . . . well, he looked better somehow. I noticed things I had never noticed before. Like, he licked his lips before he spoke, the way his muscles flexed under his shirt, and the way he looked at me like I was the only person in the world. For the first time in my life, I felt strange for staring at him; I felt self-conscious about it, and that bothered me terribly.

Now we were by the pond. It was a beautiful night. The sky was clear, showing a million glowing stars. The air was cool but not cold. Braxton was laughing, telling me about some movie he had watched recently. I was laughing, hopefully in the spots I was suppose to laugh; I couldn't know because I had yet to hear a word he had said. No, I was too busy watching his hair move with the wind. The little wrinkles beside his glowing blue eyes as he laughed. I watched his soft-looking lips move with each word he spoke.

The laughter and joy drained from his face as he slid closer to me.

"What's the matter, Addy?" His question confused me; why would he ask what was wrong with me? I looked around to see what he was talking about.

"I am fine . . ." I stopped talking when I heard the cracking and hitching of my voice. When had I started to cry? Why did I cry all the time? My own body was my worst enemy in so many ways.

I forced a laugh. "I am fine. I just am happier than I have ever been." It actually wasn't a lie but, to be honest, I didn't want to go to New York in the morning. I wanted to stay right here with the boy that I loved, forever.

"I am so glad you enjoyed tonight. Mandi and I wanted it to be very special." He looked at his hands as if it were the first time he had ever noticed them.

"I love you, Brax, I love you in ways that I shouldn't love you. I know that you have never said that you love me any more than a best friend or a sister; I don't know when it happened exactly. I think you are the sexiest boy in school, but not only for your looks; it's so much more than that. I love the little crow's feet you have by your eyes when you laugh, or the way your eyes transport me to a secret, private place that only exists to us."

The tears had taken over as I felt relief and fear at the same time. Relief for finally telling him, though it was a little more blunt than I had dreamed, and fear of what he was going to say or do.

I took a deep breath, and allowed my hair to hide my face, wanting to shrink into myself so deep I would be invisible. Silence, silence so thick I could feel it. My mind was screaming—what have you done? You are so stupid. Well, I hope you enjoyed today because you will never see him again after this!

"I am sorry." I had been able to calm the tears so that my apology came out clear and as strong as I could possibly muster.

His hand gently and softly took my chin and pulled my face towards his. His eyes were intense, and I knew he was angry with me. I looked down without moving my face, only my eyes. I wanted to take it all back, rewind back to the art gallery and start over. This was going to be the best night ever and I just ruined it.

"Do not be sorry." His voice was so low I had to look into his eyes to make sure he had actually spoken. His eyes were soft, and his face was no more than an inch from mine.

My heart almost exploded, and feelings came to life in me that I had never felt before. His lips touched mine so softly, I could have believed I had imagined it, but the electricity running through my veins proved otherwise. I couldn't look at him. I was so embarrassed. Did he mean to do that?

"Look at me, Addy." His voice was demanding but gentle. I obeyed, and, when I did, the gateway to our secret place was waiting patiently for me. I watched the light from the moon dance in his eyes. Within seconds, I was the Addyson I dreamed of being. I was beautiful, and someone that Brax could be proud to be with.

It only took the slightest move, and I was kissing him. I closed my eyes first and allowed this moment to be burned into my mind forever. Braxton slowly put his hand in my hair and his other on my cheek. I felt his hand quiver and knew he was nervous too. I opened my eyes to see his face; his eyes too are closed. His nervousness gave me some kind of self-confidence and the fumbling we were producing wasn't going to do. If he were going to wake in the morning and regret this, if this was going to be the last night I ever would spend with Braxton Carmen . . . it would be the best.

"Let me, Brax." His eyes slowly came open, and I took his face in my hands. I forcefully calmed my shaking body and steadied my eyes on his mouth. I slowed everything down and took my time with him. I kissed every inch of his lips; they were as soft as they look. I smiled against his mouth as I became more relaxed than I had thought possible.

How brave would I be? I felt confident and sure of myself. But whenever his eyes would open even in the slightest, I would feel self-conscious and scared; it was not like I had any idea of what I was doing. I just wanted him to remember it forever. I knew I would.

I slightly opened my mouth and took his bottom lip in. I waited for a sign; either a good thing or a bad thing, I waited. His hands came back to my face, and he took over again. My body stiffened from the shock of his quickness. A low, deep growl rolled from his chest before he deepened the kiss, making me melt into his arms.

My first kiss; not just with some guy that had meant nothing to me, but to the man that made me want to live. We spent the next hour exploring one another by the pond. If there were ever a question that I loved Braxton, there is no question now.

—∞—

"Just let me go with you, Addy." Braxton was begging now. He was sitting in my computer chair facing me.

Everything felt so different now. I almost felt scared of him. I was still shocked by everything that had happened that night, and couldn't stop thinking about the fact that I was leaving for New York in less than five hours.

"Braxton, it is three after midnight. I am leaving at five. You cannot go with me. Please, I am begging you to spend the rest of the time we have together."

He let his tired face rest in his hands as they tried desperately to rub the strain away from his eyes. "Then don't go, Addy, just stay here. We have so much to talk about." His voice was confusing. Did he regret what had happened at the pond? Did he just act on the spur of the moment?

I watched him, trying with everything in me, to figure out the meaning of his words.

"I have to go." The thoughts of me being a perfect size seven, with Braxton's arms perfectly around my waist, my arms around his neck, both of us happier than any other couple we knew, was clear and vivid in my mind.

I wanted that more than anything in this world. "Well, let's talk; we have a little time," I whispered without looking at him. I knew it wasn't what he wanted to hear from me. He pulled his chair closer to me. He took both of my hands into his, making me look into his eyes.

"Addy, I love you. I have loved you for a long time. You are my best friend, and I will do anything in this world for you; you know that." He broke eye contact first and looked at his feet as if he had more words down there.

My heart was breaking into a million pieces. But why? What had I expected him to say? He continued without looking at me. "I was afraid that, if you knew that I loved you as more than a sister, it would change everything between us." My eyes shot open and looked at the top of his head. Did he just say what I thought he said?

I smiled. I couldn't help myself. The words ran through my system like an addiction. "Y-you love me . . . like that?" I asked, holding my breath for his answer. Even though we had shared an amazing moment by the pond, I needed to hear him say the words. I had to hear him say it. He looked back at me but said nothing. Instead, he kissed me. I put my hands on either side of his face, "Braxton, just let me . . ." I had to take control of this, think about what I was doing and take my time.

I spent the rest of the night wordlessly expressing my feelings for Braxton, and he did the same. My entire world flipped upside down. I finally told Brax how I truly felt about him. He told me he felt the same, making so many dreams come true, all in one night. Now, I was leaving for New York in less than thirty minutes. How cruel and unexpected life could be.

—⁓—

The ride to the airport was excruciating. Braxton begged all the way there. I wished Aunt Mae had ridden with us instead of with my parents. I could tell Mom and Dad wanted me to ride with them, but they had no idea of what had happened between Brax and me; how hard this actually was. Thankfully, I know Braxton well enough that I had a conversation with Aunt Mae, just in case he asked her if he could come to New York behind my back.

My hand was in his. He was sitting up close to the wheel, his mind going a mile an hour. He would do or say anything right now to stop this from happening. I was scared of what he would do; I couldn't stand to see him like this, and normally would have done anything to stop his pain. The only thing pushing me was the dream of being a better person for him, a better person for us.

I closed my eyes and begged God for strength. He knew my heart and my reasoning. "Please, God, Please help me." I whispered to God so low I was sure Brax couldn't hear over the radio.

The airport was so busy you would think it was 6:00 p.m. instead of six in the morning. People looked excited and happy; the total opposite of me and my family. I was exhausted and emotionally drained; I felt as if I was going to pass out at any moment.

We sat in the over-sized sofa chairs not saying much of anything. Mom or Dad would spontaneously say something like "Call us every single day," and "Don't take the subway at night . . . or ever." I would nod in acknowledgment but never took my eyes off of the floor. I knew how hard this had to be on them, and my own issues with Braxton were the only thing I had running through my brain, until then.

I found the courage to look at my parents. Mom was sitting on the edge of her sofa chair as if she were ready to pounce up at any moment and pull me back to the car. Her grip on my father's hand was so tight, as if his fingers were her life support. Her eyes were blood red and the tissue in her free hand confirmed the tears she had shed. Once she noticed my eyes on her, she cleared her throat and smiled the best she could smile.

"This is going to be a great experience for you, Addy; I'm so proud of you."

I fought greatly to hold back the tears. Dad was leaned back with his ankle on his knee. His eyes too had dark circles and seemed swollen. He had a weak smile on his face, but he never blinked. His mind was far away at the moment, and I was sure he hadn't heard a word Mom had said, or even noticed me looking at him.

"Flight 117 for New York is now boarding." I felt Braxton tense up at the sound of the lady's voice over the loud speaker. I took in deep, calming breathes that seemed to quicken by the second. If I didn't slow down, I was going to hyperventilate.

My Mom was the first to hug me. Her face was close to my ear, and she spoke softly in an attempt to make her words private. "I pray that this is it, Addy. I hope this doctor can help you. I love you so much; don't forget to keep in contact with me. And if for any reason you want to come home, come home." She pulled herself away from me and the free-falling tears soaked her face. My heart caught in my throat, but I couldn't cry in front of her; it would only make it worse.

Dad was next. He squeezed me tightly—too tightly, but I didn't complain. He kissed me on my forehead and pushed away. "I love you, baby girl." and with that he quickly turned away from me. I knew he was hiding the same tears I was trying to hold in.

I turned one last time to face my Braxton. His arms were crossed over his chest, and tears were sliding down his face. He laughed out loud and looked down at his feet, shaking his head; he was trying to shake the tears from his eyes. His laugh said: I can't believe I'm crying in public. I had to laugh a little with him.

I couldn't move forward for I wasn't sure if he wanted me to hug him in front of the entire airport, not to mention my parents. When I didn't close the gap between us, his eyes searched for me. I slowly looked around the airport to try to silently communicate my thoughts with him. Recognition covered his beautiful eyes, and a look of frustration and understanding shone through. He closed the gap with only a few steps and wrapped his arms around me. I instantly felt self-conscious and wondered if he felt my fat rolls.

My parents' seeing us was nothing abnormal. To them this was something that has been going on for our entire lives. But they had no idea how things had changed. With these new feelings, this was no longer a simple hug farewell. This was extremely intimate and personal.

"I didn't know if you wanted me to hug you in public," I whispered as I stared at a lady sitting across the airport staring at us. When she noticed me looking, she retracted her eyes and planted them on the magazine in her lap. I leaned away and looked at Brax. My heart could take no more. His eyes were exhausted. His tears wouldn't stop flowing, and his words, loud enough for anyone remotely close to us to hear, begged to go with me. I broke. I cried with him.

"I will call you every day . . ." he took me back in his arms.

"Please, Addy, please." He was desperate.

". . . I swear it won't be as bad as you think . . ." I begged with him. If something didn't happen soon, I was going to back out.

My eyes wouldn't stop going to the lady in the sofa chair. Every time I looked at her she was looking at us, like we were a circus attraction. I wondered what she thought about Braxton. Did she think something had to be wrong with him?

I didn't have time to get angry at the thoughts, for Braxton had his hands on either side of my face. His shoulders were lifted as if he were putting every piece of him into the kiss. I didn't care about the lady with the magazine, the airport, my parents, or even breathing. I wanted to stay in this spot forever.

The sound of my parents gasping and whispering to one another had me pulling away from him though. I felt my face burn red. Braxton smiled at me, and I was about to tell everyone I was staying home. I picked up my bag and turned towards my family to announce it when Aunt Mae grabbed my wrist and pulled me towards the gate. I pulled against her for only a second. I turned back to look at Brax one last time, and the lady with the magazine caught my eye.

Do this, Addyson, and hopefully you will come home a third of the person you are today. People like that will not stare at you any more, and, if they do, it will be because they want to be you. That voice on the inside of me rang loud and clear. As badly as I wanted to stay with Braxton, I wanted to be pretty for him, for me, for the chance of a real life with him.

"I love you, Addyson." Braxton's voice was deep and tired.

I looked back once more to see Brax standing between my Mom and Dad. Mom had a smile on her face that was genuine. She had seen everything deeper than Dad would have. She knew things had changed between us and would have to tell Dad later.

I waved and yelled, "I love you all." I handed the man the ticket and quickly entered the gate.

—⁂—

Thank God for first class; I could hardly fit in the coach seats. Fit was not the right word; I could fit in the seat; I just couldn't get comfortable at all.

"Did you tell Mom or Dad?" I adjusted myself in my seat but didn't look at Aunt Mae. There was one thing I had failed to mention to anyone, other than Aunt Mae, one thing that would change everything. During my research on the doctor, I found that he had moved his practice back to London, his home town. Not only did I have to forge my parent's signature for a passport, but I had to spend half of my savings to have it expedited. If I was caught, well, I had no idea as to what would happen to me, I just knew it wouldn't be good.

"Hell no! That's your problem, and I don't and won't have anything to do with it!" Aunt Mae pulled her pillow and IPod out of her bag before she continued. "Not that I will not go down with you. Not to mention my brother will probably kill me. But no, I didn't say a word." She placed her earplugs in and sat back for the trip.

I smiled at her. She was right; I had no idea how much trouble I would be in, if I get caught, but nothing would stop me now. I had a plan, and if everything worked out the way it was supposed to, everything would be fine.

I placed my MP3 player on repeat and listened to the playlist Braxton had downloaded for me. Each song held a distinct memory from a time in our lives. He did think about me often. To remember these songs proved it.

I took in a deep breath and watched the Earth below me turn into a perfect picture of patchwork, like a quilt. A quilt made by the hands of God Himself. The view was breathtaking. I imagined my parents and Braxton walking out to the parking lot of the airport. I could see clearly in my mind Braxton being ambushed by my mother, and the thousands of questions she would want to ask, but wouldn't. She was the type that would browbeat answers out of you without actually asking; that made her less nosey. I giggled at the thought. Braxton's eyes came into full view on the face of my phone. I thought about last night, only hours earlier, and reminded myself that no matter what happened; this would be worth it.

CHAPTER 16

I had been sitting in the parking lot of the airport for over an hour. Addyson's parents were long gone. I could easily have gone into the airport and purchased a ticket for New York. I could easily have gone to New York and left everything here; why didn't Addy want me with her? Especially after last night, I don't understand.

Last night, less than eight hours ago, I kissed Addyson. I was right to think that everything would change because it had. Surprisingly, Mr. and Mrs. Michaels didn't say anything out of the way, but Mrs. Michaels kept smiling at me, from ear to ear, as she got into their car. I waved and smiled back. I wondered if they would still let me stay with her as much as they had done. I wondered if they would change towards me. Of course, what did it matter; she was gone and would be gone for ten months.

The airport parking lot never slowed down. There were vehicles constantly coming in and out; I felt like a part of me had just died and the world kept going. I knew I would see Addyson again, but I felt like I wouldn't. I wanted to be close to her. I wanted to hold her hand, and see her smile. I wanted her.

I have known for a while that I loved her more than a friend. I had suppressed the underlying feelings for years, to be honest. I was scared, but, not of what other people would think of me. No, I was scared that we would not work out, and I would lose her forever. I would rather have had her as the best friend forever, versus never having her around again. Now that we had taken things to another level there was no way I could turn back now.

With the turn of the key, my faithful Camero came to life. I needed to go home, I needed to sleep, but I wanted to go to Addy's house and sit by the pond. I wanted to lie in the fresh grass and relive last night. I pushed the buttons for windows to roll down and blasted the radio loud to keep me awake.

—∽—

Standing by the pond I realized I didn't want to be there. It hurt too much. I began the walk up the hill towards the house, leaving my car by the pond. The sun was high and scorching that morning. As I approached the pool gate I could see Addyson and me sitting in those lounge chairs. Her silky black hair fell around her face as I said something to make her laugh; I forced myself into her room.

Everything was exactly as we left it. I shut the door behind me and put my keys in my pocket. Standing in the middle of her room, everything around me reminded me of her, of us. I crawled into her bed and let the smell of her perfume and soap fill my insides. The confusion and pain of her being gone was overwhelming. I buried my face in her pillow and held onto it for dear, sweet, life. I let all of the emotions flow.

With my eyes closed, the vivid images of last night came clearly to my mind. I immediately began to calm down. I knew, even though she didn't say, that she was upset by the pond because she would be leaving that day. I knew in her heart she did not want to leave me. I could see her sweet face inches from mine. I could almost feel her hands in my hair and softly running across my face. I could smell the lingering fragrance of her perfume and feel the yellow, brown glow of her eyes as she stared into my spirit. When her lips touched mine, I couldn't breathe. I had never kissed someone, nor had someone kissed me, who loved me as much as she did. I was scared I would disappoint her, that I would destroy this fantasy of hers that I was so perfect. I was not perfect. When she saw the boyfriend side of me, how jealous I could be, how emotional I could be, how clingy, too clingy to be a man, I can be; would she still love me? Would she be able to handle me? Nobody is perfect.

—∽—

I woke, and the sun had already set. I pulled my tired body to the edge of the bed and held my pounding head in my hands. I feel like I haven't slept in days. The nightmares of Addyson meeting someone in New York made sleep restless and useless.

I pulled my cell out of my pocket to check for missed calls or texts from Addy. I had none. Was she having a hard time with this at all? I had wanted to call her all day, and she hadn't even sent me a basic text. Did she regret last night? Did any of it mean anything to her? Did I mean anything to her?

I took a long look around her room. The pictures of me on her corkboard, our swimming clothes in the hamper, and, in the far corner, the small painting I had bought for her so many years ago at the Apple festival. I was a part of everything in that room, how could I possibly not mean anything to her? How could she regret last night?

I stood from the bed and walked out of the room. I locked the door behind me and ran towards my car. I was going home. I was going to take a shower and get some food, and if she still hadn't called me by then, I was going to call her; we needed to talk.

CHAPTER 17

New York was nothing like North Carolina. Everyone had some place to be, and apparently, they were all late! There were more people on the street corner, waiting to cross the street, than in the whole town I lived in.

We had cabs in North Carolina, but I had never seen this many on one street, ever. Aunt Mae hailed one with a professional sounding whistle; I have to say it was kind of impressive. "Come on, Addy, move it!" Aunt Mae was almost in a dead run, trying to throw all of our bags in the back of the cab, like if we didn't hurry up, someone was going to jump in, and it was going to take off.

Aunt Mae jumped in on the passenger's side in the back seat, and crawled as fast as she could behind the driver. I jumped in and slammed the door. Apparently, either we had taken too long, or the cab driver had some place to be; he floored it so hard and fast, my back went into the seat.

"You better hold onto the . . ." Aunt Mae was trying to warn me to hold onto the hand grip above the window like she was—too late. He slammed on his brakes at a red light, and I flew into the back of the passenger's seat in front of me. The driver turned his head and looked me dead in the eye. He rolled his eyes with a look of utter disgust and mumbled something in another language. I turned beet red and pushed myself back into the seat. I looked at Aunt Mae; she was laughing. I grabbed the handle and held on for dear life. Hell, I didn't think it was too flippin' funny at all; I was scared.

At the house, Aunt Mae paid the speed demon, and started unloading the trunk. I was grabbing luggage as fast as she was throwing it at me. The trunk had barely clicked shut when the cab driver took off again, leaving black skid marks on the road behind him.

"Wow!" I said decidedly to myself.

"You get used to it, girl. It took me a while, but you really do get used to it, and now, to me, New York is the only place to live!"

Aunt Mae had lived there for almost 15 years. She had gone there with her fiancé. He worked there, and his job was extremely important to him. Apparently, his secretary was more valuable than his actual job. Two years after she had dropped her family, her job, her whole life, to live here with him, he left her for his much younger secretary. She had never allowed herself to love again.

Aunt Mae was my dad's younger sister. They looked so much alike, but acted as though they were from totally different universes. Mae was laid back and seemed to be carefree. She was content with the life she led and had more money than she knew what to do with. Dad, on the other hand, was always trying to move up the ladder. He would not be happy until he was at the top of the food chain. And, I guess there is nothing wrong with that. Mom and Dad are extremely comfortable, but far from rich. Aunt Mae acted more like my age; other than desperately missing Braxton and Mandi, I thought this should be a lot of fun.

When we walked in the front door of Mae's house, she literally slung the luggage onto the floor in the foyer. "Come on, let's go check out your room." For someone her age, she was remarkably energetic and got excited about everything. You couldn't help but be cheerful around her.

When I stepped into what would be my new home for the next ten months, it wasn't the same room I had stayed in the last time. She had redecorated the whole room. Not that there was anything wrong with it before. It had been covered in a southern country floral theme. It was pretty, but old.

Now I had a king-sized water bed, a laptop, a TV, bean bag chairs, and downright cool modern art sculptures all around. The whole room was decked out in loud, vibrant colors. I loved this. It was like something you would see on TV.

"You didn't have to do all of this for me Aunt Mae; this is so beautiful. Thank you so much!" I squealed. She hugged me. "I am so glad to have you here with me, Addy; we are really going to have a lot of fun."

I glanced around the room again. I noticed two things this time I had not noticed the first time. There was a present wrapped up with tons of ribbons on the bed, and the picture hanging on the wall. I had thought it was one of those paintings that looked like it moved, but it really was moving! It was a real fish tank, with real fish in it. How flippin' cool was that? I instantly retrieved my cell phone and took a picture of it to send to Mandi and Braxton.

"Don't forget to feed them." Aunt Mae was standing against the post of my bed with her arms crossed; she was smiling from ear to ear. I think she may have been enjoying watching me run around like an overly hyper child on Christmas morning, just as much as I was enjoying this new room.

I walked over to the bed. "Is this present for me?" I knew the answer and began ripping the paper off before she answered. It was an IPAD. My mouth hung open; I had always wanted one of those. "I got your mom and dad one too. You can actually see them while you talk to them on that thing . . . so I hear . . . sort of like a web-cam. I don't have the first idea how you do it, but you will figure it out, I am sure!"

Aunt Mae opened the curtains covering my gargantuan windows, and I gasped at the view. Just as far as I could see were bigger than life buildings, people in the hustle and bustle of their everyday lives, cars and streets that looked as if they stretched to the end of the world. It truly was a beautiful place.

I suddenly longed to have Braxton and Mandi here to share this with. It would have been perfect; I would have had everything that I needed if I had them here. No disrespect to my parents. I missed them too.

Aunt Mae and I retrieved my entire luggage and lugged it up the flight of stairs to my room. "Dinner is at seven; we are going out, so be ready, okay?" Aunt Mae didn't wait for an answer as she shut the door behind her.

I unpacked all of my stuff in a flash, hanging clothes, putting bathroom stuff away, and checking out the room in closer detail. I almost screamed when I found the bathtub! It was humongous, even to me, and there is nothing better than a delightful bubble bath and a compelling love story!

I called Braxton as I was sitting on my bed, unable to wait any longer to talk to him.

"Hey, Brax, did you get the pictures I sent?" Mandi had already responded. She agreed the fish tank was the coolest thing ever.

"I did, and I miss you." His voice still sounded down.

I guess in all of this excitement, I had sort of forgotten about everything that had happened between us the previous night and that day. Honestly, it hadn't felt real. I was sure that it had all happened, but it had crossed my mind that it was all just out of emotion and spur of the moment. A small part of me was scared to death that he would regret it, and everything would change.

After all, less than twenty-four hours ago we had told each other our feelings for each other and now I was in New York for ten months. I couldn't get Jennifer out of my mind; I even told Mandi to watch her for me. I was more than sure she would continue her pursuit of Braxton. Of course, she would, no matter what, whether I was here in New York or at home right beside him. Jennifer always got what she wanted.

Mandi might blush when Braxton complimented her, but don't think for one second she couldn't whoop some tail. It was amazing how fiery she could be. She might be small, but she could easily take care of Jennifer.

A bigger part of me thought that nothing this good could ever happen to me. I mean, what could I expect? When you're told your whole life that you are lower than scum, it's hard not to believe it. Even if you do not realize you do believe it.

"I miss you too, Brax. I was just thinking that if you were here this would be perfect." I shouldn't have said that; why the hell would I say that?

"I can be there by tomorrow afternoon, Addy." His voice sounded hopeful and even a little cheerful. "Brax, you can't come up here right now." He let out a long sigh and the sadness came back. We talked for another hour before I had to let him go and get ready for dinner. "I love you, Braxton. Try to cheer up, please, for me."

It felt so strange hearing him say he loved me. Not that he had never said it before. But now it was a whole new level of love. To be honest, something I had never imagined myself experiencing with anyone, much less with Braxton.

"I love you too, Addy; I promise I will try. Call me before bed, okay?"

I tried to picture his sweet face. "I will. Bye."

—⚉—

Even at seven o'clock at night there were more people on the street, in front of the restaurant, than there were in my whole town. In our town, the whole place shut down around nine, except for Wal-Mart. The way this place looked, these people were just getting started.

The restaurant was very dimly lit; the only light flickered from candles on the tables. There was a piano being played in the corner softly, and the little round tables, mostly for two, sat so close to each other, they must have had two hundred tables smashed into that place.

I instantly felt awkward and out of place in my Capris and t-shirt. "This is a really fancy place, Aunt Mae, you could have told me to wear something more appropriate," I said, embarrassed. She had on almost the same thing as me. "We are not here to be runway models; we are here to feed our faces! This place has the best shrimp cocktail on the planet."

When the hostess came to see us, by the pure horror and shock on her face, it was clear she agreed with me. "Two? Right this way." Aunt Mae just laughed at the lady's disapproving glare, and made a mocking face behind her back as we followed her.

Crap! I couldn't see anything in there. I was watching the pianist, and not watching where I was going, when "Watch your step!" came to my attention way too late. There was a small step down, with two steps leading to a lower level, the level the piano was on; before I knew it, I was on my face in the floor. I missed the steps altogether. "I am so sorry," I said out of shock and embarrassment.

There was a couple sitting to the right of me and I had come remarkably close to falling on their table. "Thank God you didn't land on the table; you would have broken it all to pieces!" The lady was glaring at me in her black low cut dress that fit her perfect negative four size body, and showed off every curve of her. The man with her was holding his champagne—or whatever that was—glass in front of him, not even trying to hide his laughter.

"I'm really sorry," I repeated, sure that the shine of my red face was easily seen in this darkness. I got to my feet, with Aunt Mae frantically asking if I was okay. "I will be fine. I am so sorry." I didn't mean to embarrass her. I should have been paying attention.

The hostess couldn't have cared less. She was standing at a table impatiently waiting for us to hurry up and sit down, so she could go seat more guests. I looked at the hostess. "I'm so . . ." she placed the menu down and walked off before I could finish apologizing. That's when I noticed the whole restaurant was staring at me. It was horrible. I opened my menu and sank into my chair, trying to hide from the glares.

"You shouldn't be sorry, Addy; if they would turn some damn lights on in this place, it wouldn't have happened. We can leave if you want to." I wasn't sure if she meant for just me to leave, or if she meant for both of us to leave. I knew she had to be embarrassed.

"I should have been paying attention, Aunt Mae; I was looking at the pianist, not watching where I was going. I will be fine; if you are not too embarrassed to stay and eat here, I don't mind staying," I said from behind my menu. The menu flew to the table forcefully. The unexpected movement had my already racing heart jumping into my throat.

"Don't you ever think I am embarrassed of you? It was an accident, Addy, and it could have happened to any asshole in this place!" She said this in a loud, stern whisper, glaring into my eyes. I tried my best to shake it off, and act as if nothing had happened.

We ordered our food, and she was right—it was the best shrimp cocktail I had ever eaten by far. We had sat there for over an hour talking, catching up with each other. It had been almost two years since I had seen her. Of course, all I wanted to talk about was Braxton and Mandi.

"Addy, obviously Braxton loves you just the way you are. Anybody with half of a brain and one eye can see that. So, why go through with all of this doctor stuff, if you really don't have to?" She was sincere, but she had no idea what she was saying.

"Aunt Mae, you don't understand." I laughed, but, on the inside, I wanted to cry as all of the memories flooded my brain. I began to tense up and tried hard to relax and thought of how to make her see.

"Do you realize that if it had been you who fell down those steps, those two people at that table would have tried to help you? Of course not. See, people look at me differently. If you're not overweight, you will never understand. Men hold doors open for you, while the same man would let it shut in my face. If you dropped something on the street, one or more people would try to help you gather your things, but would walk past me steadily without thinking twice. Men walk past you and smile and greet you, while they look at me with either a glare of disgust or no recognition at all. Not to mention the stares, the judgment, the whispers, and snickering."

I took a deep breath, deciding if I was going to share a terribly real and personal experience that I had been through. I felt that if there was any way I could make her understand, she would not try to talk me out of going to London, and might even help me with my parents.

101

"I was in the eighth grade. There were two boys I had gym with. I always failed gym because I refused to change my clothes in a locker room, full of perfect people, with no privacy at all. Even though I participated, the teacher insisted that is was part of the class, but anyway, Chad and Daniel were always together. They were in all kinds of sports activities, and both were very popular, but especially Chad. Other than the usual name calling, Daniel never spoke to me. But Chad would say Hi. That's about it, but it was a lot for me. He might smile at me every once in a while, and had even tried to help me with some of the activities we had to do. His actions would have been overlooked by anyone else, but to me it meant the world. He didn't stop the other people from picking on me, or call them down, he simply didn't add to it . . ."

I sat back in my seat, realizing I didn't have to whisper as I had been; we were almost the only two left in the place, the only ones left on this floor for sure. I spoke up a little as I continued.

"One day right after class, Daniel ran up to me and handed me a piece of paper. I was ready for the name calling or prank that always came with his presence. But he only said, "Chad thinks you're cute and wants you to call him tonight," and I was absolutely stunned. I went home that night and called him. Chad answered the phone, and I told him I was told he wanted me to call him. He burst out laughing, and said "Yeah, Daniel and I prank each other. We give the other's number to the ugliest people we can find, and tell them to call." I heard laughing in the background, and he hung up. I held onto the phone until the buzzing stopped, and it was just a dead line."

I watched the color drain out of my aunt's loving face, and the pity and remorse, I am so used to seeing on Braxton's face, replaced it. I had never told another soul about that; as far as I knew, apart from Daniel and Chad, no one else knew about it. Reliving it is hell.

"I want a chance for me and Braxton to have a normal life together. I want people to look at us and think: 'What a happy couple!'—not 'God, he can do so much better; what is wrong with him? If she can have him I know I can.' Do you understand?"

Mae took a while to answer, and the only words that came from her mouth were: "Yes. I do now."

—◊◊◊—

To say the least, my first day in New York had been an eventful one. I was hoping with my whole heart that this was not a sign of how this trip was going to go. I spent the rest of the night laying in my bed, in the dark, talking to Braxton until we couldn't stay awake any longer.

I didn't mention the awful things that had happened. I knew if he thought for one moment that I was having a hard time, he would have been there on the first flight out.

I was not sure why I don't want him to know about London. I knew he would be happy for me. I knew he would want to go with me, for support. But I just felt as if this were something I had to do on my own. I might find that I would regret it. But right now, I was sticking to my decision.

CHAPTER 18

Lying in my own bed for the first time in two nights, I was unusually awake. I had just got off the phone with Addyson; she had no idea how glad I was when she sent me those texts of her new room and finally called me. Her new room was breathtaking, but I couldn't help but wonder if she would like it more in New York and decide to stay longer.

"How did today go?" I was hoping she hated it there. I wanted her to say she wanted to come home, that New York was a colossal mistake.

"It's a lot different than North Carolina for sure." Her voice was so tired. I had a feeling there were some things she was not telling me, but I tried to let it go.

"I miss you, Addyson, and it's only the first day." I felt like such a girl, but I had no choice but to be honest with Addy; she would know when I was lying to her. I felt comfortable to be real with her too; that makes all the difference in the world. No one, not even my parents, had seen the real me as Addy had.

"I miss you, too. I am kind of scared about tomorrow, about the first day of school and everything. Just having you in the same school with me, makes me feel safer." Addy's words had every fiber of my being begging to go to her and protect her.

I kept her on the phone as long as I could. I could hear her falling asleep on the other end. The sound of her steady breathing told me she was sound asleep. I would have been happy to just lie there and listen to her sleep. With my eyes closed, I could imagine her lying here with her sweet face on my chest, where I could protect her from anything and everything.

"Brax . . ." Her groggy voice came through my end of the phone.

"Yeah," My voice sounded just as groggy from the lack of speaking.

"I think we are falling asleep. I guess I better go."

I closed my eyes and lied. "Yeah, I guess we are." I waited; saying bye is so hard.

"I will call you after school tomorrow. I love you, Brax."

I had to let her go. "I love you too, Addyson." I heard the phone click after we both said goodbye.

Neither of us had said a word about the previous night. I wondered if she thought about it as much as I did. Lying in my bed, it was all I could think about. It was one thing having her five miles down the street, not talking to me, but now, she was thousands of miles away and I couldn't see her, touch her, check on her, or anything. Mandi would not be there for her either. She was walking into a school that she knows nothing about, completely alone. The worst part was, there was nothing I could do about it.

I stood from the bed and walked over to my desk. I thumped the mouse of my computer and brought my desk top to life. Pulling up my music files, thousands came to view. I chose the playlist I had downloaded for Addyson's MP3 player, and clicked on play all. I stood from the desk once the music began to fill my room.

I lay back in my bed and glanced at the neon green lights of my alarm clock. It was already after two in the morning. I had to get some sleep. Tomorrow was only the second day of the next ten months.

God help me.

CHAPTER 19

The first day of school proved that the kids in New York were no different from the kids in North Carolina. The laughs, the glares, the whispers, and pointing, it was there too; but somehow it seemed worse in New York. Maybe because there were so many more people in this school than mine. This school was monumental and I spent most of my day in the halls, lost. Of course, no one cared, or even offered to help me.

At lunch, I was sitting at a table by myself staring at my orange juice, texting Braxton and Mandi. They both were in class, so they couldn't text back as fast as I could. God, I wanted to be there with them so badly. This was only my first full day here.

A girl with fire red hair came walking to the table. "Can I sit here?" She asked, and I knew she was nice—some people you could just tell.

"Sure, if you want to." I said adjusting my posture.

"My name is Caroline, according to your schedule I have next class with you." she pointed to my schedule that was laid out on the table beside my orange juice. I didn't say anything. I wanted to be with Braxton so badly I was miserable.

"I am sorry about the assholes in this school. But don't let them get you down; there are some really good people here too." As if on cue, three more people came and sat at the table with us. "Oh, shut up, Jace; I do not eat the same thing every day." A girl with long brown hair said to the guy laughing at her.

"Hi, my name is Carla. What's yours?" asked the girl following them, as she slung her tray on the table. "Addyson, but you can call me Addy; everyone else does." I said watching them all directly.

They all said hi as the first two introduced themselves to me. "I am Chloe, and that dork over there is Jace." Jace made a sardonic face at Chloe, and the rest of us laughed.

I spent the rest of my lunch getting to know them. So far they all were quite cool. But Caroline seemed to be the one I had the most in common with. Her red hair was bright red. It was thicker than hair I had ever seen before. I assumed it was naturally curly and fell perfectly around her pale face. Her eyes reminded me of Mandi's but only the color. Her eyes were big and round and as green as grass. They made her look young and innocent. I grinned to myself as the thought that she probably was wild and crazy too floated around my head.

Carla seemed shy and awkward. She was the skinniest person I had ever seen. I imagined that, if she wore a bathing suit, you could point out every single bone in her body. Her brown hair was short, and she didn't have on a stitch of makeup. Her lips were as thin as the rest of her. Her eyes seemed sunken in and almost hollow. When she spoke I had to strain to hear her.

Chloe was the total opposite of Carla. She was loud; everything about her was loud, and she didn't seem to care in the least. When she laughed, I sank down in my chair, thinking every eye in place would be on us. But no one seemed to notice at all. I guess they all were used to her. Her long hair fell to the middle of her back. It was jet black, obviously dyed, with bright spots of hot pink and white. Her mascara and eyeliner had to be equivalent to half of a container, and her eyes were as gray as a crayon. I couldn't help but stare. I imagined how pretty she would be without all that extra stuff on her. But, if that's what she wanted who was I to say any different?

Jace reminded me of every jock we had back home. Messy blonde hair, blue eyes, pretty built from the look of him, and a smile to light up a room. His perfect teeth only accented his deep dimples, and I found myself blushing when he directed that smile towards me. He wasn't my Braxton, but he was definitely cute. The one thing that made me know for sure that he was not a jock was his black-framed glasses. They made his eyes pop and gave him this exceedingly intelligent or nerdy look—but in a good way. His polo was wrinkle free along with his khakis. I could not help but giggle at the fact that he had on white tennis shoes. I totally expected penny loafers or something. Over all, he was adorable.

"This high school is the size of a college back home." I glanced down the hall we are standing in. "I haven't made it to one single class on time so far," I said, searching my schedule again, as if more information would pop up somewhere on the paper. The classes didn't last as long as ours, but they had more classes. At home, we had four classes plus lunch. Here, we had six classes plus lunch, but it was the same amount of hours in all, eight in the morning until two thirty in the afternoon.

"Come on; you are in my next class so just follow me." Caroline looped her arm through mine as we walked down the hall.

"Um, Bye!" Jace called after us, offended we hadn't said bye. Caroline threw her hand in the air and waved without even looking back at him.

"Bye Jace," I said, as she continued to pull me down the hall.

We turned right at the end of the hall, and two girls were hovering around a small girl against the lockers. My heart began to race. I knew without hearing a word of their conversation exactly what was going on. I knew the next decision I made would either make my life a lot easier here for the next ten months, or make it worse, tenfold. I fought with the decision to help the poor girl. The thought of so many people just passing by as I was picked on came to mind. I remember thinking, what did I ever do to you? Just my existence alone had offended everyone around me, and no one would help me or cared to help me; the feelings of fear, humiliation, hatred for myself, and others around me, dug deep holes of anger inside of me.

Just as we walked past the group of girls, Caroline whispered, "Don't look at them; just keep walking." I wondered if that's why nobody helped me before, if they too were just too scared to help me.

I stopped and pulled my arm from Caroline. I took a deep breath and stepped close to the bullies. "Leave her alone." I said, my voice shaking more than I wanted. The small girl didn't waste a second of time and took off running down the hall as the bullies turned to focus on me.

"Who are you?" Wow, she reminded me of Jennifer—Jennifer with a Yankee accent.

I didn't respond. The fear that was building up on the inside of me had me frozen in place. I immediately regretted this. Who did I think I was?

"I asked you a question? Who. Are. You?" The girl took a step towards me, and I instinctively took two steps back.

"Addyson." I said simply. The girl busted out laughing as if my name was the funniest thing she has ever heard.

"Dice, did she just say her name is Fattyson?" She laughed as she playfully pushed the other girl. Dice? The girls name was Dice, and she was making fun of my name? Really? Fattyson, I had to say that was original; I had never heard that one before. Dice realized that her friend wanted her to laugh at her joke and began to laugh a fake laugh.

"Addyson, let's go; we are going to be late." I heard Caroline talking, and I understood what she said. But she didn't realize that as soon as I turned my back towards these two anything could happen. She could push me down, or hit me, or trip me as I tried to walk off. I had learned over the years to never give up my back, and to wait until the bully was finished with me. Sometimes, more often than not, it prevented any physical abuse.

"Is Fattyson deaf as well as dumb?" Dice spoke this time. I didn't move a muscle. After a few more minutes of laughing, they were bored with me. "Come on, Ace. Let's go." I had to hold back a laugh. Dice and Ace, were they in some kind of gang or something? What was the deal with those names?

"Don't you ever interfere with anything we are doing ever again, Fattyson, or you will pay for it. Do you understand?" I didn't respond at all. Ace grabbed a handful of my hair and pulled my head back, forcing me to look at her. "Do you understand me?" Her spit landed on my cheek as her words were forced through clenched teeth.

"Yes." I said simply, and she forcefully pushed me away from her.

Over all, it could have been a lot worse, and I was happy with how it ended. I watched them walk away and began to breathe again. The little girl got away, and I wasn't lying in the floor bleeding: win-win.

"What the hell is wrong with you, Addy?" Caroline was standing in front of me as I rubbed the raw spot in the back of my head. "Why did you stick your nose in their business; you have no idea who they are." Caroline rambled on as I watched them turn the corner out of my sight.

"Caroline, you will never understand unless you have been bullied." I had no idea what possessed me to step in to that situation. But I know it felt fantastic to have helped another person.

In English, the first full class I had had all day, I realized that New York was way ahead of North Carolina. They expected a lot more from their students and were way ahead of curriculum here. I had a lot to do to catch up. My mind was drifting back and forth between the teacher's lesson and Brax. I wondered if he was ever scared when he was taking up for me. I wondered how he felt afterwards. Would he have stepped in for that little girl too? Of course, he would have; it's who he was. I missed him so much.

The bell sounded and the class scattered like ants. I was still packing my bag when Jace walked into the room. I was dumbfounded at how he made it to this class so fast.

"Are you crazy?"

I stopped in mid-sling. "What? How did you know about that?" I watched his face closely.

"Everyone knows, Addyson. Nobody stands up to those girls, nobody. They pick on everyone, and I mean everyone, even the jocks and cheerleaders." Jace looked behind him to see if anyone else could hear his words. "I told you Addy, you have no idea who these girls are. There are five more of them, and they are usually together."

Well, that explained the names; they were a gang. What had I got myself into? Hopefully, if I did as I was told, and didn't interfere again, I would be left alone. Or I had just made them focus on me; this was what I got for trying to help someone? No wonder no one ever helped me; what would I have done without Brax?

I spent as much time with them as I could for the rest of the day. They helped me find my classes, and instead of riding the bus, they took me home. They stayed at the house, with Aunt Mae's permission, for several hours and even ended up having dinner with us. My first day ended a lot better than it had started. I had four new friends in one day, where I only have two at home, in my whole life. I am not sure of too many things, but I was positive that my new friends were going to make this much, much easier!

CHAPTER 20

It had been over a month since Addy left for New York. Sadly, the time was not flying by for me. Her phone calls were coming less often, and when she actually did call they were getting shorter and shorter.

A couple of times, I had called her and heard some guy's voice in the background, along with others, but the guy's stood out to me for obvious reasons. It's not like she hadn't told me all about her new friends or that she was trying to hide this guy from me. But I was still madly jealous. I mean, I was jealous of all of them, even Mae. They all got to spend time with Addy every day. They saw her and could touch her if they wanted to. While all I got was to wait on the damn phone calls, and text messages.

I had thought about surprising her and just showing up one weekend. I was starting to think that maybe she was hiding something from me. I didn't understand why she didn't want me to come. Why?

The day before she left, we had spent the night making out. That sounds so horrible; it had been so much more than that to me, but I was wondering if she didn't regret it. If I had it my way, I would have been on the phone with her every free moment I had, texting every moment in between. If it was up to her, I think she could have easily gone days without calling at all.

I was not sure if I was pissed, hurt, or both. I knew the more I thought about it, the more the emotions swelled up in my chest; I had to get out and do something. Sitting in this house, by the damn phone, was driving me crazy!

—m—

Thank God Mandi was home. I had been bugging the crap out of her, I knew. But it seemed like everywhere I went Jennifer turned up, but she would never turn up at Mandi's.

"You want to go to Starbucks, and get a coffee?" Mandi was pulling her pocket book over her shoulder as she walked towards my car.

"I guess so." I laughed and shook my head as I pulled my keys back out of my pocket. She must have been expecting me; I hadn't even made it to her front door before she came outside.

"Have you heard from Addy today?" I asked, hoping she would say yes, and tell what they talked about, but hoped she said no, because I hadn't. "She texted me earlier and said that her and Caroline were going to do some sightseeing today." She was putting her seat belt on as I pulled out of her driveway.

"Did she say anything about me?" I asked, fully aware of how pathetic I sounded. I couldn't help it. "She said she missed you. And the time was going by too slow." I had a gut feeling she was lying, trying to save my feelings.

"I miss her more than she knows." I sighed and stared out of the windshield.

The parking lot of Starbucks was loaded, but we went in anyway. I ordered my usual and Mandi ordered hers. I paid for them both, and we walked to the only empty table, the one outside on the sidewalk.

"Can I talk to you honestly; I know I am asking a lot, but only between us; don't tell Addy?" Mandi looked suddenly nervous as my request sunk in. "I want you to be honest with me, Mandi, no matter what the answers are, okay? Please?" I was trying to push her into agreeing without actually giving her a choice. She sort of nodded and drank her coffee.

"Does Addy regret being with me? I mean, I do realize I have never actually, officially, asked her to be my girlfriend, but the night before she left, well, I thought it was pretty clear for both of us. She told me how much she loved me, and I didn't really have the chance to tell her everything, but if nothing else she knows I love her." I held my breath waiting for her response. I wasn't happy when she started laughing.

"Do you know what is so funny about this? And you have to know that I wouldn't be telling you this if I thought Addy wouldn't want me to. I have to be clear on that, Brax. You both are my best friends, and I will try my best to always be there for you both. But when Addy or you tell me, it's private, I will keep it private, so if you ask me something private, I will say I can't answer that, and you will need to ask her, okay?" I understood, but my mind started whirling on what it could be that she didn't want me to know. "I understand."

Her voice broke through my thoughts, and I started to focus on her instead of beating the hell out of this Jace dude. "It's so funny, Braxton, because she says the same thing to me. She is scared that you will regret that night before she left. She is scared you will change your mind, realizing it was a mistake, and then she will also lose your friendship, something that would kill her."

I sat there half relieved and half wanting to jump on a plane to New York. "What has she told you about this Jace guy?" I asked, not trying to hide my jealousy and anger.

"Honestly not much. The only real thing she has said to me about him is that he sort of reminds her of you in ways."

What did that mean? "How does he remind her of me?" The jealousy was taking over, and I was squeezing my coffee cup, so hard the lid popped off.

"He is protective of her; if she has troubles or issues, he takes up for her. But so do the three girls too. It's not in a sexual way. Brax, are you jealous of Jace?"

Why did she have to ask? What was dreadfully sad was I was jealous of them all; just because they were with Addyson. I had been totally honest with Mandi up to this point; there was no reason to lie now. "Hell, yes I am. I should be the one protecting her. I should be the one there with her, and I don't understand why she won't let me come up there, Mandi, I feel like . . . like . . . she is hiding something from me, and I think it has something to do with this Jace." His name came out of my mouth like acid. And the thought of her looking at anyone the way she looked at me was unbearable.

"It's not like that, Brax; you're letting your mind take you for a ride." I could see her sympathy. "Braxton, she doesn't call much for a lot of reasons, but the main one is she truly believes she makes you depressed. I talked to her last night, and she said she wanted to call you back after she got off the phone with me, but the sadness in your voice kills her. She said she hated telling you that you couldn't come up there. That if you begged her one more time she would give in and come home, she couldn't stand your pain; it tortures her."

She threw her cup in the trash can a few feet away without standing up. "Look, I can only imagine how hard it is on the two of you. She will be gone for a long time. The day after you two confessed your love, for one another, she leaves, but both of you knew the consequences of your actions. You both knew she was leaving. We now have less than four months before we go to New York for Christmas break. If you don't get this jealousy under control, the two of you won't make it until then. I am sorry, but it's true."

She pulled her pocket book over her shoulder, hinting she was ready to go. I stood from the table and walked towards the car. "Where to now?" I asked in a low voice, hearing her words in my mind over and over again. Christmas break, the one thing Addy agreed to; I was living for Christmas break. I couldn't wait to go to New York and spend an entire week with her.

"Addy's house." I looked at her with raised eyebrows.

"Why?" I asked curiously.

"Just do it, no questions." She grinned at me and stared out of her window.

—m—

This was the first time I had been inside Addy's room since the night she left for New York. All of the memories of that night flooded my fragile mind. Mandi walked over to Addy's desk and opened the drawer. "Addyson is very smart, Braxton; well, at least she really knows you. She said when this happens, and you start getting upset or worried to give you this . . ."

I looked at her, confused for a second, and took the book from her outstretched hands. It was Addyson's diary. "Are you sure she wants me to have this?" I asked, feeling as if I was about to intrude in an extraordinarily unforgivable way.

She laughed and shook her head. "She knew you were going to say that too." She pulled her cell phone out of her pocket. She played with it for a moment and then showed it to me.

~Braxton is a thinker, Mandi, and when the time comes, when he starts doubting my feelings, give him my diary. All of his doubts will fade. Tell him to read this, to prove I want him to have it. Trust me, he will ask if you are sure about it. Brax, I love you. Talk to you soon, Mandi, and thanks so much. ~

Addy had sent it just a week ago. "I guess she does know me." I laughed, feeling a little stupid.

"A girl who can paint your eyes, in such detail, without looking at a picture or having you in the same room at all—she knows you alright. Probably better than you do! Now come on and take me home, so you can read it." I was anxious to read it. I couldn't wait to read it. I was flipping through, scanning the pages as we walked to my car. I almost asked her to drive, but changed my mind.

I made it to Mandi's house in record time. "Call me when you need to; I'll be up late tonight." I gave Mandi a questioning look. "She said you will need to talk to me after reading it." Her green eyes glistened in the sun. I couldn't help but laugh as she belly laughed all the way to her front door. "I love you, Addy." I whispered as I backed out of Mandi's driveway.

CHAPTER 21

I had no doubts that Braxton would start questioning my feelings for him. I laughed as Mandi told me the whole story of what had happened.

After we hung up, I called Braxton, to see if he was any better. His voice sounded so good to me. If I closed my eyes I could picture his eyes, his facial expressions as he talked; his hand, not holding his phone, would be going a mile a minute or behind his head, a habit he had had since we were kids.

He was probably lying across the sofa in his room, with one leg on the sofa, and one on the table that sits in front of it. He would be all leaned back against the armrest with no shirt, no shoes, just his favorite shorts that truly looked like they deserved to be in the trash, and some snack in his lap—he honestly does eat all of the time, and stays so fit, makes me sick.

"Heeey Braxton . . ." I had a smile on my face, because if this worked, he would be a lot better now.

"Hey Baby, I miss you even more now. Why didn't you ever tell me some of these things that you wrote about me?" Well I didn't expect that question . . . "Are you there, Addy?"

I was trying to think of how to put it. "I am here; I guess the biggest reason is because I didn't think you felt the same way. I was terrified if I told you I would lose you."

Now the silence was returned. "I wish I had told you, Addyson, years ago. I just sort of thought you knew. I mean, I don't treat anyone else the way I treat you, and sure, I said I loved you like a sister, but nobody loves there sister that much . . . do they?"

I laughed, it was almost as if he had quoted my own thoughts . . . or maybe I had written that in there and he actually was. "I did think about that sometimes. But I always thought I was reading too far into things. I do miss you Braxton, and I want to talk to you so bad, but I have to go right now. I promise we will talk tonight as long as we can, until we fall asleep, okay? Please don't be angry."

I prayed he didn't ask why because I had to go to the post office that day and pick up my passport for London. My appointment was in less than two weeks, and the passport was all I lacked. I had to leave then, as they might close before I could get there.

"Okay, I'll talk to you tonight. I love you. Bye." I was trying to hurry off before he asked.

"I love you too . . . Bye." I could hear the smile on his face; it was the best sound in the world. "Addy, wait, wait, are you there?"

I had almost hung up when I heard my name again. "Yeah, I'm here." I pulled my purse over my shoulder and started downstairs.

"I never asked you officially . . . will you belong to me?" I guessed he meant would I be his girlfriend. Really? He had to ask? My heart melted as if he had just proposed marriage or something . . .

"Braxton I have always belonged to you."

—⁂—

I barely made it to the post office in time. I walked in and waited in line. I guess everyone waited until the last minute that day. They were closing in three minutes, and the line was all the way to the door. The line was moving quickly.

"What do you need?" The man behind the counter did not want to be there. Or maybe he just didn't want ME to be there. But I had noticed since I had been in New York, most people just weren't that friendly.

"My name is Addyson Michaels; I am here to pick up my passport." The man rolled his eyes at me and walked off. Like I had just asked him to walk to Canada and get me something.

He walked four feet, to a table behind him, and mine was the very first one on the stack. He walked four feet back to me. "Here." And that was my cue to get the crap out of the way for the next person.

As I was walking out of the office, I heard the same voice say, "Yes, ma'am, how are you? How can I help you today?" I turned to see a girl standing in line with a huge smile on her face. She was pretty, of course. I looked down at my passport and held it close to my heart; this was my last chance.

—⁓—

I had gotten extremely talented at this hailing a taxi cab thing. I asked the prettiest woman I could find if she would do it for me; worked every time. As I was being dropped off at the house, I noticed Jace's car was out front. I was glad to see him. He reminded me of Braxton in a way. Not looks, at all. But just the way he treated me. He was extremely protective and just wanted to make everyone around him smile.

Jace was always thinking about other people and their feelings. I genuinely liked hanging out with him. But I didn't feel the most comfortable hanging around him without Caroline, Chloe, or Carla . . . hmmm, I just realized all three of their names started with C.

When I was alone with Jace, all I did was talk about Braxton. And Jace talked about Caroline. I think he might be working up the nerve to ask me to talk to her for him. Which I didn't mind doing. I thought she liked him too. She talked about him almost as much as I talked about Braxton.

I pulled out my cell phone, right before entering the house, texted Caroline and asked her to come over. Why not? They wanted to see each other . . . I was sure.

When I walked into the house, Jace and Aunt Mae were sitting at the table playing UNO.

"Hey, you two, who is winning?" I grabbed a Diet Pepsi out of the fridge and walked back over to the table.

"She has beaten me four times already!" Jace was a little frustrated with Aunt Mae's crazy UNO skills.

I laughed at his facial expressions. Mae yelled "Five times!' As she smacked her last card down on the table. "UNO CHAMPION!" she added to rub it in a little bit more. Jace stuck his tongue out at her, then took off to the fridge to get a drink as she wildly swatted at him.

My cell phone screamed "DROID" in its bionic voice, letting me know I had a text. "Caroline is coming over, would you like to stay for dinner, Jace?" His face blushed a little just at the sound of her name. "Sure that sounds great."

Aunt Mae stood from the table after cleaning up the cards. "I am going out tonight . . . on a date. I will be home late so clean up your mess okay?" I said Aunt Mae never allowed herself to love again, but she still had . . . friends.

"Okay, we will; maybe pizza and a movie in the living room, nothing major," I said, looking at Jace for approval.

"Sounds good to me." He said finishing off his bottle of water.

—∞—

We had our pizza, and Caroline picked out some horror movie to watch, which Jace seemed to love. SAW, like . . . twenty five or something. Really? How could people watch this stuff? It was pure blood and guts all the way.

I was on one side of Jace and Caroline was on the other. I was covering my eyes so much I couldn't tell you what was actually going on. Apparently you needed to watch them ALL to know what the hell was going on anyway. I was so confused.

But they were both seriously into it. "I knew it! I knew it was her the whole time." Jace yelled.

"No way! You could have never guessed that, not in a million years," Caroline countered.

"Well guys, I hate to be a crap monkey but I am going upstairs, putting on my pajamas, getting into my bed and calling Braxton. If you want to stay, you guys can; if you don't, lock the door on your way out, okay?" After the protests and moans, they saw I wasn't changing my mind, and I headed upstairs.

It was so late, and I couldn't wait to talk to Braxton. I didn't realize the time had gone by so fast. That's one reason I am truly thankful for the three "C's" and Jace. The faster the time went by, the faster I would be home with Braxton and Mandi.

I had been talking to Braxton for over an hour when it sounded like he was about to fall asleep. I was dreaming of being at home with him, laying on his chest, with his hand on my back, falling asleep, the happiest person in the world.

That's the best part about dreams. You're never self-conscious, or worried about anything; well, at least, not in the ones you are picturing on purpose. The returning nightmare of walking up on Braxton and Jennifer making out by the pond at my house was not my choice!

Brax was talking about my diary more, asking questions and thanking me for letting him read it. If I had known it was going to make him this happy, I would have given it to him myself before I left.

"Hey, Addy, Do you have any extra blankets; I am cold in here." Jace's voice was so loud and unexpected, I about fell off of my bed. I was half asleep on top of it. "You are still awake, aren't you?" I heard Jace ask at the same time as I heard "WHAT IS HE DOING IN YOUR ROOM AT 3 IN THE MORNING!" blasting through my cell phone. I went straight into panic mode. I sat straight up in the bed. "Jace, there are blankets in the hall closet; Braxton I can explain. Caro . . ." He cut me off before I could explain anything.

"I do not want him around you any more, Addyson . . . I can't stand the thought of him getting to be with you every single day, protecting you, which I am suppose to do. I have these thoughts that are driving me insane—please, for me. I am begging you."

I don't know why I got so angry. But I did. I felt as if he didn't trust me; I felt as if he couldn't possibly know how much I loved him, even after reading my diary, if he thought for one second I would ever do anything to hurt or lose him.

"Are you still hanging around Jennifer?" I knew the answer because Mandi had already told me she was following him around like a lost dog. And he didn't seem to be doing anything about it. He wouldn't let her touch him any more. But he also hadn't told her to get lost.

He was silent for a moment. More than likely thinking about Jennifer. He knows Mandi and I talk every day. "Yes, but not . . ." This time *he* got cut off.

"Hold on a minute and don't you dare hang up." I was so pissed off I couldn't see straight. I marched down the hall and knocked on the guest room door. Without waiting on an okay to enter, I just walked in. Caroline was lying in the bed, and Jace had made a pallet on the floor.

"Jace, stand up. I am sorry it has to be this way, but I need you to do me a favor, okay?" Jace looked worried; I think he had an idea of what was going on. I put Braxton on speaker phone. "Braxton, are you there?" His anger had faded, and now I think he was embarrassed. At that moment, I didn't care; this jealousy crap was going to stop right now.

"Jace, this is my boyfriend Braxton." They both kind of mumbled uncomfortable "Nice to meet you's." Caroline was sitting straight up watching me intently. "Jace, please tell Braxton where you are sleeping." Braxton was silent.

"On the floor in the guest room." Jace looked at me as if I had lost my mind.

"Jace, please tell Braxton who else is in this room with you."

Jace's eyes floated to Caroline before he answered. "Caroline."

The last thing I was going to ask him was either going to make Jace kill me, or love me to death. "Jace, please tell the truth on this one, okay, because I know I am really putting you on the spot here, but who are you in love with?" I gave him a pleading, and sorrowful look all at the same time.

He was silent for a moment, and I looked at Caroline. Jace looked at me and then hung his head towards the floor.

"Caroline." He answered, and I watched Caroline's face turn bright red.

"You are in love with me?" Although shocked, she was also happy, and Jace could tell she was happy about it.

"I am so sorry for all of this." I didn't hang around any longer. I just walked out without looking back. I took Braxton off of speaker phone and sat on my bed. "Are you happy, Braxton?" He stayed silent for too long. "Braxton?" I said, still frustrated.

"I feel stupid Addyson. I just, I can't help it. You have no idea what I am going through." I wanted to hold him; I wanted to soothe him more than anything.

"Braxton, I know exactly what you're going through. But, unlike Jace, Jennifer is really trying to steal you from me. I have to believe that, if you wanted to be with her, you would be. But you're with me, and I trust you! I actually have a reason to be jealous, because you are so damn hot! You can't keep allowing this to torture you, please, Brax; I am begging you to trust me."

I thought about saying, 'You are the only person that has ever wanted to be with me. What makes you think anyone else would?' But I thought better of it. Even if it was the truth, Braxton would think I was degrading myself. You're not degrading yourself, when you know it's the truth.

After another hour, it is after four in the morning. He had apologized a hundred times, at least. Once I got off the phone with him, I decided I was going to go home this weekend and see him. I would surprise him. I knew I was probably making a mistake because he would do everything in his power to come back with me, and he just couldn't do that. Not to mention I would love to see Mandi and my parents. I so hoped this was not a mistake!

CHAPTER 22

The following day, after the horrible phone call, I was determined to change the way my mind worked. It was possible, right? I walked into school with a new attitude; a new start, I could do this.

"Hey Brax, where were you last night? I waited for you to come by." Mike and I had been spending a lot of time together of late. Thanks to him, I had been able to do some of the stuff I enjoyed without being miserable. We have been fishing, four wheeling, hunting, jet skiing, and we have started our own pool competition at a little place called Our Place. "Sorry, man, I went to Mandi's, and we had coffee." I adjusted my backpack and fell into stride beside him.

"Mandi, huh? Addy hasn't been gone even three months yet." Mike laughed; he knew better.

"Ha, Ha, very funny," I replied.

As if on cue, Mandi came strolling up in front of me. "Where the hell have you been? I waited for you to call last night, and you never did. Are you okay?" Mandi was concerned and pissed; it was kind of cute.

"I am fine; I didn't get off of the phone with Addy until after four in the morning." I closed my eyes as the regret of last night came rushing back into my memory. I tried to shake the images out of my mind and started to repeat, a new day, a new beginning, a new way of thinking, in my brain.

"Oh, well, that's okay then." Mandi turned in the same direction to walk with Mike and me.

"I'm Mike, by the way." Mike was irritated that I had not introduced him, but I was still fighting my own thoughts.

"Hey, I am Mandi," Mandi said, laughing under her breath. Mike fell back and came back up beside her. They talked all the way to class as I miserably thought about Addy, and how upset she had been with me last night on the phone.

Could she handle me? Was I going to lose her because I am a freak? God help me, I didn't know how to change these thoughts and feelings. I sat in my desk, and realized where I was; I had no idea how I got there. I turned in my chair and glanced back at Mandi in the back of the class; Mike was standing by her desk, still talking to her. He wasn't supposed to be in this class! I shook my head and laughed. He was interested; watch out, Mandi!

—◊◊◊—

Addy has texted me more today than she had in weeks. I was in the third period when she was in lunch, so it was harder for me to text her back. Usually we just send simple, mushy stuff like I miss you, or I love you, but that day I had a lot to say. I wanted to say I was sorry again, but I knew she would get mad. With Addyson, once something was resolved, she didn't think about it anymore, it no longer existed; so apologizing would bring something up she didn't want to think about, something she believed never happened. It was over and done with. So I wouldn't say I was sorry anymore. Tomorrow was my first football game, and I was sending messages about that more than anything. I wished she could be there. I wanted her here more than anyone else.

"We are going to get something to eat; wanna go?" Mike pointed to Mandi and signaled with his eyes that he didn't want me to go.

"Sure, I'll go." I watched the shock and disappointment cover his face and smiled widely at him.

"Good, I was hoping you would go," he said so sarcastically that Mandi had to laugh.

"I'll meet you in the parking lot after class and follow you in my car," I said, knowing Mandi would ride with Mike. I didn't wait for a response as we waved at Mandi, and walked off towards our weight lifting class.

"So, what is going on, Mike?" He knew I meant with Mandi.

"What? What do you mean?" He laughed and adjusted his bags on his back.

"Listen, Mandi is a great friend of mine. And believe it or not, I think you two would make a great couple, but don't use her, Mike. I know how you are." I gave him a serious look; all joking aside, she was not like the girls he was used to dating. I cared about this one.

All of the joking and smiling fell from his face. "Believe it or not, I am really interested in her; I really want to get to know her more." I knew he was telling the truth. Mike was not an expert liar. He told the truth, not by choice, but just simply because he was that pathetic as a liar.

"I just remembered, I can't go with you guys after school, I have that thing . . ." I smiled, without looking at him.

"Damn, I was really hoping you would go, too." Mike and I laughed out loud and entered weight lifting class.

This class was different from the rest. I had taken this class now for three years in a row. It was more of a male social gathering than it was a class. We were all extremely competitive, and though some were here for other reasons, most were here to prove he was the strongest male of our grade. Childish, maybe, but it is what it is. Plus it was an easy A.

The other thing about this class was where it was located. It sat at the farthest end of the football field. I had never been told, but my guess was it used to be a small refreshment house for the football games. When I was in there, it felt like I was no longer at school.

The strongest guy in our grade, by far, was Drake Littlejohn. The dude was massive. He was freakishly big for his age and had to work out more than he slept. His upper arms were bigger than my thighs. He was also one of the cruelest people I had ever met. He and I had gone head to head a few times over Addyson; not to mention he was one of the biggest reasons I used to refuse to play football.

"Where is your girl friend, Brax; haven't seen her around in a while." Drake was shirtless, which he liked to stay as much as possible, stretching in front of his station. A station included a bench and a set of weights, and a place for a spotter.

"You ask me that every time you see me, Drake; are you suffering from memory loss? It is a side effect of steroids." I said, setting my bag on my own bench across from Drake's.

Drake stopped mid-lunge and stared at me. "For real?"

I glanced at Mike as he shook his head and laughed out loud. "It is not; shut up, Braxton." Drake continued his lunges and waited for an answer. He was the biggest, but far from the brightest in our class.

"She is in New York, Drake, remember?" I said, changing my clothes.

"Oh, yeah, well, what is she doing in New York?" he asked for the fifth time that month.

I lay on my bench, and Mike stood behind me to spot. "Visiting the family." It was what I told everyone, since I had no other ideas as to why she was there. I had a feeling there was more to it than that, but it was speculation. She hadn't told me any other reason there would be.

"Well, hopefully, she won't come back; let New York deal with her fat ass." Drake laughed as his words hit a sore spot on my insides. I had returning nightmares, in which that very thing would indeed happen, and she would never come home, never come back to me.

I stood from the bench with such force, the bench rocked. Mike hollered, "Brax, he isn't worth it." I didn't think about who he was, or his size, or how strong he was; all I could see was pure uncontrollable anger.

Drake stood straight up and braced himself for me; I stopped only inches from his face and pointed my finger almost on his nose, like he was a two-year-old child.

"Don't you ever say that to me again! She will come home . . ." I had to believe it. I had to believe she would be home in seven months, and she would never leave me like that again.

With Drake standing over me, I blanked out for a moment as the thoughts of her living happily ever after, with some guy named Jace, in New York City came crashing through my insides. I couldn't breathe. My brain felt as if razor blades were slashing it to pieces, and I couldn't think straight. I didn't feel the initial punch from Drake, but it was enough to bring me out of my thoughts. I stumbled three feet back and ran my hand over my mouth. Bright red blood spread across the back of my arm. "You son of a bi . . ." I lunged towards him, and began to punch him where ever I could reach him.

He was bigger, but I was faster. I got in six to ten punches to his one. The only problem was his one was much more devastating than all ten of mine put together. I was not weak; I was bigger than the average junior; however, I was nothing compared to Drake.

"What the hell is wrong with the two of you? Stop it! Back the hell down right now!" Mr. Soesbee's voice boomed through the small room. I stopped and so did Drake. "Braxton, I cannot believe you are a part of this." Mr. Soesbee just looked at Drake without saying another word. I glanced back at Drake as my breathing began to come under control. He may have beat my ass, but, by God, looking at his face he knew I had been there. "If you two want to take out some aggression, fine, but save it for the football field. Tomorrow night you can take out all the rage and anger you want on them West Lincoln boys . . . GOT IT!" Drake and I both nodded our heads and sat back on our respective benches.

I looked back at Drake; I have never hated anyone in my life, even though I had more than enough reason to hate many; I had never hated anyone like I hated Drake Littlejohn.

CHAPTER 23

I was going home!

I could not contain the butterflies in my stomach. I felt like barfing. I had seen Braxton every single day of my life, almost, and I had never been this nervous to see him; nervous, or maybe anxious, maybe both.

There were two main reasons for this, one of which he knew about, and one of which he didn't—and I didn't know how well this was going to go over with him.

First, the one he knew: everything has changed between us. I would die of embarrassment if he knew how badly I just wanted to lock ourselves in my mini house, and kiss him for two solid days. I had dreamed of feeling his lips on mine for a long time. I finally experienced my first kiss with the man of my dreams, and hadn't been able to experience it again since then, really close to three months. It was my own fault I knew.

The second thing that had my stomach flip flopping around was that Caroline and Jace were coming with me, and . . . and I hadn't even told Braxton I was coming home so, needless to say, he didn't know about the surprise guests as well.

I was hoping, so bad, that when Jace and Braxton met, Braxton would realize just how much Jace loved Caroline. What did Aunt Mae say? You could have half a brain and one eye and still see how much he loved her. Jace had become an extremely loyal friend to me, and I want Braxton to like him too.

Mandi was standing on the sidewalk in front of my house as we pulled into the driveway. She was squealing and jumping up and down, clapping and throwing her fists in the air. We jumped out of the cab and straight into Mandi's car. She had come up with this great idea to surprise Braxton and my parents.

I hugged Mandi so tight she begged me to let her go.

"Mandi, this is Jace, and this is Caroline." I pointed to the love birds in the back seat. I was not picking on them; if I could have been with Braxton every day, I would be the same way, and like I would be this weekend.

"Addy has told us so much about you. It's nice to finally put a face with the name." Caroline was speaking to Mandi, but never took her eyes off of Jace. It is so sweet to see the two of them this happy.

The vision of Braxton and me, at the pond, came flooding into my veins, and suddenly my body came alive. "I don't know if I am going to be able to stick to this plan, Mandi; I want to see Braxton so bad." I was laughing, but wasn't kidding in the least.

"Just one more hour, Addy, you can do it, and it will be the best surprise EVER!" We pulled into Braxton's house. His parents were in on this too.

Braxton had his first football game that night. We were all going to show up for his game. Braxton had told Mandi that he would give anything for me to watch him play, since this was my idea, which it certainly wasn't; if the truth be told, he had always wanted to play, and I knew it.

Braxton's parents were going first. My parents were going to meet us over there when they got off work. Maybe a few minutes late, and I would be in the stands when they got there. Mandi, Jace, Caroline, and I were going to follow Braxton's parents. After the game, I would be at Brax's car waiting on him.

"It's a lot longer than an hour, Mandi! A football game last a lot longer than that . . . doesn't it?" I was talking to everyone in the car, but knew that Mandi would be the only one to answer; it would be hard for Jace or Caroline to, with their lips locked together. "Yeah, but you will SEE him." Mandi was laughing. "Yeah, but I don't want to just SEE him, Mandi I want to . . . you know . . . SEEEE him!" I was so embarrassed, but it was the truth. I wanted to be with Brax like Jace and Caroline.

Watching him play was going to be awesome; but I still wouldn't be able to touch him. It sounded awful, but the only thing that would take this horrible barf feeling away would be the moment I felt him wrapped around me; God, I couldn't wait.

Braxton's parents had always been like family to me. The tears and hugs were a display of true affection. "OOOHHH, we have missed you so much, but I must say, not as much as our son!" Braxton's mom was holding me by my shoulders, looking at me as if she hadn't seen me in years. I was waiting for her to say, you have grown up so much. But, of course, she didn't.

Mrs. Carmen was so beautiful. She was so tall I had to look up at her to see her face. She was all legs. She had long curly hair, with enormous bouncy curls that never seemed to fail her. She was always dressed in a business suit and had just the right amount of jewelry to show off her perfect manicured hands, and perfect shade of tan that she kept up all year around. I had secretly longed to look just like her for as long as I could remember. She had to have been the head cheerleader in her day, had to. But I could never have imagined her acting like Jennifer, ever. I blushed with her comment. Her statement was probably true, but also had the underlying meaning that she and her husband knew about Braxton and me.

For a second, I felt uncomfortable, with the realization that Braxton's parents might not approve of our new relationship. I mean, I knew they loved me, and they would never hurt me for anything, but what if they had dreams of a "better fit" for Braxton, like Jennifer.

I put my head down and felt myself wanting to apologize—but for what? For loving him, or for him loving me—maybe both?

Braxton's dad walked over to me. He reminded me so much of Braxton, minus his eyes; I knew what Brax was going to look like when he was older. Mr. Carmen was a devilishly handsome man but Braxton was gorgeous.

As if he could read my mind, he wrapped his arms around me tightly, having no problems fitting all of me into his immense embrace, and whispered, "We are so happy for the both of you. We love you and have wondered what has taken the two of you so long to see what every one of us already knew!?"

He leaned back holding my shoulders the exact way that Mrs. Carmen had, looking into my eyes. He was smiling with tears in his eyes, and I knew he meant every word that he was saying.

"Now, let's go give Braxton the best surprise ever." His mom squealed and looked at Mandi in approval of her plan.

—m—

The sight of the field made horrible memories flood my brain. I instantly became cautious and self-conscious. I watched, closely, every step I made, and most importantly every move anyone else made.

Everyone from school had noticed me. They laughed, pointed, whispered; I could only imagine what all they were thinking about me. I hoped Caroline and Jace could handle the ridicule. After all, I was sure people were wondering who they were.

Brax had told Jennifer I was in New York, but he only told them I was visiting my family. As far as he knew, it was the truth.

I allowed myself to daydream as I stood between Mandi and Caroline, clapping for the boys as they were being brought out on the field. Next year, God help me, I would come back to this school a different person. I would be a hundred pounds, maybe more, lighter. I would be with Braxton, and he would be able to be proud to have me as his girlfriend. I might still not be as beautiful as the cheerleaders. Let's face it, I'd never be a Barbie, but I would be me, the real me—not this.

I almost had tears forming in my eyes, as the realization came to me that I was probably the most popular kid in that school right now. I laughed. I mean, after all, I was Addyson Michaels, the most noticed, tortured, the most picked on, the fattest, the ugliest, the most likely to never have real love, the most likely to never have anything . . . but her best friend was the hottest guy in school.

The tears were forming because one day, one day, prayerfully soon, I would no longer be any of those things. I would hold my head high, proud of who I am. Not arrogant, or stupid, but comfortable in my own skin. I would be Addyson Michaels, dating the hottest boy in school!

"Braxton Carmen, Number 17, defensive linebacker." The sound of his name came from every corner of the stadium, and the whole crowd, on home side, stood and cheered, clapped, hollered, whistled; it roared through the air like a massive wave.

The tears that had threatened to form fell. He was finally doing what he had always wanted to do. I couldn't see his face well, but, God, I could see his eyes. Not clearly, but the turquoise blue I dreamed of every day and night of my life, beamed from behind his helmet, as the massive lights, reflected off of them. I had so missed him.

He ran out to the middle of the field to join his team. I could tell by his movements he was laughing. I must have snapped a hundred pictures with my cell phone.

After a few more minutes, the crowd settled to get ready for the game. I watched in astonishment as Brax stopped man after man from getting a touchdown. The people would stand and cheer his name or number. I felt like he was finally living; it was a start anyway.

My parents finally arrived almost half way through the game. We hugged and cried, laughed and talked about things, even when we should have been watching the half time show. It was a lot like the display I had with Braxton's parents. I introduced them to Jace and Caroline. So far this was turning out to be wonderful, so far.

The game was almost over. It was my cue to go to Braxton's car and wait on him. I was fully aware it might be as long as half an hour before he came. But I think this certainly did add to the surprise. Braxton had no idea what Jace and Caroline looked like so he wouldn't have a clue who they actually were.

The longer I stood there, the more I wanted to puke; why did we call them butterflies, when it was undoubtedly a puke your brains out feeling? I guess butterflies sounded better. Anyway, I no longer felt like barfing; well, I sort of still did, but not really, when I realized it wasn't Braxton walking up the hill towards me, it was Jennifer.

"Weeeelll, Addyson Michaels, I thought you had gone to New York for the rest of this year?" She stood about ten feet in front of me with her hand on her hips and a repulsed look on her face.

I am sure she was upset with the fact that I was there for Braxton's first game. She had always known I got his attention first and foremost. With me being gone, she had a much better chance of getting his attention rather than me, but there I was! I smiled at this thought.

"What the hell are you smiling at?" She snapped at me so loud, I jerked; it shocked me.

"Nothing. I just thought you would be glad to see me, Jennifer, I mean, since we had became such close friends before I left and all." If the sarcasm in my words could have cut her, she would have been damn near bleeding to death!

"Friends . . . please. I got everything I needed from you long before you left; a ticket straight to Braxton. And, for your information, Braxton and I have become very close, with you out of the way, and before long I am sure we will be the most popular couple in this school." She stepped closer, her glare intensifying, she was positively livid.

So, I guess, she didn't know about Braxton and me? For a moment, I wondered why he hadn't told her about us, or come to think of it, maybe he had, and she just couldn't care any less. Why would that have stopped her?

I thought very carefully about my response. Before I could say anything, she spoke again. "You are so pathetic, Addyson. Do you honestly think that Braxton actually cares anything about you?" Her laughter was haunting, almost as haunting as her words. "Do you not realize that Braxton is your friend because he feels sorry for you?"

I couldn't hide the pain on my face, or the sting of the tears in my eyes, the braveness that I felt just a few seconds ago had faded, and I retreated behind my hair. My face dropped to the ground, and my hair covered my face. But her words still got through to me.

"He can't stand you, Addyson; you hold him back, and pull him down to a level he doesn't belong. He deserves to be with me! You know it! Hell, you admitted it in the middle of class!" Her laughter was gone as she growled at me through clenched teeth.

She was right in my face now, with her finger in my face. I slowly raised my head to meet her gaze. I said only three words to her. "I. HATE. YOU."

I had never hated anyone in my life. Not like this. She didn't even look the same to me anymore. The hatred, ugliness, and evil that lived inside her heart made her look so disgustingly ugly to me. Anyone who could treat another person the way she had treated me our whole lives could not possibly be beautiful.

"I am fat, Jennifer, but I can . . . I will lose this weight; you are ugly to your core, and there is nothing you can do about that!"

We were almost nose to nose as the words slowly leaked out of my mouth and straight into her brain. I hit something, a nerve, and it rocked her! I watched as the emotions flooded her brain: shock that I had said it, anger at my finding the ability to say it, revenge for hurting her, pain that it was the truth, and last, loss of all control. She was about to lunge at me when his voice made her stop in her tracks.

She frantically tried to calm herself. I never moved from where I was standing. I stared into his beautiful eyes, and smiled as I saw the shock and joy; the love in his eyes for me, only me. Jennifer knew darned well that any progress she had made with Braxton, imagined or not, would be lost if he knew everything she had just said to me.

She noticed the look too, but she thought it was for her. She slung her hair around and put on her sexiest face ever. She began to walk towards him with her arms held wide open to embrace him. He never took his eyes off me, which from her stance, she must have been still assuming, were on her. After all, it would never have crossed her mind that it could possibly be for me.

"You were awesome, Braxton." Her voice trailed off as he walked straight past her.

"Thanks, Jennifer," He said, with his eyes never leaving my gaze. My heart was beating out of my chest as the man I loved with all of me came walking up to me. He kissed me. It was urgent and passionate. My eyes closed first, breaking his intense glare. Nothing else in this world mattered; the school could have blown up, and I would have been oblivious. He pulled away from me, and smiled the smile I had longed to see on his face for months now.

"Hey." He grinned.

"Hey Brax, I have so missed you," I whispered, not trying to hide my blushing face. I wrapped my arms around him and breathed in his familiar smell. I could have stayed there forever.

I opened my eyes and noticed Jennifer still standing behind us. Her face was pale, her jaw was open, and she had been rejected, big time. What could have been worse for her than not getting what she wanted, but also losing him to the one person she thought didn't deserve to breathe? It was a bitchy thing to do I know, and I shouldn't have done it, but I smiled at her! I mean a big, huge, IN YOUR FACE, smile that I could tell made her blood boil within her veins. It even crossed my mind to grab his butt in front of her. But I started turning red just thinking about it.

Jennifer stomped off; for the first time in her life . . . Jennifer Gripply was speechless.

CHAPTER 24

When the game was over, and all of my family, including Addy's parents, were there to support me, I was happy. I tried hard not to let my misery about Addy not being there ruin their happiness. They were all ready to go quite quickly. "We are going back to Addyson's house for a cook out."

God, Addyson's house, the pond, her room, the pool; there was not an inch of that place that didn't remind me of her. I missed her so much. I honestly did not think I could go there that night.

"I am going to run home and take a shower . . . then I'll be over, ok?" The smiles on all the faces made me change my mind on the last part of that sentence; I had been going to say . . . and go to bed. I couldn't do that to any of them. They all just wanted to show me they loved me, and it would have been too selfish of me to do that. I smiled and walked off towards my car.

As I walked up the hill I noticed two people standing extremely close, no, up against my car; I walked faster. As I got closer, my heart began to race out of my chest. I felt a new bolt of electricity as it shot through my veins . . . was that . . . Addyson . . . I felt the smile form; I felt the tears threatening, stinging, and begging to come out.

It was Addyson; I couldn't get to her fast enough.

I heard a voice saying something about playing a good game and realized it was Jennifer. "Thanks Jennifer," I said, and walked right past her. I couldn't take my eyes off Addyson. I walked right up to Addyson with such force; if the car had not been there, we both would have hit the ground.

I just kissed her. My mind was spinning. This was undoubtedly her; she was here. I let a moan out of my chest that took all of the stress and self pity, sorrow, and longing that I had had for weeks, out of my chest with it.

I did not want to stop. I wanted to drink her in, and stay here with her until I knew for sure she was real. God, I have missed her so. "Hey." The smile was going nowhere. God, it was so good to see her.

"Hey, Braxton. I have so missed you," she whispered. Her face was red, and her eyes were glowing their honey yellow/brown color. The sound of her voice awakened my insides, and I could feel my muscles tense under her touch, as if my whole body had just become super-sensitive.

All I wanted to do was hold her. I grabbed her and pulled her into my chest tightly. I rested my chin on the top of her head. I put one hand on her back and one hand securing her face to my chest. I wanted her to hear my heart beat; I wanted the love I felt for her to flow right out of my chest, and into her heart. I had never loved another human being like I loved her.

I pulled away from her just long enough to look at her again. I kissed her gently. Her eyes closed, cutting me off from my addiction. Her gaze, her eyes—I see my past, my future, my whole life in those honey yellow/brown eyes.

"Look at me." It came out a little forceful, ragged; my breathing was quick. I couldn't help it. She opened her eyes, and I kissed her again, a little deeper, with a little more force, trying desperately to show her how much I needed her.

Mandi and two people, I had never met before, walked up beside us, clearing their throats. "Hum . . ." Mandi cleared her throat again, louder.

"Go the hell on!" I couldn't help but laugh when Addyson's voice sounded just about as lustful as mine. She took a deep breath and smiled at me before ever breaking our gaze. "Oh, Brax, I want you to meet some people." She pulled me by my hand towards the two people I had never met before. "Brax, this is Jace, and this is Caroline."

For a moment, I wanted to hit him in the jaw! All of the torture and torments I have been dealing with came flooding back into my mind. He met my glare and never turned away. But then I noticed something, something unmistakable, that look—that look right there that he just gave Caroline; he was mad over her. I knew, because I had that same feeling for my Addy.

"Hey man, it's nice to finally meet you. I am um . . . well, sorry about the other night." I was still embarrassed about the whole thing.

"I cannot imagine what you must be going through, man; don't think twice about it." Jace reached his hand out and once our hands clapped together we embraced in a brotherly hug. I smiled at him, silently saying thank you for accepting my apology.

"It's nice to meet you too, Caroline." I grinned at her. She turned a little pink and quickly turned her eyes from mine. It doesn't bother me any more, not after reading Addyson's diary; I am proud of my eyes. I did notice that Jace had no trouble at all keeping eye contact. There was something genuine and sincere about him. I thought we could be friends.

CHAPTER 25

Why wouldn't that weekend fly by? I felt as if I had just got here and I would be leaving again in the morning. I was so clingy to Braxton; I wanted to be touching him in some way every single moment. If he sat beside me, I put my hand on his knee. If he sat in front of me, I rubbed his back. If I couldn't touch him, I was looking at him. I saw him so differently; I felt more self-conscious around him than I did before, if that was actually possible. I found myself blushing more, smiling more, laughing more. I wouldn't let myself do the initiating, though. I did not want to smother him. Truth be known; it was all a little strange. It would take a while to get used to this. I still had to tell myself over and over again—this is real; he is mine.

That day had been so gratifying. We did absolutely nothing! I did exactly what I wanted to do, and yes, I had initiated this, and was extremely pleased at his reaction . . .

So last night after the game we came back here, to my house; we hung out with our parents for a while. Mandi, Jace, and Caroline spent most of the night in the pool. Once our parents had retired, Brax joined our friends in the pool, and I took my normal position on the side with my legs dangling in. Caroline protested, begging me to come in, but Mandi knew me, and she knew exactly why I didn't want to. Water makes clothes stick to you extremely close, and a bathing suit, with all of these people around, certainly wasn't going to happen.

I felt like such a pervert staring at Braxton the entire time. I watched the beam from the porch light glisten off of his wet sculptured chest; it danced through his laughing eyes, and I felt things—well, they were just lustful.

How I wished I could have been invisible at that moment, or I could have snapped my fingers and became the beauty queen I will never be, just for one night. How glorious would it have been, if I could have seen him, touched him, been exceedingly close to him with no worries about him touching my fat; the fat on my face, my arms, my stomach especially, because none of it was there to touch!

I watched him, laughing, out loud with Jace. He threw Mandi across the pool. Caroline and Mandi tried to dunk Brax. Jace and Braxton went after both of the girls; they were squealing and laughing, and everyone was having such a fabulous time.

I was sitting on the side longing to be like Mandi and Caroline. I forced myself to laugh with them. I forced myself to look happy, and pretend that nothing was wrong at all. I would never want any of them to know what I was honestly thinking right then.

I wanted to be normal. It crossed my mind that Mandi would be a perfect match for Braxton. Honestly, I became jealous of her. In reality, Mandi and Braxton's friendship did not bother me. I wanted them to be close friends. I loved them both. I was jealous of the fact that Mandi could do those things with him, and I couldn't.

I dropped my gaze to the water, twirling around my legs, watching the waves they were making. I smiled to myself, with the thought of London, and the doctor who had promised to help me. I did have one more chance. I was one day closer!

Everyone began to climb out of the pool, exhausted from the excitement of the day. We ended the night in my room.

I took up a large part of my full sized bed by myself, so it was pretty uncomfortable for Caroline, Mandi, and I, all three to try to squeeze in. I just kept apologizing to Mandi. I was against the wall, she was beside me, and Caroline, the smallest, was hanging on to the edge for dear life.

Jace was on the floor, and Braxton was in my desk chair with his feet propped up on my desk. I don't know what was worse, Mandi having to deal with me all over her, or Brax seeing just how much bigger than the other girls I actually was.

The heavy breathing and slight snoring from Jace filled the room quickly. Even with the only light in the room coming from an extremely small desk lamp, I could still see Brax's eyes; I could feel them on me. I stared at him and made myself smile. He had a dead serious look on his face. I made an expression of concern, and he read it perfectly. He pointed to the front door.

I tried so hard to gracefully pull myself out of the wedge I was in without waking everyone up. I crawled off the foot of the bed, and the two of us walked out. Braxton grabbed the blanket I kept in the storage container by the pool. I often sat out there at night and watched the stars, which reminded me, New York didn't seem to have as many; I wonder why?

He sat on the swing, and put his hand out to me for me to sit down beside him. My mind went to Mandi. If I had been her, he could have put his legs up, and I could have lain across him, and lay on his chest, like I wanted to.

I sat beside him and took my normal position. He sat with his back against the back of the swing and I put my back against his side with my head resting on his shoulder. The arm I was resting on came around me, and I sat with his hand in both of mine. We didn't say anything. We just sat there like we had so many times before, and watched the sky for shooting stars.

Braxton's grandfather told us once that a shooting star was wished on because it was actually an angel, and if you whispered your prayer fast enough, the angel would take it straight to the Lord. I was not sure how many shooting stars I had seen, while sitting on this swing. Maybe this doctor in London would be the answer to every prayer I have ever prayed on these stars.

I am not sure when I fell asleep last night, but I was positive his actions spoke louder than any words we could have spoken. He pulled me out of that bed because he knew how I was feeling. He would have been so much more comfortable in the computer chair. But he knew I would be more comfortable out here. I fell asleep thinking about how everything he seemed to do, he was thinking of me.

—◊◊◊—

This morning I woke with Mandi in my face making silly noises. "Addyson" and she would giggle.

"What do you want, Mandi?" I wanted to throw her in the pool. Being a corpulent girl, I could throw Mandi around, probably just as easily as Braxton could; only playing around, of course. My outburst only made her worse. "I am taking them to breakfast." She was talking to me as if I was a moron or something, dragging out every single word, and I couldn't help but laugh at her. I sat up straight and stretched my whole body realizing for the first time that Braxton was gone. "Where is Braxton?" I asked, yawning and sitting Indian style. "He is in the big house; he will be out in a bit. You're not allowed to go in there." Her humongous goofy grin went unnoticed, as I blinked rapidly, trying to get my brain to function properly.

"I am taking the love birds on the grand tour of our marvelous town, and you, my dear . . ." She stood up straight and pointed at me, as if she was a teacher or a parent as she finished, ". . . have been instructed to go take a shower, put your pajamas right back on, and wait in your room until further notice."

She spoke way too fast for first thing in the morning. My brain was still trying to take in everything she had just said as I watched her wink, and skip off with that goofy-looking grin that I noticed for the first time.

I twisted around and watched her and the love birds happily walk towards Mandi's car. "Well . . ." I said to nobody as I stood from the swing and walked towards my room.

When I walked into my room, I couldn't stop the smile from plastering wide across my face. There were carnations all over the room. On my desk, there sat a book with a black ribbon wrapped around it securing a small card. The card read simply. Your turn, Love, Braxton.

My curiosity piqued as I slowly pulled the black silk ribbon from its home, and allowed it to dangle between my fingers. The hard, solid blue cover of the book gave no suggestion or hint of what it would contain. As I flipped it open, my eyes read the only few sentences on the otherwise solid white page.

> My Journal will be able to tell you how I feel for you better than I can. After reading yours, it has made so many things clear for me. And I know that we are meant to be together.
>
> I know there will be things that will probably be misunderstood. But I am trusting that you will do as I did, and put yourself in my shoes.
>
> I love you. This will prove it.
>
> Yours,
> Brax

I slowly sat in the desk chair; I read and reread his words. He wanted me to read his journal. I flipped to the first page. I didn't get to read one word on the page, when the door opened and Braxton walked in holding a tray with breakfast. He wore a giant smile on his face. I could feel the blushing red heat crawling up my neck, but managed to smile back. He pushed the door shut with his butt and set the tray on the bed. Then he quickly locked the door.

He was in his sleeping clothes too. "So you saw my gift?" He handed me a slice of apple before he lay across the bed.

"This is wonderful, Brax, the flowers, the journal; just because I gave you mine doesn't mean you have to give me yours, you do know that, right?"

I knew he knew that. I was honestly scared to death to read it. I didn't want to know if he actually thought I would be pretty, if skinny, or if he had touched a fat roll and realized how generous I actually was, or who knows what. What could I misunderstand? What would I have to put myself in his shoes to be able to, to what . . . handle it?

"I want you to read it, Addy. I don't write in it every day, but I have written in it more this year than I ever have. There are things in there that I wrote that are exactly how I felt at that moment. It answers some of the questions you had asked yourself in your diary, and your diary made everything make sense to me; please just read it, Addyson. Not today, but when you're back in New York." His eyes flashed sorrow at the words. I am sure mine did, too. He looked away from me for only a second, replaced the smile in his eyes, and finished.

"Today belongs to you and me."

I shut the book and placed it in my desk. "I will . . . I promise." I stood from the chair and walked over to the bed. I lay across the bed with my feet on the pillows, his feet were at the end of the bed, and our faces were side by side.

We spent the entire day in my room; we spent some much-needed time together. Other than when we spent an hour at a time kissing one another, it felt like it used to. We talked about everything and nothing at all.

I spent an hour just tracing his chest with my hands. Every inch of his shoulders, his neck, his face, his belly; for the first time ever I had a terrible time keeping his eye contact. His gaze was so intense, it was just powerful.

His body eventually became extremely sensitive to my touch, and I was able to make him shiver under my fingers lightly dancing on his skin.

As the sun began to set, the darkness began to take over the room, neither of us cared. For the first time, I leaned over and kissed the chill bumps on his chest as my fingers continued to lightly trace his belly. With the darkness came a little bit of self-confidence. I closed my eyes and let the emotions explode on the inside of me as I heard him suck in air, deep into his chest; from behind clenched teeth came a sound of satisfaction.

He became alive, and with speed and accuracy, his mouth met mine, urgent and lustful. He was acting like I felt on the inside. Our foreheads were tight together; his hands were tight on either side of my face. His breathing was heavy, as was mine; his eyes were closed as I watched, the almost painful expression on his face.

"Addy? Can I make love to you?" His words shot fear through every inch of my body. It all came flooding back,—who I was, what I looked like, how fat I was, and panic, self-consciousness, self-loathing. There was no way I could do that. There is no way I could get naked in front of him; his beautiful body would have to touch mine. The tears came running out before I could manage to even explain them.

"Braxton I can't . . . I want to. I want to more than you will ever know." I closed my eyes and let the words flow out of me; speaking them was just about as hard as thinking them. Even with his protesting at my eyes being closed, I couldn't force them open. I just continued to let everything flow out. The self-consciousness, the self-loathing, the fear, the panic, the fear that I wouldn't have thought I could speak. "And, and when you do see me naked, Brax, When you see how fat I actually am, I am terrified I will lose you forever."

He stopped asking me to open my eyes; he stopped everything and pulled my sobbing body into his tight embrace. He didn't say anything; he just held me. I have no idea how long I lay there in his arms. My head was resting on his chest, and his heartbeat soothed my aching insides. Years of torture and torment, self loathing, and self pity came out that night in the form of tears. Braxton never asked questions; the most he would say was, "I am right here."

I didn't think it was possible to get any closer to Braxton, but that night I had. There were no secrets anymore. There were no unspoken fears, no unspoken thoughts; he now knew everything he could possibly know about me. I told him everything from secretly wishing I could be like Mandi and Caroline, and do those things with him, to being ashamed of allowing him to fall in love with me when I knew I could not make love to him. There was only one secret that remained—London.

He never spoke. He cried with me. He would hold me tighter when I said certain things. But he hadn't spoken, until he finally said, "Addyson, I shouldn't have thrown that out so fast, anyway. It was just, well . . . I am a teenage boy and things were getting a little intense. To be honest, I want our first time to be after we are married . . . if I can wait that long, I mean."

I don't know where the hell it came from, but I smiled at him; with this huge grin on my face, I said, "What makes you think I would marry you, Braxton Carmen?" He knew I would marry him that day, but the mood lightened immediately. He had just erased all of my fears, and he knew it. "Well, wouldn't you?" He asked, laughing, knowing full well I would.

Being married wouldn't change how I felt about my body any, but we were only sixteen years old, we still had the rest of high school and college, and I still had London. I didn't say it, but my mind was thinking I want our first time to be after London.

We spent a few more hours together, laughing, loving each other. It had been the best day of my life. I had been having a lot of those lately! But soon the realization of what Sunday morning held came creeping into our minds, and Braxton, to my surprise, did not beg to go with me. He knew I wouldn't let him go.

—∞—

The goodbye at the airport was no easier than the first. As a matter of fact, it was much harder on me this time than it was on Braxton.

Sitting on the plane beside Caroline and Jace, I felt a little guilty for ignoring them all the previous day. They assured me that they had had a blast with Mandi. I envied them and their togetherness, that they had each other all the time, again; it was my own fault.

I spent hours talking to Aunt Mae once I had gotten settled back into the house. We ate dinner in that night, which she rarely did, and talked for hours about everything. Even about Braxton wanting to make love.

Aunt Mae was the only adult I had ever talked to about this much of me. And I knew no matter what I told her, it would stay safely between the two of us. "It's perfectly normal, Addyson, to want to make love to the person you love. I know you cannot see it, but Braxton can see the real you. He sees past the exterior, and is in love with who you are, not what you look like. It's a love that even people who are not overweight, rarely find. You are truly blessed."

She said it as she stood from the sofa, indicating that she was done for the night, and I should think about what she had said. I thought about every word, over and over again.

I went upstairs to my room and sat on the bed staring at the full body mirror hanging on the back of the door. I walked over to the door and locked it. I took all of my clothes off, and I stared at myself in the mirror. I watched as the massive amounts of skin flowed from what looked like every inch of my body. I held my arms straight out and watched the flab hang down. I turned to my side, and saw the disgusting image of myself looking back at me. I walked closer to the mirror allowing the angry tears to fall in silence. I stared into the image as hard as I could.

Aunt Mae was right; I couldn't see anything but the same fat person I had always hated . . . I saw me.

CHAPTER 26

Addyson had only been gone for a few hours, and I already had a longing to be with her. Rising from the sofa in my room, I placed my hat on my head and grabbed the keys to my car. I shut my bedroom door behind me, and walked through the kitchen, and living room towards the front door. "Mom, I'll be back before midnight." I didn't wait for a response; I shut the front door behind me, and walked down the driveway to my car.

"Braxton?" Her voice was almost as familiar as Addyson's; I had been spending so much time with her since Addy had gone to New York.

"Hey, Mandi." I hadn't expected to see her there. As I came closer to her, I noticed the uneasy look on her face.

"I am sorry for coming here without calling . . . honestly; I just sort of ended up here. I just needed to talk to someone, and I can't get a hold of Addy." My mind went straight to the last part; why wasn't Addy answering Mandi's call?

"I am going to Mike's, and we are going to Our Place for a couple of games of pool; you want to come too?" I dropped my hand from the driver's door and took a few steps closer.

"Well, that is sort of my problem—Mike, I mean." I had known Mike most of my life. I knew he was somewhat of a player, but he would never physically hurt anyone. For some reason, the way Mandi looked and was acting, those crazy thoughts began to flood my mind.

"What did he do to you?" I felt anger rising as the runaway images continued to run wild.

"Oh, no! Brax, it's nothing like that." She giggled as she walked to the other side of my car and got in. "Ok," I said to myself. I felt stupid for allowing myself to ever think something so ridiculous about Mike. But if that wasn't what was going on then why was she acting so strange? I calmed my mind and entered the driver's side of the car.

"What is going on?" I didn't bother starting the car yet. I needed her to talk first and get whatever was going on out in the open.

"I think I am falling in love with him." Mandi dropped her face towards her lap as if she was totally embarrassed about what she had just admitted. Relief came immediately. I sat back, relaxed, and laughed. "Well, what is so bad about that?" I asked, confused.

Mandi silently stared at her shaky hands in her lap without saying a word. I leaned in only an inch, and saw the silent tears that streaked her face.

"Mandi, what is going on?" I placed my hand on her shoulder, and she jerked, as if she had just noticed where she was, and that I was in the car with her. I retracted my hand quickly, completely unaware of what to do. My heart was breaking for her, and I didn't even know why.

"I was in seventh grade. He made me feel amazing, like I was the most beautiful girl in the world. I loved him. I would do anything for him. I lied for him; I lied to everyone—my parents, my friends, the teachers, myself . . . everyone. I trusted him because I was supposed to, after all, he was the grown up. A grown-up doesn't lie; a grown-up would never hurt a kid . . ." She looked at me, and her green eyes became livid with anger. I was desperately trying to understand what she was saying, but I didn't say a word.

She searched my eyes, but somehow I knew she wasn't looking at me. She was seeing the person she was talking about, the time she was reliving in her mind. The anger began to drain, and the silent tears became vocal, and she shook from the sobs. I didn't know what to do, what to say, I was lost. Before I could frantically come up with something to say to her, she spoke again.

"He said I was special. That he had never had a student like me before. He said he loved me in a special way, a way that he had never loved another student before. He even said he could never live without me. He explained how much trouble he would get into, if other teachers or my parents knew how much he loved me. So, I had to swear to keep his love for me a secret, and I did. I never told a single soul about him, about us." She took in a deep, calming breath and sat back in the seat. She cleared her throat and ran her hand through her hair.

"First, it was just kissing; you know, making out basically. I was so amazed that a remarkably handsome man would find me attractive. I mean he was so gorgeous. He wasn't the normal creepy, ugly, pedophile. He was so attractive. He made me feel special, lucky even." She looked at me again; she looked exhausted and drained of all energy.

"Then one day half way through the year, I decided to surprise him at his house." She closed her eyes and laughed through the tears, shaking her head to the memories. "His son, my own age, one of my own classmates, answered the door and asked me what the hell I was doing at his house." The laughter faded, she didn't blink as the images played in front of her eyes.

"His wife came to the door moments later and asked me if I was ok. She asked me if I needed help. I guess the look of total destruction and heartbreak wasn't hidden on my face. I was so young, Braxton; I couldn't think reasonably. No, instead I asked if that was his address. As soon as I did, a look of knowing and understanding stamped itself on the lady's face. Back then I had no idea what it meant, but as I got older, I realized that he had done it before, and she stayed with him anyway. I realize that her heart too was shattering into a thousand pieces." She leaned forward and rubbed her face with both hands.

"The wife said no, but the son said yes, that it was, in fact, his address. The mother gave her son a disgusted look, and the son shot a confused look towards his mother. I didn't know what to do next; like I said, I was so young. I simply walked away. The walk became a fast walk, and before long it was an all out sprint for my house. I decided not to talk to anyone; instead, I would talk to him at school the next day, I would find out what was going on, and why he had not told me that Harrison was his son. But that would never happen. The next day at school, it was announced that due to family emergencies he would no longer be our teacher; that he and his family had to move out of state." Mandi glanced out of the window and watched the leaves float around the yard.

"What happened? Did you ever see him again? Did you tell anyone?" I placed my hand over hers and held it tight as she prepared to finish her story.

"I had no choice but to tell my parents. See, the day before I went to his house, I had allowed him to make love to me. I was terrified out of my mind, and honestly didn't want to do it, but he said he wouldn't love me anymore if I didn't prove my love to him. I thought it was what couples were supposed to do. Truth be known, there was a part of me that knew that things between us weren't right. I knew that teachers and students shouldn't be doing the things we were doing. But another part of me wanted to believe that I really was special. That a handsome man could love me, and I wanted to believe that when I was older we would get married and be together forever." Mandi finally looked back at me.

"But the fairy tale ended quickly when one day he just disappeared. Seeing his family made a lot of things real for me, and one of them was that I was the stupidest person alive. I was a whore, and a slut, and completely stupid for ever believing that someone could love me like that. I was happy letting him go; I was happy that no one else knew and that I would never have to see him again . . . until I started having massive abdominal pains. I had no choice but to have my mother take me to the doctor, and once the examination was over, it was revealed to my parents that their thirteen-year-old daughter was not a virgin. I had a major bladder infection along with a urinary tract infection that had produced a yeast infection, as well. I had no choice but to tell my parents. Once my father found out all the details he was livid. He called the police and the ball started rolling right there." Mandi squeezed my hand and released it before placing both of her hands in her lap and closing her eyes.

"It was almost a year later before the court date. I had to testify in front of a court room full of strangers, but the worst part was my parents. I had to explain every detail of the relationship between him and I, while my parents listened intently. My dad has never looked at me the same, and I have never looked at love the same." Mandi turned her whole body towards me, and I turned towards her. "I thought all of that was behind me, but the feeling Mike has made come alive in me again, I honestly didn't think was possible, making me realize that it is still very raw inside of me." She stopped for a response, but all I had was a ton of questions, questions I wasn't sure I should ask.

"What happened to the teacher?" I said quietly, watching her for a sign that I was asking too much.

"Because of my age, it was still considered rape, but I tried to make it clear that I was willing, to an extent. He was sentenced to fifteen years in the State pen. His wife and Harrison moved back to Michigan where her family lives. He is supposed to get out in eleven years. I have been told that he may get out earlier due to good behavior, a chance for early parole.

"My parents spent thousands of dollars sending me to therapists who tried to make me believe that I was raped, that I wasn't willing, and that none of it was my fault, that I wasn't stupid, nor was there anything wrong with me. I finally understood that the only way I was to get away from those people was to agree with them." Mandi slid back in her chair, breaking eye contact with me.

"I can't honestly say that I don't believe that it was my own stupidity that caused it to happen, but I can honestly say that it changed my heart forever. I have a very hard time with affection of any kind, and as much as I like Mike, I honestly don't know that I could be . . . a normal, I guess, girl friend to him."

Everything made sense now. I realized that it wasn't anything Mike had done to her; it was her own past that had her in shambles. She was scared that she would have to do certain things to keep Mike around. "Have you talked to Mike?" I asked as soothingly as I could.

"No! I have never told another soul about this, Brax, and you have to swear you will not say anything to him about it. I just needed to tell someone for some reason; I need help with this, and you're his best friend, maybe you could help me." Mandi's phone rang, making us both jump.

"Hello. I'm actually here with Brax right now. I will. I called you earlier to talk to you actually, and I will talk to you later, but right now I have to go meet with Mike; remember I told you about him? I will . . . I promise. Ok, bye." Mandi shut her phone and returned it to her pocket.

"That was Addy, she said for you to call her later and she loves you." I couldn't help but wonder what Addy thought about Mandi and me spending so much time together alone. I was not so sure I would like it if it was the other way around.

Looking back at Mandi, there was no way I could abandon her now. Something between us had changed now; we have been friends, but this made me respect her even more. "Mandi, everything will work out for the best. You have to believe that. When you are ready, and only when you are ready, you need to tell Mike everything you have told me. He will understand. I am always here, and I will help you anyway I can, but I have to say, you cannot let the past, and past events stop you from possibly falling in love with someone, regardless if it is Mike or someone else, you have a right to be happy; you deserve to be happy."

She didn't say anything right away. She slowly nodded her head in agreement, and finally said, "You know you're right. I am not going to let my chance of happiness, whether it is with Mike or not, pass me by. It's time to get rid of this fear that follows me around. Thank you, Brax, thanks for listening . . ." She leaned over and hugged me tight. I squeezed her back, and tried to make her feel the respect I had for her.

"Are you ready to go see Mike?" I sat back in my seat and so did Mandi. I smiled at her as she let out a deep breath, as if the weight of the world had been lifted from her shoulders, and she smiled in return. "Let's go!"

CHAPTER 27

I was finally on the plane to London. I sat back in my comfortable chair by the window and prepared myself for the seven and half hour-long flight.

I had so much going through my mind. I hadn't told my parents. I was too afraid they would flip out, and not let me go. I am going no matter what the consequences are. Braxton and the thought of what this was going to do for us, and Aunt Mae sticking her neck on the line for me, for she had agreed not to tell Dad, pushed me even harder to go through with this. Calling my parents every day and keeping up the act of being in New York might be tricky, but hopefully not. Mandi, I wished she was coming with me; I would have given anything to have her there with me right then.

I scrambled through my backpack for my IPod, a pencil and paper for doodles, and Braxton's journal. I had not read one word of it, for the fear was still there in the back of my mind. Every time I would work up the courage to read it, I would shut it, and put it away, after rereading the sentences he had written directly to me.

I opened the book again, working up my nerve, determined to read it this time.

June

School is finally out. It's hard to believe I will be a junior grade next year. I am about to head to Addyson's house; we are leaving for the beach in the morning. This is my favorite time of the year. VACATION. The one with the

Michaels is always the best. I know Addy doesn't have much fun. She won't go swimming in the pools, or lazy rivers; she will not get in the ocean with us. She doesn't eat the different cuisines our parents are famous for wanting to try, although some I refuse to eat too. She will not let me have any kind of physical contact with her in public, but only at the beach; back at the beach house she will. Last year, under Pier 14, I had thought about trying to kiss her, but I knew she wouldn't allow it. She loves me like family, like friends, nothing more, and nothing less. I mean, if she did love me any more than that, she wouldn't be making me look at every girl that looks my way on the beach, would she? Constantly saying, she would be suitable for you, or she is pretty, or look at her.

Those girls are pretty. But I don't love any of them. I think this year I am going to kiss her under the pier. I am just going to do it, and see what happens. Worse case, she laughs at me.

I read this entry over and over. He had written this last summer, or four months ago, which meant he wanted to kiss me last summer, a year ago. Well, he didn't either summer. I remember standing under that pier with him. I remember him acting strange, but I thought he was just tired.

I made him look at every girl who drooled over him, because I honestly felt as if he felt obligated to stay with me his whole vacation. I mean, our parents came together to my family beach house. I had no idea he had felt that way for at least a year; I had questioned some of the things he said and did, but I wouldn't allow myself to believe any of it; I just didn't think it was possible.

"Would you like refreshments?" The flight attendant's voice rocked me back to reality. I looked at her with a bewildered look, and finally had the sense to speak. "Oh yes, please." I grabbed a can of Sprite Zero; it was the only diet thing to chose from, gross, and a small plastic cup of ice, off of the tray.

"Thank you very much." My southern drawl was thick compared to her English accent. I couldn't wait to get back to the book. So far so good! I had not read a word that made me want to kill him or myself . . . yet . . . reading on.

June

Our first beach trip, with the Michaels, was better than ever. Instead of just staying at the beach and doing our regular thing, this year I had my own car. Addy and I went to places we didn't normally get to visit. We hit Charleston, North Myrtle Beach, Cherry Grove; we even spent a little time in Florence visiting one of my cousins. I probably wouldn't have gone, but I had to show off my car. Mom and Dad surprised me with it right before we left. I had wanted a Black Chevy Camero since the first time I watched Transformers. It's a bad car! I am sorry to say I didn't have the guts to kiss her . . . again. I almost did at a restaurant I took her to in Charleston; we sat right on the ocean. It was unquestionably the perfect setting. I got too nervous and spilled my drink all over her. Kind of killed the mood; I even think that if I had not done that, the way she was staring into my eyes, she would have let me. Sometimes when she looks at me, I think she loves me back. Then other times, because of things she does, I don't think she wants me to even touch her. I don't know. Maybe next year?

I stared out of the window of the plane, looking at the patchwork of God's creation below. I remembered that day. He was so nervous. I laughed out loud remembering the look on his face.

I was searching his eyes for a clue of what the hell was going on with him. He was so handsome that day, his eyes were glowing more than usual because of the shirt he had on, and the sunlight bouncing off of the ocean; they were just radiant.

He had pulled his little metal chair over to my side of the table so that we could face the water together. The sun would be setting soon. I watched the people walking on the ocean as they laughed, and lived their everyday lives, oblivious to my staring.

I remember asking him, "Beautiful isn't it?" without ever turning to look at him. He said yes in a voice deeper than usual, and a moment later I had soda running down my legs. I stood up, trying to swat it off. Why we do that? Like we think if we swat at the wet area fast enough it will magically be dry; anyway, it looked like I had peed in my pants. I mean perfectly. I couldn't help but burst out laughing, and secretly thanked God I had my windbreaker in the car. Brax didn't laugh; I didn't understand why that day, he smiled, but he should have laughed. It was funny—maybe you had to have been there—but now I saw the problem. He had been going to kiss me.

After he ran to the car and got my jacket out of the back seat, I tied the arms around my waist letting the rest cover my "accident". We walked out with his arm around my shoulders, but he never said a word about any of this.

It floored me that he would have been nervous around me. Up until a few months ago, I never thought he could ever, ever, think of me any differently than a sister, or best friend, then to have read this and found out that he had loved me, that way, for at least this long; Aunt Mae was right. I was blessed.

—∽—

I must have fallen asleep. The calm soothing voice over the intercom woke me. "Please fasten your seatbelts and prepare for landing." Already? I must have slept for at least four hours.

Fifteen minutes later the plane had landed at Heathrow, about fifteen miles from central London. I then found myself taking an underground train to my destination, a beautiful Bed and Breakfast, compliments of dear Doctor himself.

The underground train was a first. We had nothing like this in North Carolina. It was sort of like the subway in New York, but Aunt Mae had refused to allow me to take it. That made this even more fun! Everyone here was so polite. I felt extremely under-dressed. Everyone around me was dressed in business type attire, and me, of course, there I was in my Capris and T-shirt.

Finally, I arrived at the Bed and Breakfast. I could not believe how beautiful it was. This place was gigantic. The whole place looked as if it was being swallowed up by flowers and vines. But not in an un-kept way; it truly was beautiful.

A lady, maybe in her later sixties, came running out of the front door. She was trying to get my bags as she spoke.

"How do you do? Welcome to the Belmont Lodge, dearie." she had grabbed a bag in each hand, leaving me with my pocketbook and book-bag. She turned, and began to walk towards the house before I could protest.

"Doc said you would be here about this time. Watch your step, dearie, and he was right; you're right on time. Your room is on the ground floor; it has a double bed and your own door to the patio . . ." I was yet to be able to speak to her for she never missed a beat. I was wondering when she was going to breathe. ". . . you have a beautiful view of the garden! HOUSE RULES: breakfast is served between seven and ten in the morning; you can smoke outside, not inside . . ." She stopped dead in her tracks and turned towards me. "You don't smoke do you, dearie?" I quickly shook my head no and was about to tell her I was only sixteen years old when she cut me off.

"Check out is at ten in the morning, and be sure to leave your key in the room. You have Internet connection and T.V. There is no air-conditioning, but we do have heat . . ." Her words trailed off as my mind wrapped around all of the information.

Did she just say they had no air conditioning? What? I continued to follow her around the house as she constantly talked at an enormous speed, and I was desperately trying to remember everything she had said to me.

The way she was talking, I wasn't going to see her again after this . . . ever. I still had not seen any other people in the house other than the two of us, and I was suddenly scared. Was I seriously going to be truly alone, for two weeks, in a place I had never set foot in?

The lady quickly turned towards me and handed me a business card. She smiled the sweetest smile, reminding me of Aunt B on that old television show, Andy Griffith. "Call me if you need me, dearie." She was walking out of the door, before I could even say goodbye, when she quickly turned back, remembering something she had forgot to say. "You will have a friend tomorrow; her name is, um . . . Elizabeth Johnson . . . She will be staying for at least one night; you will make your first friend!" She was happy with herself for remembering. Then, just like that, she was gone.

I stood in the middle of the living room, or at least what we would have called the living room in the States, and stared at everything around me. I walked out to the garden and sat on the wooden chair and looked out at the beautiful view.

"Elizabeth Johnson . . ." I whispered to myself. Well, at least, I wouldn't be utterly alone. I hope so badly she would be compassionate. So far, everyone in London had been so polite and kind . . . hmm. I wished I could say the same about New York.

I called Braxton the same time I would have, had I been in New York. He did not know the difference. I wanted to tell him. I wanted to tell him I was in London, I mean *flippin' London*, so bad. I wanted to tell him why I was there, and what this could mean, but I didn't.

I was terribly afraid that he would try to talk me out of it for some reason. I didn't know; I thought he would be happy about it! Wouldn't he?

It didn't truly matter; it didn't matter what anyone thought about it; tomorrow was my first consultation.

—∽—

As promised, breakfast was ready at seven in the morning. I grabbed a cup of orange juice, and a muffin looking thing, and ran out to the cab that had already been waiting on me for five minutes.

I handed him the address for the doctor's office. This cab ride was much different to the one in New York. This was actually pleasant. I didn't dare blink! I watched as the gargantuan buildings flashed by. Everything was so . . . so antique looking.

The drive had only taken ten minutes, and I was extremely disappointed it was over. I had to ask the cab driver which building I was suppose to go into. He pointed to the one to the right of me.

"Thank you very much."

I shut the door as I heard the man reply, "Cheers!" He quickly drove away.

"Cheers—like in the movies," I whispered, grinning.

The inside of the doctor's office looked like any other I had ever been in. Mind you, I have been in a lot, and for this very reason. I had to fill out a stack of paperwork before I could go any further. Lots of the questions they asked, I didn't know, and I darned well couldn't call mom and dad. So, I called Aunt Mae. Thankfully she knew about our family history.

After a half hour, of paper work I finally got to see the Doctor. He had all of my history; my past results of every test that had ever been run on me. But he made it clear that to him those papers meant nothing; he was starting from the bottom.

For the next two hours, he asked me questions. It felt like thousands of them. He asked me about my eating habits, what I ate, when I ate, exercises, daily activities, stress levels, depression, on and on and on . . . I answered each one honestly.

The next hour was consumed with taking blood, and every x-ray and scan known to man. I did a stress test on a treadmill; I thought I was going to die. I cried through that one. When he finally told the nurses I could stop, every inch of me hurt. I knew I was going to be sore in the morning. Finally, we were done. Thank you, Jesus.

"It will take between seven and nine days to get all of these results back. Once I have had an opportunity to carefully examine each one, I will call you back in for your last consultation. We will discuss treatment, assuming there is one, and then I will send you back home."

My heart fell when he said assuming there is one. I had not even considered that there might not be. He noticed my expression.

"Don't worry, Addyson, everything will be okay." He tried to reassure me. "I am regarded as the best for a reason." His grin and warm hand on my shoulder did nothing for my hopes.

—∽∾—

Back at the Lodge I was thinking about everything that had happened that day. I had not even thought about there not being a treatment. My mind tortured me with the doctor's words.

Again, I had not seen another person in this house at all. I remembered "Aunt B" saying that a girl my own age would be there today. But I still hadn't seen her.

I talked to Mandi for a long time, while sitting on the patio. I missed her. How fabulous would it have been, if she was there with me? To have someone who could help me through this. If the doctor told me he couldn't help me, I was not going to want to be alone. I would be devastated. After all, this was my last chance.

I was taking pictures of the sun setting over the garden when a cab pulled into the Lodge. I watched as a girl, about my age, looked right at me. She didn't have anything but a book bag from what I could tell. And 'Aunt B' came running out of the house to greet her.

I couldn't hear what they were saying, but I had a pretty clear idea. And 'Aunt B' didn't seem to know what to think about not having luggage to carry.

I went back into my room and sat on my bed. After her speedy grand tour, I would go introduce myself. I could so use someone to talk to right then. The real question was, would she want someone to talk to?

I heard the door right next to mine shut closed, then footsteps heading towards the living room. She was almost finished. I walked out my door and waited in the hall to see the girl when she came back to her room. After a few more minutes, she came back down the hall towards me.

"Hi, my name is Addyson Michaels. You must be Elizabeth Johnson?" I waited to see how she was going to accept me.

"How did you know my name?" She was suspicious, and I noticed for the first time that she had healed scars all over her. Maybe she was running from someone?

"I am sorry. The lady who runs the house told me you would be coming today, and that we were about the same age." I looked away from her; I figured if she was going to be the type to be hateful, it would be coming now.

"Nice to meet you." She was still a little uneasy, but she smiled at me.

"I was wondering if you would like to hang out on the patio for a while; I mean, after you get settled and all?" I asked, sounding downright pathetic. I couldn't help it.

To my surprise she said, "Sure."

After talking for a few hours on the patio, I found out that our lives were not so different. We both have our own terrible stories to share. She told me all about her dad being an alcoholic after her mother had an "accident", but she never told me any details. She told me about the scars, and how her own father, in his drunken rage, would beat her and abuse her in ways that a father never should. I cried for her. But she never shed a tear. She was so strong . . . I wanted to be like her. And suddenly the torment and torture I had been through my whole life no longer seems that severe.

After a while, I was calling her Liz, and she was calling me Addy. It was as if we had been friends forever. I was so grateful to have her there. We had the run of the house. We went a little . . . well . . . wild. We had the radio blaring and were dancing on the furniture, using what-knots as microphones, I felt like a carefree kid again. Liz was the first person I had ever acted like this with, other than Braxton.

We ended up both staying in her room that night. She told me all about James and Alex and her dilemma. I didn't tell her this, but I secretly hoped she hooked up with Alex. He reminded me of my Braxton in a way. He was so protective of her.

I told her all about Braxton, Jennifer, Mandi, the reason I was here and the doctor's appointment—my last chance. I wished Mandi could meet Liz. If Mandi and Braxton could have been there, I would have had everything I needed.

CHAPTER 28

That day had been a lovely day. When I talked to Addyson that morning, she sounded better than she had ever since she had been in New York. Hearing her sound happy made me have a better day. She hadn't been in the very best of moods over the past few weeks. She wouldn't tell me what was wrong, so I stopped asking. I had to believe that if she needed me she would let me know what was going on and tell me to come to her.

I stayed at Mike's house the previous night. There is something about staying in someone else's house that makes you feel uncomfortable about being the first one walking around in the morning. I would have hated to wake up the whole house.

Instead, I put my shirt on over my jeans and slid my shoes on quickly and headed out the front door to my car. It was hot outside that morning. My black car seemed to react to heat like an oven. I opened the door, and prepared for the wave of heat that would hit me. I sat inside and rolled down both windows.

Heading down highway sixteen, the overwhelming thought to go straight to the airport, with nothing but the shirt on my back, wouldn't leave me be. How surprised Addy would be if I just showed up on her door step in New York? I could spend the week with her, have lunch with her, Jace and Caroline, and spend my nights holding her. I was sure Mae wouldn't mind in the least.

I turned left into McDonald's parking lot and turned the car off. I had only missed one day of school that year, they could live without me for one football game, and my parents would understand, I thought. I smiled to myself; this certainly could work.

I ran my hand through my messy hair, only to push it around in a different mess. "New York." I whispered as I pulled myself out of the car and towards the entrance to McDonalds. Breakfast, airport, and New York; sounded like a plan.

Walking into the dive, I couldn't have been more excited. A group of girls was coming out of the building, so I decide to hold the door open for them.

"Thank You," the tall one in the middle said, smiling a lighting white smile in my direction. I looked over my sunglasses directly into her set of ocean blue eyes. She stopped walking abruptly, making the girl behind her run into her. "Your eyes are the most beautiful color I have ever seen." Her bikini top and booty shorts had not gone un-noticed, especially from the car filled with guys waiting in the drive-thru.

"Thanks, yours are pretty too." I pulled my shades back up to cover my eyes and began to walk into the building when her French nails dug into my arm.

"Wait! What's your name?" The girl asked, not letting me go.

"Braxton." I replied simply, not too happy with the moon-shaped marks being imprinted on my arm. I gently pulled my arm from her grasp and looked from my arm to her.

"I am sorry; I didn't mean to do that. I just wanted to know your name." Her face flashed red. "Braxton." I smiled and confirmed.

"Nice to meet you, Braxton." Her hips suddenly began to move in an extremely seductive way. I couldn't say that she wasn't attractive; she was. But I genuinely don't want to embarrass her in front of her friends. I thought it best to stop this before it went any further. "I am dating someone," I said simply and left the girl standing alone in front of the door.

After a few moments, once I felt it was safe that she was gone, I looked back towards the door. She and her group of friends were standing outside talking to the one person that could kill my positive mood. The one person I never wanted to see—Drake.

His eyes met mine, and he pointed towards me. The girl looked back at me as Drake spoke. I could hear her laughter through the door and inside the building. She placed her hand over her mouth and shook her head before looking back at me. What the hell was so funny? What was Drake saying to her?

I turned back around and moved a step closer in line. Scanning the menu, I decided to get two sausage biscuits, two hash browns, and a cinnamon roll. The person in front of me was leaving, and it was my turn. Before I could tell the man my order, I felt a tap on my shoulder. I know who it is; what the hell did he want? I turned to face him.

"Hey Drake," I said before even turning all the way around. It was Drake, but the girl was with him, as well.

"Brax, please tell this girl that you are dating Addyson Michaels." He was visibly holding back a laugh. "For some reason, she doesn't seem to believe me." the girl was waiting with curiosity for my answer.

"Hold on."

I faced the man behind the counter and placed my order. I was shaking from the anger rising inside of me. It is taking an enormous amount of self-control not to hit Drake and cuss the girl out. Once my receipt was given to me, the man took off like lighting to begin to fill the tray with my breakfast.

I turned back as calmly as possible to face Drake and his new-found friend. I lifted my sunglasses and placed them on the top of my head. I needed her to see into my eyes; she had to see that what I was going to tell her was one hundred percent the truth. I stepped so close to the girl I literally heard the intake of air in her throat.

"Yes, I am dating Addyson Michaels. I love her with every fiber of my being, and one day I plan to marry her. I belong to her, and she to me. Do you have a problem with that?" I couldn't control the anger that was leaking through my voice, and seeping into my eyes. My hands were shaking again.

Speechless, the girl began to stutter words to Drake. Drake laughed out loud as the girl almost ran out of the building.

"Your order is ready, sir." The man said from behind the counter.

"You're an asshole, Drake." I turned and retrieved my food.

Taking the tray to the drink station, I began to fill my cup full of Coca Cola. What was the point in all of that? Maybe to embarrass me, or the girl, or both of us; only God knew with Drake, what his intentions were. "What an ass." I whispered one last time as I snapped the lid on my drink.

"Addy is really lucky to have you. I hope one day I will find someone just like you." Marina had been standing beside me the whole time. I hadn't noticed her until then. Marina was another overweight girl in our school. If I was not mistaken, she was a year behind us. She got picked on, but not as badly as Addy. As a matter of fact, to me, she looked like she had lost some weight. I noticed she was eating a fruit and yogurt cup for breakfast. Good for her.

"Sorry for my language." I placed my drink on my tray and turned to walk back towards my table. "I am the lucky one; see ya around." I sat at the first table by the window. Drake and three of his friends sat in the far corner to my left. I kept my eye on them, waiting for something to be said, but nothing ever was.

Ten minutes later I was in my car and on my way to the house. I wondered what my parents would say about me going to New York. The hard truth of the matter was, I was broke, and had to get money from them. Hopefully, I would be on my way to New York, to my Addyson, within the day.

CHAPTER 29

The morning already proved it was going to be a better day than yesterday. I was so grateful I would not be alone all day. Now I had Liz—for today at least.

At breakfast, that morning, which consisted of bowls of cereal and orange juice for both of us, she mentioned that today featured an extraordinary London tradition, and she was going to show me around. I couldn't wait.

"Liz, where are we going?" My voice mirrored the excitement I couldn't hide on my face. Apparently, it was a surprise, for she wouldn't even drop me a hint. "You'll see. Now look over there; that is Tower Bridge!" She giggled as the view took my breath away.

Like everything else in London, it was monumental and extravagant, lacking no detail, and utterly breathtaking. "Everything is so much more amazing when you see it in person." I was talking slowly as my eyes were drinking in the image of the bridge.

The double decker bus, another first for me, was beginning to slow down, when hundreds of thousands of people began to come into view. Normally, I would begin to panic at this number of people in one place; I would hide behind my hair, and usually hold onto Brax for dear life, but not this time.

As far as my eyes could see there were people of every race, every culture, every shape, every size; how could I possibly stand out in this crowd, right?

"There must be a million people here?" I was desperately trying to see what was going on. Children on the bus came alive with laughter and squeals of anticipation. Parents became instantly more alert, grabbing their children's hands and spouting off 'stay close' rules.

"This is the Mayor's Thames Festival. This happens every single year. The festival begins at Westminster Bridge and closes down busy streets all the way here, to the bridge and beyond. It's a festival for the Arts!" She was smiling from ear to ear with her revelation, knowing I love any art, proud of the obvious shock on my face.

We hurried off of the bus as we slid, her a little easier than me, through the massive crowds of people. The smell of food filled the air; I don't think there was anything you could ever want, that wasn't here on these streets. From fresh-spawned cotton candy, to any cultural traditions, even the American favorite, Hot Dogs. But I was told that there was the 'feast on the bridge' and that's where all the delicious food smells was coming from.

Every inch of the grounds was taken by someone entertaining with something. Right in front of us was a massive crowd, watching this B-Boy in the middle of the street, dancing, and throwing his body in ways I didn't even think was possible.

To our left was a group of kids ranging from what looks like four years old to maybe seventeen, putting on a Tae Kwon Do demonstration; the way they moved, it was almost as if they were dancing.

To our right, well . . . was dancing; on a stage people were dancing the Jive, people from all corners of the world. This was truly staggering.

Liz and I spent the entire day at the festival, watching remarkable people do extraordinary things. When I thought it couldn't get any better than this . . . it did! The night festival began. As the sun faded away to sleep for the night, the streets came alive in a whole new way. I would think the whole of London would be lit up by the light shows and parades dancing through the streets. But the best part, in Liz's opinion, was about to come, the fireworks from the very middle of the river.

"COME ON!" Liz had to scream over the crowds and the music, laughter, and enthusiasm. She pulled me by hand, and we made our way to the edge of the bridge. "THIS IS AMAZING!" I screamed back.

Suddenly the loud boom of the fireworks stole everyone's attention. The blues and yellows, red and greens, spewed out over the sky, leaving a mirror image over the waters. With every boom came a new vision of color and beauty. Every person watching let out oohs and ahhs, as the show seemed to last forever.

I stood there with the reflection of the display dancing in my eyes. I wanted to remember this day forever. It had been a day full of music from every genre, dancing from every culture, street arts from clowns to B Boy dancers, river races with crafts of all shapes and sizes, carnival and parades, pyrotechnics, art installations, massed choirs so enormous they could have taken up an entire football field in America, and food and feasting. People were even wearing what they called "salad hats," which, is exactly what it sounds like—hats made of veggies. The finale was a magical illuminated Night Carnival that stretched all along the banks of the Thames, followed by a fireworks display fired from the center of the river itself! I felt alive! I felt as if, for the first time in my life, I was living.

After the show, Liz and I both allowed our adrenaline to fade, and with that came the exhaustion. We both agreed it was time to go back to our Lodge. As we were walking back to the bus stop, laughing and joking around, I accidentally bumped, pretty hard, into a girl about my age. It wasn't the first time it had happened; also it had happened to me all night long. It is literally elbow to elbow in most areas, but it was totally accidental.

"I am so sorry. I didn't mean to." I sounded like a recording by now, and most people had smiled or nodded confirming that, hey, it happens, and went on about their business. But I quickly realized that this girl wasn't going to let it go, by the look that came across her face. Once she saw who had done it, the familiar flash of pure hate came into her eyes, and I knew what was coming.

I tried so hard to get away. I lowered my head and began to move quickly through the crowd. I ignored the yells of "Hey, fat girl, I am talking to you!" or "Bitch, I said stop!" as I knew that Liz had no idea of what was going on, and wanted desperately to get onto the bus and leave all of this, that was sure to happen, behind.

Without warning, I hit the pavement, hard, landing on my backside and my elbows. I felt the stinging pain shoot through both of my arms and sat up grabbing both of my elbows. Not to mention the terrible pain coming from my butt bone. All of the embarrassment and shame came flooding back into my system, the same feelings I had two years ago at that football game. She had grabbed me by the back of my shirt and pulled me firm to the ground.

I was still sitting on the ground and looked up as I felt cold soda and ice cover my head, face, and chest. "I SAID STOP, FATSO!" She was screaming, half because of the crowd and half because she was ticked off after pouring her drink over the top of my already aching body.

"I really didn't mean to bump into you; it was an accident." I became scared, as I realized that this girl was with four more girls, and I wasn't sure if those boys staring at me were with them or just watching the new show.

I knew I had to get to my feet. Her towering over me like that was putting me at a frightfully distressing disadvantage, and if I wanted a chance to get away I have to get up.

I began to turn my body to get on all fours, when a blunt force caught my rear end with such speed, I flew straight forward, eating the pavement below me. I felt the road-rash forming on my face. I didn't know how bad it was, but my bottom lip, chin, cheek, and forehead were on fire.

I gave up. I let the sobs come and let these people see the fat girl broken; after all, that's what they wanted, right? They wanted to see the fat girl suffer for . . . for what? For being fat? They wanted to hurt me and make me hate myself, or make sure I knew how much they hated me. They wanted me to have nightmares, and be scared of them; they needed me to know that they are superior and perfect, they wanted to break me. Why else would they do it?

I finally rose to my feet without anyone touching me or saying anything for a long moment. When I turned to face the girl I had no emotion. I had no fear, no pain, no sorrow or embarrassment, no shame, not even hatred. I felt the blood dripping onto my shirt. I never flinched; I never raised my hand to touch it. In my mind, I could imagine how awful it undoubtedly was. Now, not only was I the fat girl, but the fat girl with the scarred-up face; I imagined the worst.

The girls gasped as the laughs faded. They had looked at me, and when I saw the look in their eyes, it must have been as awful as I imagined. Most of the girls turned pale, and were telling the leader: "That's enough, Brandi. Leave her alone!" I noticed the look of horror in Brandi's eyes, for a moment; I could imagine her saying, "What have I done?" just by the look on her face. But the sorrow and regret is often taken over by anger. I was not sure if it was anger at me for existing, or at themselves for the realization of whom or what they actually were. But it never failed. She raised her hand back to smack me across the burnt side of my face when she was cut off quickly.

"If you touch her again, so help me God, I will destroy you!" Liz didn't scream but growled it through clenched teeth. Everyone around had no problem at all hearing her.

"Liz, please let's just go," I begged her. Liz didn't need any of this. She still had never told me why she was in London to begin with. But I had a strong feeling it wasn't good, and she did not need to deal with stuff like this.

I found a new respect, not for myself, but for Liz and suddenly wanted to protect her. I walked closer to Liz, so I could see her face. There was fire in her eyes, as if all of the past that she had lived came flowing through her veins. There was disgust on her face, and she was fearless, and everyone standing there knew it.

"COME ON GIRLS, ARE YOU GOING TO LET THESE TWO JUMP ME?" Brandi was giggling nervously. With her wrist still held in a death grip by Liz, pure fear came over her face, and her girls began to step back a few feet. One girl even said, "We told you to leave her alone, Brandi." They eventually turned away and walked off, leaving Brandi totally alone.

Liz didn't need ME to protect her; Brandi was the one in need now! For the first time, I remembered where we were. I noticed a pretty decent sized crowd was watching us. No one, not one adult, tried to step in or break this conflict up; everyone was waiting for Liz. I was getting a little worried too, for Brandi.

Brandi was getting more terrified by the second. The anticipation of Liz's reaction was getting intense, as Brandi realized promptly that she was utterly alone. The adults weren't even going to help her—that was clear. Liz had still not spoken or removed her death grip from Brandi's wrist and with every moment that went by, Brandi became more frantic.

Everyone was holding their breath, including me, just waiting; when Liz finally spoke.

"How does it feel? How does it feel to be zeroed in on, pointed out of a group of people, and embarrassed, humiliated, degraded, and abused? How does it feel to want to shrink out of your skin, to become invisible, and run screaming in pain and shame, panic and despair?"

Liz slung Brandi's wrist out of her hand like she was infested with a disease, it was already turning blue from the hold for so long, and Liz finished. "Everyone here knows who you really are on the inside. Everyone here knows that you are not as perfect as you appear. Everybody standing here, with their eyes on you, now takes you for what you really are—a monster."

Brandi began to cry at the meaning of each word Liz laid on her. Brandi turned pale as she stuttered and tried with everything she had to retaliate on Liz, but ended with a weak and unpretentious . . . "BITCH!"

Brandi turned quickly to run off, and ran hard into one of the boys who had been standing by her the whole time. "Dustin, let's go!" she tried to get the handsome boy by the arm and pull him off with her. He stood as still as a statue. Her face blanked again, and in a much lower, more pleading voice, she begged, "Dustin, please let's go." It almost sounded like a question.

Liz and I both stood shocked at his reply: "I am taking them home." Dustin, Brandi, Liz, and I all about jumped out of our skin at the booming sound of applause, the whoops and hollers, cheers and whistles, for none of us had noticed that the crowd had tripled in size.

Brandi screamed from her public rejection and humiliation as the laughs, points, sneers, and glares had changed from me to her. I looked at Liz as she began to come back from somewhere in the past, in her mind, from some dark, horrible place, and with tears of gratitude and appreciation for my new found friend, I hugged her as tight as I could.

At first she tensed up from my embrace, still raw from the memories and emotions she had just relived and unleashed, but soon she relaxed as the tears of accomplishment slid down her face.

"Thank you so much Liz," was all I could say. From out of the crowd came an older man with a first aid kit. "My name is Doctor Brownfield; may I take a look at your face?" His eyes were soft, kind, and caring. "Sure."

The crowd began to hover around Liz, shaking her hand like she was the hero of London. Even though she was a musician and played in front of vast crowds, this was different, and the overflow of people was a little too uncomfortable. Our new friend Dustin must have realized this because he protectively stood in front of Liz keeping the crowd away as the doctor finished examining my face.

"Lucky for you, it really looked much worse than it actually is. Once I cleaned the dirt and debris from the area, I can see you really only seem to have a small cut on your eyebrow, which is where all of the blood was coming from . . . and a few scratches on your cheek and chin. Your lip is busted pretty well though. Just keep it clean, washing with warm soapy water at least twice a day. You shouldn't even scar, hopefully." He gave me a slight grin as he walked away, not waiting for a thank you or anything.

"Can I take the two of you home?" Dustin asked, realizing the doctor was finished with me. Liz and I looked at each other for the other's approval. She finally nodded at me and said, "Let's get out of here!"

—∿—

Once we reached the Lodge we couldn't thank Dustin enough for bringing us home. He was so kind and polite and devilishly attractive with his English accent, and deep green eyes. I wasn't sure if it was a crush forming for Liz or just a respect for her actions, but his smile lingered with his gaze as he looked at her.

"I am sorry about everything Brandi did tonight; I am sorry I was with her, and I am sorry I didn't stop her." He looked straight at me begging for forgiveness with his voice and his eyes.

"Thank You," Liz and I said in unison. He smiled, knowing I accepted his apology and that Liz did, as well.

I followed Liz into the house, suddenly sore from head to toe. I wanted to shower and go to bed. We talked for about thirty more minutes, telling each other our goodnights and headed to our separate showers.

I stood in the hot shower, feeling the new stings of freshly-broken flesh, realizing I had scrapes on my knees, as well. My elbows burned, as did my face. My bones were tired. I crawled into the nice, fluffy bed allowing myself to sink deep into the feather pillows, surrounded by softness and comfort.

I began to drift off quickly as I remembered, this was the first day I had not texted or called Braxton, and the second day I had not texted or called Mandi or my parents.

CHAPTER 30

Midnight had come and gone with not so much as a single text message from Addyson. It was taking everything inside of me not to call her or text her, but I felt like I shouldn't always be the one to initiate a conversation. It would be gratifying to know that she was thinking about me sometimes, too.

Earlier that day I had received a phone call from Mr. Michaels. He called me just in time; he stopped me from going to New York. If someone had told me, six months ago, that Addyson would run off to England, by herself, without so much as a word to anyone at all, I would have laughed in his face.

Turning over in my bed, I reached over to my night stand and checked for a text message again. There was nothing, not one word, like the rest of the day. I turned onto my back and scratched my chest as the thoughts of the fear in Mr. Michaels voice rang clear in my mind.

"Did you know about this, Braxton? What the hell is going on here?"

I cut him off; I had no idea what he was talking about. "Slow down, Mr. Michaels. What is going on? Is Addy okay?" I had been sitting at the kitchen table with my parents going over my plans for New York. I think they were about to agree to let me go.

"Addyson is in London; I can't get my sister to answer the phone, but I am almost positive that Addyson is there alone." I thought for a second that he was joking. Addyson would never do something like this, ever.

After a long moment, I finally replied. "Mr. Michaels, I swear to you I had no idea, and still am confused as hell, to be honest with you." My mom was rapidly asking what was wrong as the panic in my voice was rising. My father cupped her hand in his and whispered, "Let him get off the phone first."

Mr. Michaels knew as much as I did, which was precisely nothing. After five more minutes of telling each other to call with any new information, the call was over. I relayed the information I had to my parents, and we sat silently staring at the table. "I guess I am not going to New York, but thanks anyway." I stood from the table and walked to my room.

I have been in there ever since, waiting by the phone. Mandi knew; I bet she had known since the beginning, and she didn't tell me. I was so angry with her I couldn't bring myself to call her and question her about it. I knew I would lose my temper and say things I would later regret. I would call her in the morning when, hopefully, I was a lot calmer.

Sometime after two in the morning, still without anything from Addy, I fell asleep. I tossed and turned all night long, until finally, at four in the morning I gave up and turned on the television. The nightmares were intolerable. The nightmares of Addyson Michaels, the girl I grew up with, the girl I fell in love with, the girl I have known my whole life, the nightmares of Addyson never coming home. The Addyson I thought I knew never existed to begin with.

CHAPTER 31

I guess I should have been keeping my priorities straight for the last two days, understanding that keeping the lie up at home, with Braxton, Mandi, and my parents was a little more serious than sightseeing!

"Have you lost your mind? What am I supposed to do now, Addyson Dawn Michaels? Tell me! I have dodged, avoided, and jumped through hoops to avoid your parent's phone calls! Now they are threatening to come up here. I am not lying for you, Addyson; I told you that, from the start. I told you, if they called me, I would tell them to call your cell phone. What now, tell me?"

Aunt Mae wouldn't let me get a word in; I would attempt to apologize, or tell her I would figure this out, but I gave up after the last time she cut me off. After at least five more minutes of deserved screaming at me, I finally was able to speak.

"Aunt Mae, you're right; I am sorry. I will fix this somehow. I am going to call them, and if something happens, I will tell them the truth, making sure they know that I really didn't give you much of a choice." It was the truth; I would have come to London with or without her help or approval. If she had told my dad when I first told her, I would have never made it here and for that I owe her forever.

"Addyson, it doesn't matter what you say. I am the adult here. You were my responsibility, and I let you go half way around the world, at sixteen, and by yourself!" She let a deep, long sigh out of her lungs as if to wash the worry away, or accepting her words herself, realizing that she couldn't do anything about it now.

"Addy, I wanted you to go, I understood, and still do understand why you wanted to go. But I honestly thought you were responsible enough to be there. Maybe I was wrong. If something had happened to you yesterday, my brother would never forgive me! Now call your parents. I love you, Addy. Good luck; you're going to need it!" She hung up before I could even tell her I loved her back.

I sat there on my bed, running over the possibilities of what could happen with my parents. I knew I had been selfish with Braxton, taking advantage of my parents' trust, and now putting Aunt Mae's trust from my parents in jeopardy.

Here, goes nothing, I thought. At this time of the day, my mom would be at the office. I called her desk.

"Hi mom." I tried to sound as excited as possible. I prepared myself for mom's wrath; I knew it was coming. "Addyson Dawn Michaels, where the hell have you been?" If she had not been at work, she would have made my ear drums ring, screaming into the phone. Instead, it was terribly slow, stern, and red-hot angry. I am not sure which was worse.

What was my plan? I had it, practiced it from every single angle that she could have come at me. But when I heard the worry, the anger, and fear in her voice, I couldn't remember anything.

"Well, I have been, you know, with school, and homework, friends . . ." She cut me off and said something, an angle I had not thought of:

"That's funny; it's the weekend, and neither Caroline nor Jace have seen you at all! Now, Addyson, what is your next lie?"

I had not thought about Mom calling either of them. I had totally forgotten about both of their parents requiring our home number, among other things, before they could come to North Carolina with me. Damn caller ID! Caroline's mom and Jace's mom, both, had called to talk to my parents to make sure that the visit was okay with them, or perhaps to make sure that it was true.

I was so busted; the only thing left to do was tell the truth. "Mom, I am in London." I was expecting to hear screaming now, office or not, cussing even, but I was totally shocked at what she said next.

"We know." I couldn't register what she was saying. I let my face and body relax from the tensing up I had been doing, and finally let the words sink in.

"How?" She sighed, but the disappointment coming through her words was worse than the anger she had earlier.

"We check the VISA card often, Addyson, to see what you are spending, and honestly, to make sure you are not going crazy with it. When you pay for something, the statement tells what has been purchased, how much it cost, and the location. Your Oyster Card showed up in London. Your father and I both thought it must have been a mistake, or maybe the main office of the transportation system in New York was in London. Do you know why, Addy; do you know why we would consider something so ridiculously stupid? Because, your father and I knew that our Addyson would never lie to us. Our baby would never deceive us, and take advantage of our trust. You would never do the things that you would have to do to pull off something as dangerous, and just plain stupid, as this."

I heard her voice crack, and the disappointment and heartache went to my core. I broke into sobs, too. "I don't blame you for being upset with me. Let me explain . . ." I spent the next few minutes telling her the whole truth. I told her everything about the doctor. Originally the doctor had, in fact, been in New York. But due to his family being in England he moved back home and opened an office there. Once I read his articles and his world-recognized ability to help unexplained weight gain and obesity, there was no question in my mind that I had to come to England. I explained how he had talked to me personally before I even went to New York and that he was so confident in his abilities that he paid for the plane tickets, the lodge, and even said, if he couldn't help me, the consultations too would be free. Mom was surprisingly quiet as I continued to explain the trip here, not telling Braxton or Mandi, about Aunt Mae begging me to tell them, even yesterday at the festival. "A miracle, Mom. He is my miracle."

"When are you coming home?" She was still upset, but with the truth came a little bit of understanding. "As soon as the doctor calls me in for my final consultation; then he will send me home." I was terrified she wouldn't let me stay long enough to hear the results.

"We will talk more about this when you get home. By the way, when you leave London you are to come straight home to North Carolina, and I want you to think very hard about this question I am about to ask you. Do not answer me now. No, think about it; think about it long and hard." She was silent for a few seconds before she finally asked me the question.

"When have your daddy and I ever not done everything we could do to help you with this weight problem, Addyson? We have spent hundreds of thousands of dollars on medicines, treatments, gyms, diet plans, an underground pool, and more. What made you think that you couldn't tell us the truth and that we wouldn't do everything in our power to make it happen? You would have not gone by yourself, which is, honestly, the worst part about all of this! Think about that, I want to hear the answer. I love you, Addyson, and I expect to see you in no more than seven days."

"I love you too, Mom." I sat in the silence of my room, a tear rolling down my face, every word mom said was the truth. The only thing I could tell her was how terribly afraid I was she would not let me come; she was right, and that's what made it so terrible.

—∿—

"Hey Brax—" This phone call was no different from the ones with Aunt Mae or Mom. Braxton cut me off, asking where I was, why he hasn't heard from me since early yesterday morning; it was the very same questions on repeat, just another person.

I knew once I told him the truth, one of two things was going to happen. He would either be happy, which I doubted very seriously, or highly pissed the hell off; which is exactly what happened.

"Why wouldn't you tell me? Why wouldn't you want me to come with you, to be there with you and support you through this? Your mom and dad would have let you go, Addyson, and somewhere in your heart you know that. And them knowing that I would be there with you the whole time—they probably would have actually been happy about it!" He went on scolding me like for another solid hour. He was asking questions, and I was giving mostly short yes and no answers; it was all I actually had time to say, anyway: Don't you trust me?—Yes. Don't you want me there?—Yes. Did anyone else go with you?—No. The questions went on and on and on.

Why is it that words—well, specific words, the truth—can hurt worse than an actual physical beating? I guess because the pain of a beating doesn't linger on in your mind. You forget about how awful physical pain hurts; otherwise women would never have more than one child. Words, on the other hand, sink in deep; they stay in your heart and mind, eating away at your insides, especially when the words come from the people you love the most in your life. When you're told through hurt and pain, knowing full well it's your entire fault, that's when it hurts the most.

I told Braxton everything: Where I am staying, about the doctor visit, the festival—minus Brandi and the ride home from the hot English guy N about Liz, and everything that she had been through, too. "I know what I did was wrong, Braxton. I know I should have told you all the truth. But in my mind, this is it. This is my last chance. I hope you understand when I say that, if I could do it all over again, I would do it all the same way. Only because, I know I am here; I know I will have the last consultation with the doctor. I know I am about to be a different person, or at least on my way. I am very sorry I hurt you, but this is just as much for you as it is for me."

To my utter surprise, Braxton did not argue with me at all. "I understand; I don't agree with it, or even understand it fully, but I understand what you were thinking, and why." I knew he meant it. He wasn't angry any more. He was still hurt and probably would have trust issues with me for a long time, until I prove to him that I do not usually lie to him, but, overall, before we got off the phone, he was almost back to normal. I got off the phone and sent him two dozen pictures on his cell phone. He replied to almost all of them. I sent pictures of London, the festival, the lodge, and Liz. The last text he sent me shocked me, but made me smile.

~Everything is going to be OK, Addy, regardless of how stupid it was to go alone. I am proud of you for your bravery. I love you. ~

—⁓—

It was after noon before I came out of my room for the first time. I realized that Liz had not been by or anything. I wanted to go check on her and tell her about my morning. You know, honestly, I knew I had a lot of making up to do to a bunch of people, and I honestly did feel crappy for hurting them. At the same time, I felt relief. Like a building had been lifted off of my shoulders and I could come out of hiding, so to speak.

I knocked on Liz's door. I didn't hear any movement or sounds at all in her room. I checked inside the house, the garden; I couldn't find her anywhere. I walked back to her room and knocked again—nothing. I slowly opened the door. "Liz?" I walked on in when I saw her bed made, and her key lying on top of the bed spread. The rooms were empty and quiet, clean and perfect, like no one had ever been there at all. I walked into her bathroom. I don't know why; I knew she was gone, but for some reason I just had to make sure, even though the door was wide open and the light was off. I turned to walk out and noticed a piece of paper lying flat on the chest of drawers.

Addyson,

    I am sorry I had to go without saying goodbye in person. But something came up, and I had to go right away. I waited as long as I could, but you never came down for breakfast. At 10:15, I had to go. I hope you are alright. I am leaving my phone number and address, and I hope that we will keep in touch. I actually had a fantastic time with you. I needed to "let go"; it's been way too long.

Your Friend
Elizabeth Johnson

    I smiled as the tears ran down my face. I knew in my heart that I would never see her again. But I would call and write for sure. Just as fast as she had walked into my life, she was gone.

CHAPTER 32

The more I dwelt on the facts, the more I did not understand Addyson and her way of thinking. My sixteen-year-old girlfriend was in London, by herself, so she said, and would be there for another four days.

I was ecstatic when Mr. Michaels told me that they were making her come back to North Carolina after the consultation, and not back to New York. Yesterday, all of her stuff from Mae's was shipped back here. I smiled the whole time the truck driver was unloading it.

I was trying to stay angry; I wanted to be angry with her, and I had a right to be angry. She had been lying to me for at least three months, maybe longer, yet somehow, for some reason, I couldn't stay angry with her.

Maybe it was because I had been with her so many times during her torments. I have watched her cry, when we were much younger, and withdraw even more from the world. Hell, I have cried for her. If this doctor could help her, if he truly was as good as he said, then this would change everything for her. It wouldn't change how I felt about her, but it would change things for me too. She would allow me to do more things with her. She would allow me to touch her like I dreamed of doing. I was not being a pervert, I was being honest and honestly, what guy doesn't think about sexual intimacy with his girl?

"Let's go." Mike jumped from the sofa and was heading towards my car.

"Where are we going?" I stood from the patio chair and walked through our garage.

"Mandi's, where else?" I let out a sigh of frustration and shook my head. I pulled the keys out of my pocket and grabbed my T-shirt off of my dad's motorcycle. "I'm going to drop you off and come back here." I pulled my shirt down over my jeans and slid into the driver's seat.

Mike plopped in his seat, slamming his door too hard for my liking.

"Stop slamming my door, and put on your seat belt." Another thing I have to tell him to do every single time we get in the car.

"Ok man, sorry." Mike looked like a wounded puppy as he pulled his belt over his chest. I guess I did snap his head off.

"Look, I didn't mean to be so rude. I-I just need a break." I sat back in my seat, trying to adjust myself. "Brax, you have been acting so strange for the last couple of days. I know you have a lot on your mind with Addy and all, but don't take it out on me." Mike crossed his arms over his chest and glared at me full force.

"I said I was sorry; can we drop it?" I sent him an intense look, and then forced my eyes back to the road.

"Drop it? Sure I will drop it. That's just like you, Brax; you jump all over me then you don't want to talk about what is really going on with you." His door opened, and he jumped out before I even got the car in park. Mandi came bouncing out of her house with a smile on her face. Mike slammed his door shut and began to walk towards her. The shaking sound of the window rattling in his door made my blood boil inside of my veins. I jumped out of the car with one foot inside and one foot on the ground, holding my door open.

"What the hell is wrong with you Mike? I have asked you a million times to stop slamming my damn door!" Mandi pulled away from Mike and looked between the two of us. "If you can't respect my car, then don't get back in it!" I sat in the car and slammed the door hard. As I put the car in reverse, Mike came running to the window.

"Me slam the door? What did you just do?" His hands were on my window, and he was bent down to eye level with me.

"It's my damn car!" I screamed. Mike laughed and stood straight up, throwing his hands in the air then back to his sides.

"You know what, you know what, and you are flippin crazy! I come to your house every single day, I have dinner with you, I spend time with you, and all to make sure that you're not lonely. And this, this is the thanks I get!" He bent back down to eye level before he finished, "You know what, and we are finished. Don't call me, don't come by my house. It's over between us." My eyes almost popped out of my head at his words.

"No, no, you can't break it off with me; I am breaking it off with you. I am finished, don't call me, and don't come by my house!" I jumped back out of the car. "You are the crazy one, I can get better friends, ones that will treat me right and respect my car!"

The sudden outburst of laughter from Mandi made us both stop in our tracks. I was breathing hard; Mike was red as beet with his arms crossed over his chest, and his nose held, literally, in the air. We both looked at Mandi, "What is so funny?" we both asked in unison.

It took several minutes for Mandi to catch her breath and speak. "The two of you, that's what." She bent over with her hands on her knees and let out another belly laugh. "M-my God . . ." She laughed for minutes longer. Holding her belly and taking in several deep breaths, she continued, "The two of you are like a couple. You act just like a couple, you sound like one too." Her laughter overtook her again as Mike, and I protested with all the male testosterone we could muster.

"The hell we do!" Mike puffed out his chest and slammed his hands deep in his pockets. I thought about the whole argument and what was said. I ran my hand through my hair and watched my feet as I turned back towards my car. She was right, we did sound like a couple. I couldn't help but laugh as the sound of Mandi's belly laugh continued to fill the air.

"What the hell are you laughing at?" Mike pointed towards me and looked back at Mandi.

"She is right; we did sound like a couple." I crossed my arms and leaned against the hood of my car.

"You did, you really did. Epic!" Mandi stood straight up and pulled her cell phone from her pocket. "But the best part is, I have it all right here on my phone!" She held the phone high in the air and waved it at Mike and me.

"Oh hell no!" Mike took off running after Mandi as she screamed and laughed all the way inside the house.

—◊◊◊—

"Are you going to tell us what is wrong, Brax; you know we only want to help if we can." Mandi put her legs back over Mike's as he flipped through the channels of the television. Mike put his hand out and rubbed the bottom of Mandi's leg without even looking at her. He has no idea what he has, and neither did she.

"I really don't think you want to hear what I have to say." I stood from the sofa chair in Mandi's living room and walked to the bay windows. The sun was still up, but not for long. Six months ago I would have been on my way to Addyson's house to walk around the pond with her. We would have had dinner with her parents, maybe played a board game or two with them, and then walked around the pond. The pond was our special place. Neither of us had said it; we just knew it, but anytime we had something serious to talk about, it always happened at the pond. Sometimes we would do nothing but laugh and joke. I can barely hear her laughter any more in my memories. Over the last few days, I had wondered if I would ever get my Addyson back—if my Addyson ever actually existed.

I turned back towards Mike and Mandi. Mike was holding Mandi's hand, and they both were staring at me. That simple act of holding hands, they had no idea how remarkable that certainly was. I walked back towards them and sat on the edge of the sofa chair.

"You two remind me of what I try not to think about. You can kiss each other anytime you feel like it." I pointed to Mike and continued, "You can run your hands through her hair, or tell her you love her in person. You can look into her eyes as you speak to her. You can hold her hand." The look of confusion come across clear on Mike's face, but Mandi understood me perfectly. "I am jealous of the fact that the two of you have each other. When Addyson is thousands of miles away, doing God only knows what, while I am stuck here with the tortures of my own imagination." I turned the threatening tears into anger and forcefully stood from the sofa chair.

Before either could respond I walked towards the front door. "Don't be sorry for being in love; I don't want the two of you to change for anyone, especially me. I just need a break; I need to go home."

I shut the door behind me and almost ran to my car. I wasn't fast enough. Mandi came running out, leaving her door wide open.

"Brax!" As bad as I wanted to ignore her and fly out of the driveway, I just couldn't do that to her. I rolled my window down and let her speak. "I understand, Braxton, and I am really sorry for you. But one thing you need to understand is the Addyson that left North Carolina is the same Addyson that will return. She did this, all of this, for both of you. She knows you love her no matter what, and she realizes how blessed she is to have you. But the cold, hard fact, whether anyone believes it or not, is she knows that without being a smaller version of who she is, the two of you will have a hard time making it." She paused to make sure I was listening. My mind went to Drake and the girl in McDonalds. That would have never happened had Addyson been, well, smaller. "Stop being so damn selfish, stop with the pity party, and stupidity; for God sake, grow up! If you want to be there for her, then be there. If you want to love her regardless, then do it! I love you, Braxton, you are one of my best friends, and I would do anything to help you. But this one is all on you!" She smiled slightly and slowly walked back into her house.

I sat in her driveway for fifteen minutes thinking about what she had said. As bad as I hated to admit it, most of it was true. It didn't take long to decide what I was going to do next. I pulled out of her driveway and called my mom. No, I knew exactly what I needed to do.

CHAPTER 33

The last few days had been so horrible. I sat. I waited. The phone didn't ring enough. I even called my voice-mail, often, just to make sure it was still working. I had been the one fussing at Braxton for not calling me enough! I kept him on the phone for hours on end. I didn't leave the lodge. I stayed in my room, or in the garden, all day long.

I have been waiting for Braxton to call me when he got out of school. I still hadn't heard from him, and he would have been out of school for at least an hour by now. I had been staring out into the garden so much I knew how many leaves were on the ivy plant crawling up the post. I knew how many cracks were in the wooden table. I was unreservedly bored out of my mind.

I would never have told another soul this, but I had sat on this patio reliving the last night I spent with Braxton. His turquoise eyes, the heat between us, running my fingers lightly over his beautiful tan chest, God I missed his lips, and I couldn't wait to get home to him.

I sat there daydreaming about the day that I would be confident enough to allow him to touch me back. I dreamed of the day that my belly would be flat, legs and arms toned, and my jaw sharply defined. Me; the real me behind this horrible irremovable mask. I couldn't wait to have the same passion that Braxton had.

What would Braxton think then? If he loved me now, and he obviously did, what about when I had a gorgeous body with confidence, self esteem, and the ability to drive him crazy! I would be seductive with no fear, with the same needs he had; the only difference would be I would share the need for his touch. I would not care where he touched me or what he saw, but would want him to feel all of me, and see all of me, the way I see and want him. I couldn't wait.

I heard the car door shut, but never looked up. I was in heaven right then, with a clear picture of Braxton's beautiful, powerful, seductive, and sexy as hell crystal clear blue eyes. I was living in the moment. With my eyes closed and mind engulfed in Braxton; my body was in London, but my heart was in North Carolina with Brax.

"Addy." His voice was so deep, soft, and heavy. Hmmm, I wanted to lie in his arms and stay there. "Addyson." I smiled to myself remembering his glare and the intensity of his lust, as he asked me to make love to him. What would it be like when I was the real me? I imagined his hands on my face, "Addy!"

"I miss you, Braxton." I whispered to myself. If only I could have stayed right there in that perfect vision, it felt so real; I would stay out here until I went home. I could even hear him as clear as day. I missed his voice and didn't even know it. I snuggled further into my chair. I heard a light chuckling.

My eyes popped open, and I sat up straight, worried, and a little startled, and downright pissed for being bothered. Here, I was lusting over visions of my half-naked boyfriend in my mind, and the gardener was like staring at me or something! My eyes quickly surveyed the area around me. I turned all the way around and looked straight into the same turquoise eyes I have been dreaming of for days, my Braxton's.

I cried, of course, damn crybaby, and stood from my chair with force. I reached him before he had a chance to say hi; I kissed him, so lightly, just wanting to feel his soft, sweet lips against mine. I had my eyes open and wouldn't break his eye contact. I hungered for his eyes. I wanted him to take me to our place. In his gaze, I was who I am supposed to be. He sees who I so desperately beg God to be. I am his Addyson.

I kissed him deeper, wanting that deep groan from him, that signal of satisfaction and completeness. I ran my hands under his shirt and felt his bare tanned chest. His gaze began to get distant. I snaked my arms around his waist and ran my nails from his shoulder blades down to his waist, and that did it. His eyes closed, and the sound I wanted to hear came out of his chest and against my own lips. I nuzzled his neck and smiled intently, happy with myself for getting what I wanted.

"Hi" I said unable to hide the smile on my face; you could clearly hear it in my voice, happiness. He laughed, and I heard the sound rumble in his chest as his arms wrapped around me, and it was over. All of the usual things came flooding back into me, and I gently pulled away. So that, he wouldn't notice, I quickly grabbed his hand, trying to guide him. "Come on, I want to show you around the lodge, and maybe we could go to town for a while. I haven't left the house in five days."

He quickly pulled me back to him and kissed me again, hard, deep, and passionate. It was needy and powerful, making me close my eyes. I lost all strength to deny him, or push him away. I wanted to feel him this close, more than anything, even over my self-loathing. I let him wrap his arms around me. I let him touch my face without looking down and shying away, it was a struggle, but I was determined to stay there with him. It was an eternal fight that too many go through. I felt the tears slide down the side of my face, betraying me; I didn't want Braxton to know; I didn't want to talk about it. I didn't want to say it to him.

"What's the matter, baby?" His voice was tender, but he never stopped kissing my lips lightly, pulling his body closer to mine with every intense move. I felt him. I couldn't help it; he was a man and some things they just can't hide. I immediately felt nervous and guilty at the same time. I wanted to, you know, please him; but I was scared out of my mind to go any further than this. But we had talked about this, right? We had talked about what . . . wait, I was letting my mind ruin this moment for me. Shut up and just enjoy him!

"Look at me, Addy, please." His voice was pleading and breathless.

"I am just so happy to see you, Brax." I smiled or tried to.

"I love you Addyson."

Those were the last words spoken between us, other than the intense conversation we were having with our bodies, showing each other how much we loved each other.

My phone was on the patio, ringing. After the third ring, my mind snapped back into this world, back from our own, and I pulled away to grab the phone.

"The doctor," I actually said to myself. "Hello!" I just knew I was too late.

"Addyson Michaels?" The thick sound of her English accent came clearly through the phone.

"Yes?" I replied, happy to have caught the call.

"This is Dr. Melton's office; we have your results and need to see you first thing in the morning at 8:00am."

Why wasn't she happy? Did she not realize what this meant? Maybe she knew the results; maybe, she knew he couldn't help me.

"I will be there!" I have been thinking positively and speaking positively; I am not going to stop now! "See you then, cheers."

I shut my phone, unable to contain my emotions and squealed "8:00AM BRAX, 8.A.M." I laughed and ran to him, wrapping my arms around his waist, resting my face on his shoulder. "This is it, this is it, Brax, my last chance; it's almost here!"

I allowed the secret vision of me to come into my mind. She was laughing and dancing, jumping up and down ready to come out. I smiled so big my face was hurting; laughter was coming out from somewhere deep inside of me. I hadn't noticed him holding me, his arms around my waist, as best he could, and nothing could kill this for me. Nothing came into my mind but the vision of the new me.

—∾—

We were early to the doctor's office. I was so nervous, for as soon as the cab pulled up to the place, my thoughts went to assuming there was a treatment like Dr. Melton had said, and I scolded myself for even allowing my brain to whisper those words.

There was a treatment. This was the best doctor for unexplained obesity in the entire world. This was my prayer that the angels have taken to the Lord. This was all I have ever wanted. This was it; this was my chance for a normal life with Braxton Carmen.

We were sitting in the waiting room; my legs were jumpy, and Brax looked sorry for me. I tried to smile at him. Did he know how much this meant to me? How could he? He knew what I have been through, but it was not the same. There was so much that goes on in a tortured mind, so many secrets, so many little things that normal-sized people don't realize and just take for granted. I didn't think he could possibly understand.

"Addyson Michaels?" I jumped out of the seat before she finished my name and was almost to her before she could shut the folder file she was reading my name from. She was just standing there; what are we waiting on? I thought about leaving her standing there and going to find the doctor myself.

I looked at her and realized she was staring at Braxton; she kind of smiled, turned a little red, and began to sway from side to side . . . really? Not now.

"Brax, come on, I swear I can't leave you alone for two minutes and people want to jump your bones!" The nurse's face dropped to the floor from a mixture of my bluntness, her utter embarrassment, and her complete shock that he was with me. "Yeah, he belongs to me" I said, past ready to go see the doctor.

Brax walked up beside me. "Really? You don't notice this everywhere you go?" I whispered to him under my breath as we followed the nurse about fifteen feet behind her, down a long corridor. "No, Addy, I have told you a hundred times I only see you." He smiled his heart-melting smile and leaned in for a quick kiss.

The nurse was standing to the side, holding the folder file inside the door, pointing that this was our room. She never took her eyes off the floor. I couldn't help it, I thought to myself; and that's where you need to keep your eyes, on me or down, and off my Braxton.

The doctor was waiting on me as I walked in the door. By the serious, glum, look on his face, my world began to shatter. I was shaking as I grabbed Braxton's arm, and held onto him for dear life. "I am here, Addy." I was so grateful he was.

When the doctor finally looked at us both; his eyes went from me to Braxton and back to me, his eyebrow rose up, and a smirk came across his face. I wondered what he was thinking. He shook Braxton's hand and asked us to sit down. I was going to throw up. I could feel it in my throat. He started speaking. I heard something about: sorry it took so long, a million tests, blood, and then my eyes shot to him like rubber-bands when I heard, "SO, I have good news and bad news."

"The good news is . . ." I was holding my breath—breathe Addyson just breathe! "I most certainly can help you!" His face went wide with a grin showing all of his perfect white teeth, and I burst out crying. I was laughing; I wanted to smack him for making me wait this long. I wanted to kiss Braxton, but most of all I was so extremely grateful. I thanked him a hundred times if I thanked him once. And every time I thanked him I would thank God for sending me to him.

"Addyson there are six major hormones found in meat. Three are naturally occurring—Oestraliol, Peoesterone and Testosterone. And three that are synthetic-Zeranol, Trenbolone, and Melengstrol." He sat on his little round black stool and faced me.

"The American USDA and FDA claim the hormones to be safe. However, the European Union's Scientific Committee of Veterinary

Measures Relating to Public Health believes they pose a potential risk to human health." Dr. Melton was cleaning his little round glasses with a white towel as he continued. "Most of the issues are most often found in women, especially pregnant women, and unborn children, amongst other people. But we see the most in women and children." Hurry up already! I was going to have a stroke; I just knew it, right here on the table!

"According to your eating habits, and meal records you should not have consumed enough to virtually hurt you or affect you. However, we have found that your body thoroughly rejects or is allergic to one of the most common hormones found in meat of all kinds, Melengstrol."

Rejects, allergic, okay; my mind was going to implode! "If we had not found this, had you gone as long as five more years without this diagnosis, you would be a full blown diabetic, and possibly have cancer in your female organs." I sat absorbing all of his words, trying my best to make sense of them.

"So you're telling me you can help me, for sure, that I am allergic to hormones put into meats? What will I have to do? Just stop eating meat?"

His laugh was kind, not mocking. "It will not be necessary. I will put you on a prescription that you will take three times a day, unfortunately, for the rest of your life. But I will go as far as to say that within the first six months of being on this medication, combined with the Acia berry blend of natural fruits from all over the world, MonaVie, cleaning your system fully, you will be at least fifty to sixty pounds lighter, with in the first year. Maybe less, and you will be at your ideal weight!"

Braxton was the one to jump up and hug me. He was laughing, and when he pulled back and let me see his beautiful blue eyes, the tears rolling down his face were tears of pure happiness for me. I leaned in and kissed him, still in pure shock.

I quickly looked at the doctor, remembering. "But what about the bad news?" His face was serious now, watching Braxton and me together. I was scared. I didn't want him to say the medicine will kill me eventually, or the medication was a hundred thousand dollars a bottle, or I already had cancer, or what? Just say it!

"You will have to pay me now . . . I found the answer!" Once the shock wore off, I began to laugh hysterically at this cruel man, getting enjoyment from my discomfort. He handed me a little paper cup with an orange pill in it, smaller than a baby aspirin. So this was it? This was the thing that was going to help me. This was what I had prayed for, dreamed of, begged for, my entire life—a little orange pill. "Start taking them today." Doc handed me a full bottle of my new life drug.

As Braxton and I walked out of that doctor's office, I was calling my parents, and he was calling his. We were leaving for North Carolina in the morning.

CHAPTER 34

Lying in the lodge, holding Addyson as she slept, only one thing came to mind. She was, in fact, the girl she had always been. I didn't know why I allowed myself to worry about such childish things, but I had.

Quietly sliding from between the sheets, I walked outside onto the patio. It was much cooler here than it was at home. I knew people who would have given a left arm to be there in London. I wished I had come earlier, and we could have spent some time together here. Just this patio alone was a remarkably romantic place; maybe we will come back one day.

"Brax?" Addy's voice reached me before I saw her. Her long black hair made her face look pale in this light.

"Can't sleep either?" I said, motioning for her to sit beside me.

"I'll be right there." She vanished back into the darkness of the room.

Focusing on the gardens, I couldn't ignore the slightly eerie feeling that something was lurking behind the tall mounds of Ivy. I laughed to myself as I rubbed the growing chill bumps spreading across my chest and shoulders. This was simply a mixture of my imagination and too many horror movies.

"Here you go."

I jumped a little, not expecting Addy to be back so soon. I looked at the cup in her hand with a skeptical glance.

"Just try it," she said. "After a few days, hot tea grows on you." She took a sip of her tea and sat close to me on the bench. "It's just part of being here, I guess." Her fingers glided over the bare skin of my back inducing more chills, chills of a different kind. She has no idea how much I had missed her.

I took a small sip of the tea, knowing I wasn't going to like it. I preferred sweet tea with ice and a ton of sugar. I hated to admit it wasn't that dreadful. "Pretty decent, actually" I said, as she smiled in acknowledgment.

We sat for several minutes looking off into the garden. The moon was the only light you could see, making the gardens look dark and dangerous. I took Addyson's hand in mine and held it tightly. This simple action of affection I had missed so much.

"Addy, can I ask you a question?" I sat back in the bench and turned towards her.

"Of course you can." She placed her tea on the table and gave me all of her attention.

I thought for a moment about how to ask my question. "If the doctor hadn't been able to help you, would you have ever allowed me to make love to you?" I wasn't as embarrassed as I thought I would be. Talking to Addy about anything had always been easy, but now I thought it might be different, it wasn't.

She looked at me for a long moment before answering me. I could see her face turning red, even in the dark. "I know I would have, eventually. The real question is would you have waited for me?"

I immediately felt offended. She should know that I would do anything for her. If I have learned anything over the last few months, I have learned not to assume things. "What exactly do you mean?" I asked with as little emotion as possible.

"I mean, you're a guy. Guys have, well, needs; more than girls do. From the girls I have talked to, most of them do it to keep their guy. If they don't give it up, then they lose the guy." Addyson looked down at her hands; I wondered what she was thinking.

"I am not like other guys, Addy, you know that. Besides, I would do anything for you, or not do anything for you." I laughed, I felt stupid for being so goofy, but goofy or not it was the truth. "There is one thing that I cannot handle though. There is one thing that will tear us apart faster than anything else." Her eyes grew large as she waited for me to continue. I knew I had to finish, but I was afraid of her response. "What Braxton, tell me."

I took both of her hands in mine and leaned forward. She needed to know I wasn't threatening her, or that I wasn't trying to bring up past things, but I knew she needed to hear me. "Don't ever lie to me again;

about anything, ever." Addy knew in her heart that I wasn't being mean towards her, only telling her the truth.

"I promise Brax, no matter what, I will never lie to you again."

The next several hours went by in a flash. I told her all about Mike and Mandi from my point of view. Though Mandi had told Addyson all about her side, I told Addyson all about Mike's side. They truly were perfect for one another. It would be nice to hang out together when we got home.

Addyson told me about the festival that she and Liz went to and the remarkable things she had seen here. "I said that if I had to do it all over again, I would. I would Brax, but this time I would have asked you to come with me, even to New York. This experience has changed my life forever." Addy sat up and looked into my eyes to finish. "I have learned that no matter how scared I am, and no matter the consequences, I can do anything. I don't have to have you protect me." My heart almost broke at her words. It's not like I wanted her to need my protection; I wanted her to need me in general. As if she could read my mind she said, "I want you to always be there, because I love you, but not because I have to have you around." I understood exactly what she meant.

"Look." I turned my head in the direction she pointed. The sun rising up over the gardens relinquished the eerie feeling and brought a feeling of peace and beauty. The colors of the flowers, just seconds earlier hidden, began to come alive in my view. Purples, reds, oranges, and the lavish green that dominated the entire yard could take your breath away.

"Let's go home." I said, before kissing her until the sun had fully risen over us, and the lodge I would never forget.

CHAPTER 35

I had been home for three months. In three simple months, I had lost thirty five pounds. It doesn't sound like a lot, but to me it was three pants sizes and a fresh start to the new me. Already my life had changed so much, and I still had a long way to go.

Jennifer was the only person who didn't have something pleasant to say. Most of the cheerleaders, regardless of Jennifer's protesting, had become friends with me. Of course, Mandi is still my best friend, and I would choose her over anyone.

My wardrobe had tripled in size, and my mother and I had the most fun shopping for new clothes. I wore everything from vests to bathing suits, yes, even bathing suits! I felt beautiful, mostly because of Braxton, but beautiful none the less.

My parents had trust issues with me for obvious reasons. Even though I deserved it, I still would get extremely irritated with them for not allowing me to do the things I always did before. Simple stuff like go to the library or to the college park to feed the ducks. As long as Braxton was with me, they never questioned me; otherwise, I had to call when I got there and had to be home before ten at night.

Braxton could see the biggest changes in me, because he knew me better than anyone else. I allowed him to hold me and touch me more without feeling too self-conscious. It was still there some, but not as severe.

Every day, when I woke up, I looked at me in the mirror. I found myself wanting to keep my nails painted, wear makeup, and actually cared about what was in style or not. With self esteem came a wanting to take care of myself even better. I actually enjoyed it.

I am still a little scared but for totally different reasons. There are things about me that I am learning to change, things that I have dealt with my whole life. I still hide behind my hair sometimes, but stop as soon as I catch myself doing it. The compliments I received were almost as hard to handle as the ridicule, simply because it was all foreign to me. Certain people still made me nervous, but rarely did terrible things happen to me. Some still made smart remarks; some would always see me as Fattyson. There was nothing I can do about that.

Now, I spent my time trying to be the best girl friend I could be to Braxton. I wanted to make him laugh; make him smile, be the reason he is happy. When I have lost fifty or more pounds, I felt like I would be comfortable in my own skin, completely comfortable, and honestly proud of who I was.

—◊◊◊—

Eleventh Grade was almost over. It had been eight months since my trip to London. I had lost seventy-five pounds! I still had a ways to go. But I had gone from a size twenty-four to a size fourteen in pants! I would even get into a bathing suit. It's a one piece, but a bathing suit none the less, and in front of people!

Needless to say, my whole life had changed. The teasing had stopped; all except Jennifer. She just hated me; she would never get Braxton from me.

I had spent every moment with Brax. We were extremely public now. He would have always had it that way, bless his heart, but now I was just as public. I participated in social activities, parties, football games—only to see Braxton play really, but I was no longer scared to go.

I was treated differently. By everyone, even teachers, but especially by boys. Boys went out of their way to help me. I was extremely popular for all of the right reasons. Not that this was my intention, but I was not mad about it either.

Mandi was my best friend and always came first, but now I had a lot of girlfriends. But the weirdest part of all of this was the attention from boys! I would never have done anything to hurt Braxton; there wasn't a boy in this school I would choose over him, but it felt fantastic to be stared at, asked out (and they all know I am with Braxton), winked at, flirted with, even grabbed once—which got the boy a bloody nose. It wasn't Braxton either; it was me who busted it!

I felt sorry for Braxton. He now knew what I had felt for all of those years, watching girls hit on him right in front of me. Of course, it still bothered me, but women no longer approached him when I was with him. After all, it was no longer hard to believe he was with me. I was looking forward to my new life. I was looking forward to senior year. I was looking forward to everything now.

I know, right now, I am living my life to the fullest! And loving every second of it!

Never give up!

Addyson Michaels.

PROLOGUE

My Life in her Hands
Braxton's Story
Part two of the My Life series

Sometimes I wish she had never gone to London. Addyson has changed a lot. I mean she is still my Addyson. She still stares into my eyes making me feel like the only man alive, the only person who matters to her.

It took a while. I watched it all happen right in front of my eyes. She began to fade, to disappear. At first it was only her body, transforming into this beautiful creation. I am not going to lie, she is hot. I loved her before, so you know I am not a pig! But her curves are showing, her confidence is growing, her self esteem is at an all-time high, and the things she can do to me!

Her touch is different, her kiss is different, and her words are more direct; sometimes I think her number one goal is to drive me crazy. She pushes me sometimes; I love every minute of it! She lets me hold her now. She lets me touch her back and her sides. The first time I wrapped my arms all the way around her waist, and pulled her against me, she cried.

I have been there for all of her firsts. So many marvelous things have happened. It's like watching a caterpillar turn into a beautiful, free butterfly. But there have been a few unpleasant things too. There have been some changes in me. Things I never expected. I was protective of her before because she was being put through hell. Now I am protective of her trying my best to keep her. I have always been a little jealous, but nothing serious; minus Jace, but what can you expect? She was thousands of miles away in New York, and I heard the guy's voice at three in the morning, in her bedroom. Give me a break. But I now know what real jealousy is, and it is hell. It is the worst thing ever. If I don't change soon, I will lose her over my own stupidity.

God Help me.

Summary

I am the most popular girl in school. Every person in my school knows me by name. But before you allow your mind to paint the image of the most beautiful and flawless girl in school, without a single imperfection, let me finish.

I am also the fattest girl in school. My celebrity status comes from the complete opposite of your previous image, to what I am. I am sixteen years old, five feet six inches tall and weigh two hundred and forty five pounds.

Does the rest of me really matter? Like the fact, that I have perfect silky black hair, with very few pimple scars or blemishes on my face, and the wildest honey yellow/brown eyes you have ever seen? Nope, the rest doesn't matter at all. I am the most popular . . . to pick on, tease, laugh at, pull pranks, ridicule, degrade, and humiliate. Every person knows me by name, and extremely few have passed up the opportunity to torture me.

To deepen this widely known status, my best friend, Braxton Carmen, also just happens to be the hottest, most sought after guy in our school. He is not a part of every sport in the school, and he doesn't walk around arrogant and acting like a self righteous moron. No, he is just Brax. We have known each other our whole lives; our mothers were best friends since grade school, and we are more like brother and sister. Brax is extremely protective and that keeps the torture to a minimum, at least when he is around.

Problem is just a few months ago my feelings have began to change from best friend/ sibling mode to, well, I think I am in love with him. Wouldn't you be? He is the cause of everything right in my life. But for the first time in our lives, I may have to let him go. This will be the hardest thing I have ever had to do. But first let me start from the beginning—well, at least from where everything changed.

I am Addyson Michaels, and this is my story . . .

COMMENTS FROM REAL PEOPLE ON WATTPAD. THE VERSION ON WATTPAD HAS 20 CHAPTERS.

What a great book! I can't wait to read the second part. You really get to experience the feelings that Addyson and every other girl who is or has been obese has felt. It's a shame that how they are treated isn't fictional. "Never give up!"—**Mary, 32, Texas USA-**

I love the way you ended this story!!! It's like an entire life lesson. I'm not like fat or anything, but I'm bigger than other girls, because I have a lot of curves. It really makes me feel self conscious a lot and I hate it. This story made me realize how bad some people have it, and I feel grateful for my body the way it is!!! Thank you!—**Karategurl1998, unknown age and location-**

That was the most amazing and sweet book I have ever read. They were so cute and I really hope I will find someone like Braxton. You can't understand what reading this incredible book did to me. I have the same problem too, I am overweight and when I read this book everything became clear for me. You gave me the strength to begin to lose pounds and to believe that everything will be alright. Soon I will walk with my head up and happy with someone like Braxton who loves me entirely and with all his heart. I knew you experienced it because the way you wrote it showed that you know what I and other over weight girls experience and feel. You know I will read and reread your story again and again because it gives me strength and when I feel bad I will be ok when I read this and I will write you soon and will tell you that I found my Braxton. Love you . . . really love you for writing this beautiful, touching, and very real story. Thank you.—**Mariana, 23, Bulgaria-**

*Update on Mariana**—I began to lose weight because of your amazing book. I have now lost 36 pounds. I have many more to lose but it is something big for me, you gave me strength. Love you*

I am so glad you told me about this story. I am in absolute love with it already. The concept is very realistic and like something no one has really wrote about on here (Wattpad). I can tell it is going to be an emotional and hard journey through this book and I am excited every step of the way! It's beautifully written and flows perfectly together. You've added just enough detail without boring the reader and yet, you leave me wanting more! I am most certainly reading on!—**Ciaran, 18, Grand Isle LA-**

Best book on Wattpad!!!—**Singdanceposesmile34, unknown age and location-**